# PRAISE

## CHASING

"Prepare to laugh, cry, and pray as you inhale each poignant word of this stunning debut novel. Simply unforgettable!"

—Patti Lacy, author of *An Irishwoman's Tale,* 2008 *Forward Magazine* Book of the Year Finalist, and *What the Bayou Saw*

"CHASING LILACS is the kind of coming-of-age story that sticks to you beyond the last page. Unforgettable characters, surprising plot twists, and a setting so Southern you'll fall in love with Texas. Carla Stewart is a new talent to watch!"

—Mary E. DeMuth, author of *Daisy Chain* and *A Slow Burn*

"Carla Stewart writes a tender story with such emotional impact, you will hope, fear, cry, and rejoice with her characters. Readers will find themselves cheering Sammie on through her ordeals as she seeks love and forgiveness."

—Janelle Mowery, author of *Love Finds You in Silver City, Idaho*

"Gripping! Nostalgic and filled with bittersweet memories, Carla Stewart's CHASING LILACS captured my imagination, and my heart, from the moment I started reading."

—Elizabeth Ludwig, award-winning author and speaker

"Endearing characters, twists that propel the story ever forward, and soul-searching questions combine to create a heart-tugging tale of self-reflection and inward growth. Carla Stewart's CHASING LILACS carried me away to 1950s small-town Texas…and I wanted to stay. I highly recommend this insightful, mesmerizing coming-of-age tale."

—Kim Vogel Sawyer, bestselling author of *My Heart Remembers*

"Carla Stewart's debut novel, CHASING LILACS, is a deeply emotional masterpiece. Witty dialogue and normal teen antics nicely balance the thought-provoking introspection and dramatic storyline. Young Sammie, the heroine, is both a normal kid and wise beyond her years. Reminiscent of slower-paced days gone by, CHASING LILACS takes you back to days forgotten and leaves you inspired."

—Vickie McDonough, award-winning author of 18 books and novellas, including the Texas Boardinghouse Brides series

"It's the fifties—Elvis is on the radio, summer is in the air, and a young girl tries to understand the mystery that is her mother. Like its heroine, Sammie Tucker, this gripping and emotional debut will find its way into your heart."

—Shelley Adina, Christy finalist and award-winning author of the All About Us series

"Guilt and redemption are at the soul of this heartwarming tale of a little girl searching for her mother's love. Carla takes us back to a simpler time and a simpler place with wit, wisdom, and insight. God bless her."

—Charles W. Sasser, author of *God in the Foxhole* and *Arctic Homestead*

"Carla Stewart has crafted a wonderful story in the style of *To Kill a Mockingbird* with compelling characters you will care about."

—Margaret Daley, award-winning, multi-published author in the Christian romance genre

"A remarkable debut novel. Carla Stewart cleverly captures the stark simplicity of a young girl's voice with all the masterful qualities of powerful prose. Unforgettable."

—Susan Meissner, author of *The Shape of Mercy*

# Chasing Lilacs

*A Novel*

## CARLA STEWART

New York   Boston   Nashville

Copyright © 2010 by Carla Stewart
All rights reserved. Except as permitted under the U.S. Copyright Act of 1976, no part of this publication may be reproduced, distributed, or transmitted in any form or by any means, or stored in a database or retrieval system, without the prior written permission of the publisher.

Unless otherwise indicated, Scriptures are taken from the
King James Version of the Bible.

FaithWords
Hachette Book Group
237 Park Avenue
New York, NY 10017
www.faithwords.com

Printed in the United States of America

First Edition: June 2010
10   9   8   7   6   5   4   3   2   1

FaithWords is a division of Hachette Book Group, Inc.
The FaithWords name and logo are trademarks of
Hachette Book Group, Inc.

Library of Congress Cataloging-in-Publication Data

Stewart, Carla.
    Chasing lilacs / by Carla Stewart.—1st ed.
        p. cm.
    ISBN 978-0-446-55655-2
    1. Mothers and daughters—Fiction.   2. Mothers—Death—Fiction.
3. Suicide—Fiction.   I. Title.
    PS3619.T4937C47 2010
    813'.6—dc22
                                                              2009027122

*To my dad, Mike Brune, and in memory of my mom, Pat Brune.*
*You taught me to believe: first in Jesus, then in myself.*
*You are loved.*

ACKNOWLEDGMENTS

I HAD THE GOOD FORTUNE of growing up in a place similar to Graham Camp. The days were carefree and the summers long. Even then, I had a deep curiosity about things whispered when no one thought I was listening. Thankfully, the events in *Chasing Lilacs* never truly happened—they are only the what-ifs birthed in my imagination.

I'm grateful to my parents, Pat and Mike Brune, who gave me a childhood worth remembering. For Donna and Marsha, you are cherished. Nothing compares to having sisters who are also my friends.

Although writing is a solitary calling, this book would not exist without the many people who've shaped my life and my writing. To name each of you would be a whole 'nother book. Still, many of you stand out and have awed me by your gifts of encouragement.

The Crossroads Writers and Tulsa Night Writers—you saw my beginning pages and offered gentle, but invaluable critique. Carolyn Steele, your wisdom and willingness to pore over the many drafts of this book make me indebted to you always.

ACFW (American Christian Fiction Writers). When I attended my first conference in 2006, it was like stepping into writers' heaven. A special thanks to Mary DeMuth—your affirmation renewed my passion for this story. Chip MacGregor, your honesty and wise counsel set me on the right path. Lissa Halls Johnson, your insights and tough love made this a much better book. Thank you all.

Sandra Bishop. Words fail me. I am so blessed to have someone who "gets" my writing and who has worked tirelessly on my behalf.

Myra Johnson, Kim Sawyer, Cindy Hays, fellow WIN members, and those who cheered and prayed in the shadows—I'm honored by your unfailing support.

My editor, Anne Horch, her assistant, Katie Schaber, and the entire team at FaithWords—your belief in this story and attention to every detail humbles me.

My "family" at Community Worship Center—you may never know this side of heaven the impact of your prayers and hugs. This journey has been made brighter because of you.

Max, my husband, my best friend—you've filled my life with love and laughter. Your faith in my writing dream overwhelms and sustains me. And for our ever-growing family—Andy, Amy, Brett, Cindy, Scott, Denice, James, Allison, and our six amazing grandchildren—this book is for all of you.

None of this would have been possible without my Savior, Jesus Christ. For giving me unspeakable joy, I offer up my praise. May all the glory be yours.

## [ ONE ]

THAT JUNE, RIGHT AFTER I finished sixth grade, Norm MacLemore's nephew came to Texas for a visit. Benny Ray Johnson brought home a new Edsel. And Mama tried to take her life for the first time.

We lived at Graham Camp then—a petroleum plant with company housing. A spot in the Panhandle of Texas where the blue of the sky hurt your eyes and the wind bent the prairie grass into an endless silk carpet as far as you could see in every direction. God's country, some people called it. While it may be true that God created that corner of the world, it crossed my young mind that he must have been looking the other way when it came to Mama. Why else would Mama's spells, as Daddy called them, drive her deeper into her quilts? Lights out. Shades drawn.

Her spell that June had gone on longer than most, and she seemed to be slipping farther away. I hoped my being out of school might snap her out of it, and I had no trouble inventing excuses to linger in the house and be of some use to Mama. Mostly, she let me fetch her things. An ice bag for her headache. Another one of those pills from the brown bottle.

I tiptoed in and out with her requests and studied her for signs of improvement. With every smile or pat on my hand, my insides lurched. *Maybe today she'll suggest we bake a cake. Or take a walk down to Willy Bailey's store.* I would have settled for just having her sit with me on the couch and watch television.

Please don't get me wrong. Mama was the primary thing on my mind, but a few days into the summer, I began to get restless. Itchy. As I scribbled ideas for the newspaper my best friend, Tuwana Johnson, and I planned to write, my mind drifted, wondering what the next three months would hold. When the floorboards creaked beside me, I looked up, startled to see Mama shuffling into the front room. A little flutter came into my chest. Mama's robe hung limp on her thin frame, the belt trailing behind.

My gaze traveled to her face, searching for signs that the fog had lifted. One look at her eyes and I knew nothing had changed. Flat. Muddy. Looking at me, but not really seeing me.

"Hi, Mama. You want to watch *Queen for a Day*?" I kept my voice light, airy, and made room for her on the couch beside me.

She flopped down. "Not those wretched stories. It would give me a headache all over again. No television."

"You're feeling better, then? No headache?"

She fiddled with the button on the cushion. "Not exactly."

Her answer could have gone either way. Not exactly better. Or not exactly a headache. A huge silence hung between us.

Before I could think of something else to say, the back door slammed and Daddy came in. Even without seeing him, I knew the routine. Hard hat on the hook by the back door. The plunk of the metal lunch box on the kitchen counter. Then Daddy clomped through in his steel-toed boots and appeared in the kitchen doorway.

"Hey, Rita. Good to see you up." He leaned over and brushed his lips across Mama's cheek.

She dipped her head away and pushed herself up from the couch, whisked around the end, and pattered to the bathroom. Not a single word.

When Daddy winked at me, I couldn't tell if he was trying to cheer me up or cover the disappointing welcome from Mama.

Mama came from the bathroom and stood, feet apart, robe gaping over the same nightgown she'd worn all week. Her fingers curled, white-knuckled, around the brown pill bottle.

"I'm out of pills." She held out the bottle.

"You know, sugar, I could take tomorrow off. Take you into Mandeville and see Doc." He put his arm around her slumping shoulders, but she shrugged him off.

"I don't need to see Doc. I need my pills."

"Seems to me they ain't doing much good. Maybe Doc could give you a different brand or something...."

She shoved the bottle into Daddy's calloused hand. "And what am I supposed to do until tomorrow?" Her eyes darted around, jerky little movements. "Please. Take Sammie with you. Just get them."

She backed up the few paces to her room, then turned and shut the door.

Daddy thumped me on the arm. "You up for a root-beer float?"

In other words, we were going into town to get Mama's pills and could stop at the Dairy Cream on the way home.

He didn't say anything the whole twelve miles, just tapped his fingers on the steering wheel, his eyes aimed straight ahead. I counted rusty brown cows with white faces and wished Mama had some physical thing wrong, like a broken leg or appendicitis, so we could say, "Just two more weeks and she'll be good as new." But deep down I knew it was something else. I just didn't know what.

In the waiting room, I thumbed through a dog-eared *Highlights* magazine while Daddy went into Doc's office. When they came out, Daddy put the refilled bottle in his shirt pocket, and Doc handed me a peppermint stick. "Take good care of your mother, Sammie."

I should have taken Doc's advice.

But the next morning, Daddy told me Mama needed to rest. "Go on and have some fun."

Sunshine peeked through the window above the kitchen sink. It didn't really take any convincing on Daddy's part. I slipped on my Keds and took off. Sweet, dewy grass and a drift of rose scent gave me a heady feeling as I walked the two streets over to Tuwana's. When she opened the door, the smell of peanut butter cookies floated out. Delicate, sugary sensations tickled my nose. Tuwana flounced into the kitchen and snitched us each a cookie. I took tiny bites and let each morsel melt in my mouth.

I thanked Mrs. Johnson and licked my lips around a stray crumb. She smiled through pink lipstick and told me it was nothing, that she was glad to see me. Wiping her hands on a starched, dotted-Swiss apron, she turned back to the cookies.

Tara and Tommie Sue, Tuwana's little sisters, giggled above the blare of the television. Through the organdy curtains that billowed out from the window breeze, the sun scattered dust motes. I just stood there, soaking up the clatter, until Tuwana dragged me out onto the front porch. We painted our fingernails, then our toenails, and between it all, talked about a lot of nothing.

When the noon whistle shrilled through every inch of Graham Camp, it surprised me that the whole morning had flown by. Not once had I thought about Mama.

Running into the wind, my hair streamed behind me as I cut through the Barneses' backyard, darted past a row of tin garages, and zipped into the house. I took a second to catch my breath and listen for Mama, but the hum of the Frigidaire was all I heard. I went to the bathroom, flushed, and reached for the faucet to wash my hands. That's when I noticed the brown pill bottle on the back of the toilet.

The lid lay off to the side. I picked it up to screw it back on, thinking Mama had been careless when she took her last dose. The bottle was empty. I scanned the bathroom. No other bottles. No other pills laying around.

A tingle zipped up my spine. I raced into Mama's room, shadowy and stale, and squinted to make out her body curled under her quilt—asleep, it looked like. I touched her lightly on the shoulder.

"Mama, wake up. It's time for lunch."

She didn't move.

I gave her a little shake, not wanting her to yell at me if she had another headache.

Nothing.

A knot formed in my throat. Her mouth sagged toward the pillow, her face ghostly white. I moved the quilt and lifted her hand, but it flopped back against the sheet. *Check her pulse.*

I looked around, wondering if someone had said the words or if I had just thought them. *Check her pulse.* How? What did Miss Good from health class teach us? Which side of the wrist? Thumb on the inside of the wrist. No, maybe it was the index finger. *Think. Think. Think.*

*Forget the pulse. Check her breathing.* I leaned down close, hoping to hear some air coming from Mama's mouth. My own heart banged against my chest, filling my ears with its thump, thump, and I knew it was useless. Even if Mama were breathing, I would never hear it.

I flew out the back door, ducked under the clothesline, and tore through Goldie Kuykendall's yard. Not even bothering to knock, I ran in and yelled, "Goldie! Help!"

Goldie listened to my blubbering and picked up the telephone. "We've got an emergency over at the Tuckers'. Get Joe straight-away. . . . Tell him his wife swallowed a bottle of pills."

She hung up and made another phone call. Then another. A ticking clock in my head screamed "Hurry!" but the next thing I knew, Goldie grabbed my hand and rushed us across our backyards to my house.

Already, like some strange magic, neighbors appeared, whisper-ing, asking what had happened. I broke loose from Goldie's grip, and as I raced up the steps to the front door, I heard Daddy's Chevy screech to a halt. Red-faced from working in the boiler room at the plant, he stormed past me. Goldie took my hand and whispered, "Wait." In no time, the screen door swung open, nearly knocking me down. Daddy stepped out carrying Mama. He put her in the car and ducked into the backseat beside her. Brother Henry from the Hilltop Church got behind the wheel and roared off.

A sweaty, sick feeling came over me, and the faces of those gath-ered on our lawn blurred. My thoughts jumbled as I caught the words *crying shame, poor Sammie, mercy sakes*. I waited for someone to say that Mama was alive, that everything would be all right, but no one did. Then a horrible thought crept in. Doc told me to take care of Mama. Why, oh why, hadn't I done what he said? I tried to swallow, but my throat had shut itself off, and I knew why.

It was all my fault.

## TWO

A TERRIBLE SHAKING STARTED SOMEWHERE deep inside, cold and trembly. Goldie's arm around my shoulders steadied me but didn't stop the clammy breakout on my scalp and neck. She sat beside me on the couch in her front room and held me.

"Take it easy. I know you're scared." She held me close, her arms sturdy around me. She smelled of disinfectant and something woody or earthy. I leaned against her, gulping in buckets of air, letting her soft bosom cushion me.

Gradually my breaths returned to normal, and I eased away from her. A zigzaggy scratch stung on my arm, smeared with crusty blood.

Goldie noticed it too. "Gracious, you've got a nasty scrape. What happened?"

I shrugged and had the faintest recollection of running by Goldie's rosebush screaming for help. Now the jagged line brought back the reminder of Mama. I sucked in another big breath and shivered. Goldie went to her kitchen and brought back a wet rag and a small brown bottle with a skull and crossbones on the label. Gently, she washed my arm.

"Just a bit more, Sammie." She blew on my arm, then painted a red streak of "monkey blood" on the scratch. My shoulders hunched together. It burned like fire.

We both blew on it, and before I could think, I blurted out, "Do you think Mama was breathing?"

Goldie's Buster Brown hair swayed across her round-as-the-moon face. She nodded in a way that could have meant anything. She patted me on the cheek, her green eyes drooping at the corners, and I could tell she really didn't know.

After that, she hovered around me, brushing the hair out of my eyes one minute, straightening up the *Baptist Messenger* magazines on the end table the next. A honky-tonk song crackled over the Philco radio, and Goldie walked over to fine-tune the static from Hank Williams's "Cold, Cold Heart."

Just as she straightened up, the phone rang. Two short jangles. One long. My body stiffened as Goldie and I looked at each other.

*Daddy? So soon?* My stomach knotted up.

Goldie's thick fingers fumbled with the receiver, her voice croaky as she answered. Her face didn't show anything as she listened and then motioned for me to come over.

Gripping the phone, I said hello.

"She's holding her own, Sis," Daddy said on the other end.

My breath whooshed out.

He went on. "I'll be staying the night, to be here when she wakes up. I think Goldie'll be all right with you staying there. Don't worry. I'll see you in the morning." Click.

*Alive. Mama's alive.* I stared into the receiver. It was good news, wasn't it? But what did he mean "holding her own"? Holding her own what? I hung up, my feet planted to the floor. In my head, Mama's arms and legs dangled like a marionette's from Daddy's arms. Daddy's face had no expression, just his jaw clamped tight, like the wooden Indian we'd once seen at a filling station.

"What did he say?" Goldie's voice brought me back.

"She's holding her own. He's staying at the hospital until she wakes up." Well, that was something anyway—thinking she'd wake up. "He thought I could stay here until then."

"Praise be. Yes, of course you can stay here. Thank you, Jesus." She squeezed me tightly, then held me out at arm's length. "You must be starved. I'm fixing us some soup, and then you can help me with those critters out there." She motioned toward the back of the house, to the aviary attached to her porch. I nodded, glad to have something to keep my mind off Mama hanging by a string in some strange hospital room.

After stirring the chicken noodle soup Goldie made, I couldn't take a single bite. Bits of the pale chicken popped to the top every time I moved the spoon, and the smell made me sick. I tried a saltine cracker, which felt like gravel in my throat. I pushed my bowl away, and Goldie didn't mention it, just tossed her head toward the aviary.

She held the door for me, and together we entered the porch work area. A pine-plank table sat along the wall with rows of feed sacks propped beside it. A screen door led into the aviary. There were box cages full of flapping, colorful parakeets whistling and chirping, louder than a flock of spooked blackbirds. The cages lined one whole wall, rows stacked upon one another with space between each one. I counted eight across and five high and multiplied them in my head. Forty cages. Each one had a tray that slid out so we could remove the soiled newspaper. A faint smell, like cat pee, filled the air.

Goldie handed me a stack of newspapers. "New liners for the cages after I pull the dirty ones out." She went to work.

"It's my fault, you know," I said to the room in general. The parakeets twittered louder now that we'd riled them. "Do you think it's my fault, Goldie?" I shouted above the aviary racket. "You know…Mama taking those pills?"

"Lord, have mercy. Where'd you ever get a cockeyed notion like that?" She threw a used newspaper into an empty feed sack.

"Daddy didn't want to get the pills for her. He said she needed to try something else for those spells she gets. If I'd stayed home this morning—"

"No one's going to be putting blame." Her green eyes peered into mine. "Things happen. If we were meant to understand it all, we wouldn't be needing the Almighty, now would we?"

"You mean God?"

"Sammie Tucker, listen to me. God loves your mother the same as you and me. He created each and every one of us, and no two people on this green earth are exactly alike. We all got our own ways, and to go figuring out the mind of someone else is a plumb waste of time. Your mama's gonna be just fine." She went back to yanking the smelly papers from the trays.

I wanted to believe her, really I did, but *holding her own* and *just fine* didn't sound like the same thing to me. And that picture in my head of Mama dangling by a wire darted in and out no matter how much I tried to stop it. No, it was definitely my fault, and tomorrow, when Daddy brought Mama home, I knew what I had to do. Protect Mama. Make her well. Doc said to take care of her, and that's exactly what I would do.

But when Daddy picked me up at Goldie's early the next morning, he didn't bring Mama. He told us she woke up and could state her name and knew that it was June 1958. He thanked Goldie for putting up with me and took me home.

My insides itched to know about Mama, but Daddy seemed off in some other world.

"How is she?" I blurted out, louder than I intended.

"Doing better. Fair to middlin', I'd say." He disappeared into the bathroom. While the water ran in the bath and he clanged around shaving and what all, a million questions played ping-pong in my head. My feet wouldn't stay still. I tapped one foot, arms crossed, waiting for Daddy. Why hadn't Mama come home with him? Why was he in such an all-fired hurry to get cleaned up?

He came out, a piece of red-dotted toilet paper stuck on his chin, and disappeared into his bedroom. I watched from the doorway as Daddy threw some of Mama's things into a suitcase and snapped it shut. Straightening, he motioned for us to go outside.

We sat on the cement steps of the porch, the morning sun filtering through the trees and making kaleidoscope patterns at our feet.

"Mama's gonna need some help." He took a pack of Camels from his shirt pocket and fished one out. He tapped one end on his silver lighter before cupping his hand around the cigarette and lighting up. A puff of smoke drifted by as he inhaled.

"Help? What kind of help?"

Bent over with his arms resting on his knees, he didn't look at me, just took a long drag and stared off into the distance.

"A hospital. Wichita Falls. She'll spend three weeks talking to a doctor—a psychiatrist—going to group sessions and something called ECT. It's where Zeb Thornton took his wife, Mabel, a while back. Even though it's a couple hundred miles from here, it's a good place, from what he said."

"Three weeks?" Tears gathered behind my eyelids. I gazed up at the sky, willing them to drain back into my head. "And so far away. What will they do to her? It won't hurt, will it?"

"No, just help her get better." Daddy stubbed the cigarette in the Folgers can beside the porch. "I called your aunt Vadine."

"Why?" Something seemed off, like he hadn't told me

everything. Maybe Mama wasn't going to be all right. What if something else was wrong? Must be something horrible or he wouldn't have called Aunt Vadine.

"As your mama's only real kin, I thought she ought to know." He dug in his pocket for another Camel. "I asked her to come and stay a few days."

My insides tumbled about. "It's not like I need a babysitter, you know, if that's what you're thinking." Please, not Aunt Vadine.

"I've got evening shift next week and then graveyards. Don't want you being alone so much."

"Don't worry about that. Tuwana and I are working on our summer newspaper. We decided to call it the *Dandelion Times*. Oh, and Goldie said she could use my help just about any time with her parakeets. She's been keen, teaching me all about them. Aunt Vadine will be the one sitting in the house by herself."

"Glad you got things to do. Besides, she can't come. She got herself a new waitress job at one of them new twenty-four-hour truck stops."

"That's a relief." I puffed out my cheeks and let out a long breath.

"Why's that?" He flipped his smoke into the can.

"She's practically a stranger, that's all." And scary, I wanted to tell him, remembering the pinch she gave me for putting my elbows on the table the last time we saw her.

"She's family though." He picked up Mama's suitcase and walked to the Chevy. "Goldie said she'd be around if you need anything. See you tonight." He gave me a wink and got in the front seat.

"Tell Mama I love her."

"Will do."

The car eased down the street, a streak of sun bouncing from the back window. Half of me wanted to run after him and beg to go with him, but the other half stood frozen, unable to think or move.

"Gotcha." A poke in my ribs startled me.

I whirled around and faced Tuwana, her blue eyes as round as marbles.

"Don't scare me like that!" I glared at her.

"Sorry. I thought you'd like some company."

"It's not that. Right now I'm just a little bumfuzzled."

"Your mom. She's going to be all right, isn't she?" Tuwana cocked her head the way our dog Patch used to when he wanted to play.

The world went into slow motion, Tuwana standing there waiting for an answer and me wanting to say, *Oh sure, any minute now she'll be her old self.*

Instead of words coming out, tears trickled from my eyes. Blinking, I tried to hold them back, but they spilled out, running down my cheeks, tasting salty in my mouth and making my nose drip. Tuwana's skinny arm wrapped around my shoulders, and together we walked to the porch. She pushed me into a sitting position.

"So, tell me about your mother. When's she coming back?"

My eyebrows scrunched. "Three weeks. There's a special doctor and something called ECT, whatever that is."

"Shock treatments. That's what Mother says people get when they have a nervous breakdown."

"A nervous breakdown?" I looked hard at Tuwana. "Is that what you think? She didn't go nuts and fly apart. Not even close. She took some pills."

"Maybe she did that before you found her. The flying apart thing."

"Are you crazy? Mama's not like that." Who did Tuwana think she was, scaring me like that?

"I wonder how they do them." Tuwana hugged her knees to her chest.

"Do what?"

"Shock treatments. Do you think they poke them with needles or something?"

"Who knows?" My stomach got a sick feeling. *Shock treatments? Needles?* Whatever they were, they sounded awful.

"Maybe they plunge them into tubs of ice water or hook them up to electricity."

"Stop it! Daddy said they don't hurt." My face felt hot. "Why would you even say such a thing?"

"Don't get your panties in a wad. I didn't mean anything by it."

Gritting my teeth, I turned to Tuwana. "Daddy would've said if Mama had a nervous breakdown. He didn't. She needs help, that's all. Daddy wouldn't lie about something like that." My eyelid twitched, but I wouldn't back down from looking at Tuwana. "I'm upset, and you would be too if it was your mother."

"You're right. Sorry." She looked away and then patted me on the shoulder. "Hey, I'd better go. Catch you later."

Being right didn't change the sinking feeling I had inside. What if they hurt Mama? Shutting my eyes, I tried to remember her smiling and laughing, but nothing came. Squinching my eyes tighter, her arms and legs dangled like a rag doll, flashing like a jerky movie behind my eyelids. The way her hair hung over Daddy's arm and her skin had the color of chalk flickered in and out of my head.

I wrapped my arms around my knees and rocked back and forth on the porch steps. I tried to picture her in a frilly apron like Alice Johnson wore or combing my hair the way I'd seen Mrs. Johnson do with Tuwana and her sisters. No matter how hard I tried, the same pictures came. Mama curled into a ball in a dark room.

Mama with her eyes wild, her robe hanging open. *Your fault. You should have...*

Tears built up again and dropped on my legs. Only this time something had shifted in my head. Why couldn't I have a normal mother? One who loved me the way Mrs. Johnson loved her girls. One who didn't swallow a bottle of pills and get sent off for shock treatments.

## THREE

THAT NIGHT DADDY CAME in late and slipped quietly into my room. Half-asleep, I mumbled, "How's Mama? Is she mad at me for not staying home?"

Daddy leaned over and tucked a loose strand of hair behind my ear. "Not that I'm aware. Sleep tight." His lips brushed my forehead, then he padded away in his stocking feet into his own room.

Every chance I got the next day, I asked Daddy questions about what the place in Wichita Falls was like. Did Mama have to wear a hospital gown? Would she get to come home and visit? Could we go see her? I hung on the kitchen counter, asking even more questions while Daddy smeared mustard on a piece of bread and slapped on a slice of bologna. "When does she start her treatment? Will she take pills or shots?"

"They didn't give me the treatment schedule. It's not a regular hospital, so the patients wear their normal clothes." He filled his thermos with coffee.

"That's good." Since Mama's regular clothes the last month had been a terry-cloth robe and nightgown, I couldn't really picture her. Daddy had packed her a suitcase though.

He screwed the lid onto the thermos. "There's also a nice court-yard with benches, and some of the other patients were feeding the squirrels when I left."

"Did Mama like it? Did she want to feed the squirrels?"

"Not while I was there. You sure are full of questions." He snapped the lid on his lunch box and looked at me. "This ain't no time to be brooding about your mama, so I want to get something straight. Mama's in the right place, and you've got the whole summer, so I want you outdoors having fun." He thumped me on the arm and left for his evening shift at the plant.

I didn't want Daddy to think I was brooding, and he was right about having the whole summer. So Tuwana and I started working on our newspaper like we planned.

On the walk to her house, a curlicue of smoke lifted above the trees on my left. The top of a high chain-link fence surrounding the gasoline plant came into view beyond the camp. Inside the fence, gray buildings with rows and rows of windows had smokestacks at the ends pointing up like Roman candles. Near the front, great white balls of steel, taller than three houses, huddled together. Containers of some kind. Engine noises and hissing sounds filled the air—refining natural gas, Daddy said. He told me underground pipes brought the gas in where it went through a series of boiling, compressing, and cooling like the biggest science experiment you ever saw. From there it went through an underground maze to another plant that made gasoline, the kind you get at the filling station. Daddy worked crazy shifts, a week of daylights, then a week of evenings, then graveyards, but he said it sure as heck beat working on the oil rigs.

Tuwana dragged out her mother's Royal typewriter, and we set it up outside on a scratchy green army blanket.

She hunched over, pecking the keys, while I dictated what to write and spelled words for her. One *m* in *Siamese* for the article about the Zyskowskis' new kittens for sale. Five dollars each.

"I wish you'd let me type the stencil," I said after spelling the sixth word for her. "I'm the one who wants to be a newspaper reporter."

"It's my mother's typewriter from when she went to steno school, so I do the typing, okay?"

She plunked away, and every three or four pecks, she tilted her head, first one way and then the other. I ignored her and stretched out my legs. Leaning back on my elbows, I let the sun warm my face. Puffy white clouds drifted past. A dragon. An elephant. A ship with pointy ends like the Vikings sailed. My mind drifted too with the *tap-tap-tap* in the background. When it stopped, I glanced over at Tuwana.

"Tuwana, what happened to your hair?"

"It's about time you noticed. You've been here thirty minutes and not one word."

"Well, what happened to it?"

"This, you may be pleased to know, is a poodle cut. Mother gave me a Toni perm last night. It's the latest thing. Don't you love it?"

"Well, it's perky, like a poodle, I guess, if that's what you were going for."

"You oughta have my mom cut your hair and give you a Toni. Then we'd be the most popular girls in seventh grade."

"I could cut my hair, frizz it up, and wear nothing but my birthday suit to school, and I still wouldn't be popular." The image of me streaking in the nude made me shudder. *Gross.*

"You're too serious, Miss Nose-in-a-book."

"I prefer to think of myself as creative and introspective." I threw out the last word from our sixth-grade vocabulary list and liked the way it rolled off my tongue.

"Boring, you mean. Just like this dumb paper. What we need around here is some excitement."

"As in..."

Tuwana spent the next thirty minutes talking about boys and her mother's idea that she should try out for cheerleader in junior high since all the cheerleaders were popular. And just for the record, I didn't mind a bit. The sun soaked into my skin, and while Tuwana twittered, I thought about what Goldie said about no two people on this earth being alike.

As far as me and Tuwana, she got that right. I was a plain vanilla wafer, and Tuwana was like a squirt of whipped cream.

After Tuwana finished typing, I gathered up the stencil and my notebook and took the long way home—down the blacktop road that split Graham Camp in half. Once I'd counted every one of the houses. Seventy-two divided up into nine rows. All the exact same box shape with cement porches and a ribbon of sidewalk rolling out to the street. Belinda and Melinda Zyskowski skipped rope as I passed by. *"Cinderella, dressed in yellow."* Poppy Brady, Fritz's new wife, sprayed the garden hose on the hollyhocks in her front yard, and Doobie Thornton whizzed by on his Vespa. He waved and beeped the horn.

Graham Camp. Not even a dot on the Texas map. Besides the houses, we had a playground on one end next to the community hall. Across the main entrance, we had Bailey's store and the Hilltop Church. The only thing missing was a school, so we rode the bus twelve miles to Mandeville, which did get its own little dot on the map.

At home I turned on the television, but the reception was off. Wavy lines swam across the screen, so I got up to adjust the rabbit ears, then sat back on the couch and picked at the scab on my arm from where I'd scratched it on the rosebush. At first I didn't think about much of anything, but that jingle with the Toni twins came on. Why would Tuwana think I'd want her mother to give me a Toni perm? You didn't just pick any old mom to give you the latest hairdo. Mama should be the one helping me decide about my hair and whether I wanted to be a cheerleader. No, definitely not cheerleading, but I would like it if Mama would cut my bangs or buy me a ribbon for my hair once in a while. That's what mothers do. They don't swallow pills and get shock treatments.

With my fingernail, I scraped at another piece of the scab on my arm. A drop of blood popped up, so I spit on my finger and smeared it away. Another drop came, and I watched it ooze toward my hand. My eyes got that hot feeling before tears come. A tear splatted on my arm, mixing with the blood. What would it be like to have a mother like Alice Johnson? Not exactly like her, but one who cared about my hair and baked cookies for no reason? When my nose started dripping, I got up to get a Kleenex.

The door to Mama and Daddy's room stood half open. I thought of finding Mama that day, her body curled into a parenthesis under the quilt. Her red hair tangled around her pale face, dotty with freckles. The prickly feeling I got when I couldn't wake her. Taking a deep breath, I pushed the door open.

Emptiness filled the room. Mama's quilt, folded at the end of the bed, drew me toward it. The blue and green and pastel patches sewn together were the Dresden Plate pattern, Mama once told me. I took the quilt in my hands and sat cross-legged on the bed, outlining the stitches with my fingertips. I slipped the quilt around my shoulders. It felt cold, like the underside of a pillow you turn over on a hot summer night. Mama's lilac cologne drifted up, but mostly it reminded me of stale morning breath.

What good had this quilt done Mama? None that I could tell. She'd swallowed the pills anyway.

I threw it off and left it in a jumble. That's when I saw the book lying on the nightstand on Mama's side, laid out flat, like she'd half-read it. *Gone with the Wind*. Mama's favorite book.

I picked it up and carried it to my room, feeling like I'd snitched a piece of licorice from Willy Bailey's store. Maybe Mama wouldn't mind. I took down the High Plains Bank calendar thumbtacked above my desk and, beginning with the day Daddy took Mama to the hospital, made an X for each day she'd been gone. Two so far. According to Daddy, Mama would be home in nineteen days. I flipped to the back of *Gone with the Wind*. One thousand and twenty-four pages. Dividing in my head, it came to fifty-four pages a day. Wouldn't Mama be surprised that I read her favorite book?

On my bed, I doubled the pillow behind my head and opened the book.

*"Scarlett O'Hara was not beautiful, but men seldom realized it when caught by her charm as the Tarleton twins were...."*

Scarlett had decided on a plan to win Ashley Wilkes away from Melanie when I looked to see how many pages I'd read. Seventy-six the first night!

I thought about Scarlett and how she went after what she wanted. That's what I should do: come up with a plan. Gathering Pedro, my lumpy, stuffed dog, in one arm and the book in the other, I lay on top of my chenille spread and thought about Mama. She used to make cookies like Alice Johnson, only Mama made the cutout sugar kind. Once she made me a dress, plaid with a ruffle on the bottom and long sashes for a bow in the back. Once. A long time ago. A lump came in my throat.

When Mama came home, I would help her cook and tell her my dream of being on the school paper. She would laugh at the things Tuwana told me, and we would pick out my school clothes from the Montgomery Ward catalog. My new Mama, after being shocked back to her real self, would talk to me about those things you can't talk about with a dad. You know, the things from the fifth-grade film when they sent the boys to the gym for an hour. It hadn't happened to me yet, but Mamas know. They just know.

Other things too, like makeup and what to get Daddy for Christmas.

Most of all, she would love me just because.

## FOUR

T UWANA AND I made arrangements to use the mimeograph machine at the plant office. Mrs. Ford ran the office and half the plant. Daddy always joked that when Mrs. Ford goes, there goes the plant. She was terribly nice, plump, and could talk on the phone and type at the same time. She told us to come on Tuesday, so that morning, I headed over to Tuwana's. As I passed the row of tin garages in the middle of her block, her dad, Benny Ray Johnson, lay under their rusty Studebaker with his boots sticking out. He was whistling "The Tennessee Waltz" and making an awful racket under the car. Tuwana waved and tossed a bag of garbage into the incinerator next to the garages.

*Whoosh.* The burning gas of the incinerator caught the paper sack on fire followed by an S curl of smoke. Day and night, the jets burned, waiting to crisp our garbage the minute we pitched it in. It reminded me of the lake of fire and eternal torment Brother Henry preached about.

Two years before, I gave my life to Jesus after one of Brother Henry's hellfire and damnation sermons, which was practically every week, but one particular Sunday, it got my attention. Jesus didn't call my name like Brother Henry said he would, but I got a choked up feeling in my throat that I took to be Jesus. Later, when Irene Flanagan started playing "I Surrender All," I went forward. Funny, but all this time later, I still remember the polka-dotted shirtwaist Mrs. Flanagan wore that day and the sun fanning through the window like melted butter and me right in it.

Tuwana pranced over to me, and I could tell something was up. "You'll never guess what happened! Our prayers have been answered." Her voice had an electric sound to it, and for a minute I thought it might have something to do with Brother Henry or the prayer chain.

"What prayers?"

"Our prayers for some excitement. You'll never guess, so I'll just tell you. Two words. *Cly MacLemore.*"

"Huh?" Sometimes Tuwana made no sense at all.

"MacLemore. Norm MacLemore's nephew. He's visiting from California. Can you believe it? Excitement with a capital *X*."

"I have no idea what you're talking about." We started toward her house.

"Fourteen years old. And from California, did I tell you that?"

Tuwana opened the back door and hollered to her mother that we were going to the plant office now. All the way over, Tuwana chattered about this being the best thing since bobby socks and that we simply had to figure out how to meet him.

Mrs. Ford waved us into the office and showed us how to put the stencil on the machine, then flipped a switch and went back to her typewriter. *Clackety-clack.* Warm, inky-smelling papers rolled off the drum. Fifty sheets. We gave Mrs. Ford the first copy, free of charge, since she let us use the mimeograph.

"The *Dandelion Times*. Catchy title. Y'all musta gotten your inspiration from my yard. Wall-to-wall dandelions!" Her eyes crinkled up when she laughed, and dots of sweat beaded up along her upper lip. She pulled a hanky from the front of her blouse and patted her face.

We thanked her and left, going door-to-door selling the papers for ten cents apiece. Every other word out of Tuwana's mouth was something about coming up with a spectacular plan to meet Cly MacLemore. "Come on, Sammie—since you're so creative, you think of something."

"I'm not very interested in boys. I told you that. If you're meant to meet him, you will. *Que sera, sera.*"

Tuwana made a face and huffed off to the next house.

We'd each made eighty cents by the time we got to the Mac-Lemores' street. Slim Wallace's truck sat in front of his house across from Norm and Eva's, so I started up his sidewalk.

"Not Mr. Wallace." Tuwana's fingernails dug into my arm. "Mother says he's disgusting."

"We're just selling papers. It's not like we're going in or anything. And besides, what's wrong with Mr. Wallace?"

"He's a murderer, that's what."

Sometimes Tuwana came up with the weirdest things, but this was one I hadn't heard before. Mr. Wallace lived by himself, I knew that. He always came to church and sat alone on the back row, slipping out before the last amen. He was quiet and a little rough looking, but a killer? Not likely. I marched up his sidewalk and knocked.

"Yes, what may I do for you, young lady?" Mr. Wallace had a kind face and cloudy gray eyes.

"I'm Sammie Tucker. My friend Tuwana and I are selling our camp newspaper, the *Dandelion Times*. We thought you might like one. Ten cents."

"Certainly. I'll take two." He pulled a quarter from his gray work pants.

"You don't have to buy two 'cuz there's two of us." I held the quarter out to him.

"I'll send one to my daughter. She'll get a kick out of it."

"Thanks." I handed him two copies. "Thanks a lot, Mr. Wallace."

When I turned around, feeling pretty smug, Tuwana stood in the middle of the street like she'd been caught in a game of freeze tag.

"Look, a quarter. Your mean old Mr. Wallace bought two papers." I waved it in front of her, but she was staring across the street. A faded green Rambler with a California license plate was parked half on the grass beside the MacLemores'.

She grabbed my arm and talked through her teeth. "There he is. Sitting on the porch. Oh my gosh, how do I look?" Unfrozen now, she fluffed her poodle hair.

A guy who looked older than us sat hunched over on the steps. He had greasy black hair combed back at the sides with a V dipping down his forehead. His black leather jacket looked melting hot.

"Oh, he is so cool. Did you see him blowing smoke rings? Don't look now, but he's staring right at us." Her voice quivered with excitement.

"Here's your big chance. See if he wants to buy a paper." I stepped toward the MacLemores' and saw that an extension cord hooked to a tan plastic radio snaked out the screen door. "Jailhouse Rock" blared from the slatted speaker.

"Excuse me." Tuwana squeaked out a giggle.

The guy moved his shoulders in time to the music. "Who are you?"

"Tuwana Johnson. And this is Sammie Tucker."

"Crazy. A girl named Sam." He had on rolled-up Levi's. Loafers. No socks. A wrinkled white undershirt under the leather jacket. Sunlight bounced from the silver do-dads on the collar.

I stuck out my hand. "Pleased to meet you."

"No need for the formality, cat."

"My name's Sammie, not cat."

"Just an expression. Didn't mean to rattle your cage." He tossed the stub of his cigarette into the grass.

Tuwana stood, her eyes as round as saucers. "'Rattle your cage'? You are soooo funny."

Elvis still crooned through the radio. "Elvis…" Tuwana's eyelids fluttered like a mosquito had flown into her pupil. "Don't you just love him?"

"He's all right. Bossin' cat the way he strums his guitar."

"You must be the MacLemores' nephew." I got right to the point. All that worry about meeting him, and here he was, in the flesh. A hood. That's what Daddy would call him.

Tuwana prattled on about writing a summer newspaper and how we'd be glad to show him around Graham Camp. In the middle of our telling him about our Fourth of July picnic, the screen door burst open and a man stepped out. His bald head sat right on his shoulders, which sloped down to arms as big as tree trunks. Squinty eyes set close together glared at us.

"Junior, I'm leaving." He pitched a canvas duffel toward the Rambler and turned to Cly, or was it Junior? Maybe we'd met the wrong relative. For Tuwana's sake, I hoped so.

Then Norm MacLemore came out on the porch, nearly tripping on the extension cord. He swore under his breath. "Don't take any wooden nickels." Norm shook hands with the man I didn't know. "I'll straighten the boy out for you."

"See ya, Pop." Cly stepped toward the thick-bodied man and held out his hand.

Instead of shaking hands, the man narrowed his eyes at Cly. Stone-cold blue eyes. His lip curled up on one side. "Keep your sorry self outta trouble."

A painful look crossed Cly's face, and for a minute I thought he might be going to cry. It lasted for only a flash, and then he looked down at the grass.

His dad stalked to the Rambler, got in, and clanked down the street without looking back.

"Grass needs mowing," Norm said to Cly. To us he said, "Don't think he'll be needing your help." He kicked the radio and stormed into the house. Static hissed from the speaker.

Swooping up the radio, Cly started up the steps.

"Wait a minute." I held out a paper. "We'd like you to have this—Junior, wasn't it? No charge."

"Thanks. Junior's what my family calls me. Friends call me Cly, short for Clyburn. After him." He cocked his head in the direction the Rambler had taken.

"Fine. We'll call you Cly." I gave him a wobbly smile, anxious to get away. "Maybe we'll see you around. How long you staying?"

"According to my old man, until I show some gratitude and change my attitude." He glanced at the *Dandelion Times*.

"What's wrong with your attitude?" Tuwana asked.

"That's what I say. What's wrong with my attitude?" He snorted and looked over his shoulder at the screen door.

Tuwana flashed him a big smile. "Mother says attitude is everything. Clothes, hair, the way you talk...That's why she thinks I'd be a great cheerleader. You know, the way I've never met a stranger. Like you, Cly. I knew right away we'd hit it off."

"I...I'd better go...see what Norm wants me to do." He disappeared into the house, leaving us stranded on the front lawn.

Tuwana lifted her shoulders. "Now what?"

One thing I knew: I didn't want to sell any more papers, so I suggested we go over to Willy's store for a Coke. I jiggled the change in my pocket and took off.

Overhead, the sun beat down, hot as blue blazes. Wavy air

drifted up from the gooey tar on the highway as we trudged in silence. Not even the anticipation of an icy Grapette from the soda cooler in the back of Willy's store could erase the memory of the look Cly's father had given him.

I'd seen that look before—in Mama's eyes the night my baby sister died.

## FIVE

GOPHER'S POND SAT IN the middle of a cow pasture a few miles from Graham Camp. The Chevy bumped along the ruts to take Daddy and me to his favorite fishing hole, his treat for both of us surviving the first week without Mama. Secretly, I suspected he didn't want to spend time in our empty house, and that was fine with me. I spent all the time I could over at Tuwana's or helping Goldie with the aviary.

When we got to the pond, the sun glowed red in the west with streaks of purple splitting the sky. Long shadows fell on the mossy pond as Daddy tied the red and white float on my fishing line. He smiled while I threaded a squirmy night crawler onto my hook, then set the can of worms between us.

I got the first bite but no fish, and he handed over the coffee can for me to dig out another worm. After I threw my line back out, I sat cross-legged on a clump of grass and looked at Daddy.

"What do you think Mama's doing right now?"

"Don't rightly know. Maybe playing a game of checkers in the game room."

"Who would she play checkers with?"

"Other patients, I guess. Maybe one of the attendants. She's probably thinking about you right now. . . . 'I wonder what Sammie's doing.' I bet that's crossed her mind."

"You think?"

"I don't think. I know."

Daddy's fishing pole jumped and bent toward the pond. He stood up and started reeling in the line. He smiled when he pulled a tail-flipping, whiskery fish from the water.

"Look at that, would you? A fine little mud cat. A one-pounder, I'd say." He put it on a stringer and lowered it into the edge of the murky water. Before he baited his hook, he took a box of matches from the tackle box and lit the Coleman lantern. The wick sputtered and took off, a bright circle in the fading evening light.

When he threw his line back out, I quizzed him some more. "Another thing I've been wondering. What do you know about Mr. Wallace?"

"Slim?" He had a surprised look on his face.

"Tuwana says he murdered someone."

"Is that a fact? Can't recall ever hearing that yarn down at the plant, but Slim spent a lot of years out in the oil field. Rough stuff happens out there—things you and Tuwana are too young to be fretting over." He shifted his boots and sat up straighter. "Could be it's just a tall tale someone invented to entertain themselves. Whoa, Sam, your float went under. Start turning the reel; pull up the slack."

My armpits started sweating. The line went tight, nearly yanking the pole from my hands. Slow. Steady. I turned the reel and pulled in the fish—a whopper, Daddy said. He grabbed it in his outstretched hand and asked me for the needle-nose pliers to remove the hook. When he put it on the stringer, I could tell it was at least six inches longer than the one Daddy'd caught. Its back, as slippery as a salamander, glistened in the lantern's glow.

Thirty minutes later, after neither one of us got another nibble, Daddy said we ought to be getting back. He packed up the tackle box, blew out the lantern, and put our catfish in a wet gunnysack in the trunk.

On the ride home I asked Daddy if working in the oil field was the same as working on the rigs I'd heard him talk about.

"There's lot of different jobs, but yes, the rigs are the main thing, minding them day and night when the gushers come in."

"Were you out minding a rig when my baby sister died?"

Daddy didn't answer for a long time. I wasn't even sure he heard me, but after a while, he said, "I didn't reckon you remembered that."

"I remember a lot of things." A fuzzy picture came into my head of Mama holding a baby, me standing beside her. Before we came to Graham Camp. A baby named Sylvia.

"Do you think Mama still misses Sylvia?"

"I'm sure she does." Daddy's hands gripped the steering wheel. "You don't forget your own flesh and blood."

"Do you miss her?"

"Every day of my life, but I don't let it get me like it does your mama. That's what keeps her so worked up all the time. Reckon that's one of the things she's talking to the doctors about."

He kept his eyes on the road but reached over and patted me on the knee. "I got me a fine girl right here. Ain't too bad a fisherman either." He pulled into the drive and parked in front of our tin garage. "Think you'd like to learn how to clean a fish?"

I wrinkled my nose. "I guess so."

That night I wrote my first letter to Mama, a long rambling lot about Tuwana wanting to be a cheerleader and our first edition of the *Dandelion Times*. I wrote a whole page about Goldie and her favorite parakeet, Lady Aster, who Goldie said was the top of the pecking order. When I thought about mentioning Cly, I chickened out. Mostly because of that look his dad gave him and the creepy way it reminded me of Mama after Sylvia died. Disgust. That's what I'd seen. Disappointment. Was Mama disappointed that I was the one who lived and Sylvia didn't?

After I sealed the envelope and wrote Mama's name on the front, I put on my green pj's, switched off the lamp, and slid between my bedsheets. Moonlight sprinkled through gauzy curtains, so I opened the window and rested my chin on the sill. Leaves fluttered like butterflies playing tag above me. A cloud glided across the moon, hiding the light.

Sylvia. We never talked about her. Ever. If her name popped up, the room would go quiet as a morning fog and Mama would quickly jump onto another subject. Daddy might think I didn't remember the night Sylvia died, but I never stopped thinking about it.

Whooping cough. That's what Mama said she had. Poor baby. Barking like a puppy.

I had kissed her chubby, round cheeks. "Shoo, get away from her." Mama pushed me away and picked up my squirming sister. She coughed even more—sharp yips that came from inside her tiny chest. Mama held her on her hip and jiggled the phone buttons under the receiver. "Come on, blast it, start working." Back and forth, she paced from the phone to the window looking for Daddy to come home, until I thought she might wear out the floorboards. Snow globs stuck to the window screen, and a fierce wind howled outside our front room.

"Where is he? Why doesn't he come home?" She tried the phone again.

Huddled in Daddy's chair with my knees drawn up, I peeked at Mama and tried to think of something to do, something to make Mama happy, to help Sylvia. When I got a washrag from the bathroom and brought it for Sylvia's diaper change, water dripped on the floor.

"Now look what you've done." Mama threw one of Sylvia's tiny blankets on the floor to mop up the drips. "Do something. Just stay out of the way."

In my coloring book, I stayed in the lines on a horse picture and printed my name around the edges of the paper. Twice on each side. When I showed Mama, she waved me away and started changing Sylvia's gown. Lying there naked, a dent the size of a thumbprint sucked in every time Sylvia opened her mouth to take a breath. When Mama got the clean gown on Sylvia, she gathered her up and held her tight, shuffling over to try the phone again.

The wind made a flapping noise in the chimney, and snow completely covered the window screen. Still, Mama paced across the floor, back and forth. Sylvia's cough got weaker and weaker until all I could hear were sucking noises in her tiny chest. Mama sat on the couch and rocked back and forth, kissing Sylvia's face even after it turned blue and her dimpled fists went limp. When I stood beside them, Mama squinted her eyes at me. Flashes of contempt. I wished I had been the one who died. Not Sylvia.

The cloud slid past the Graham Camp moon lighting up the butterfly leaves again. A coyote howled in the canyons away from the camp. Closer, another coyote answered. A long, moaning howl. I shivered and closed the window. Then I crawled back into bed and hid under the covers.

## [ SIX ]

WHEN DADDY HAD GRAVEYARDS the next week, he came home and slept in the mornings, which meant I had to creep around quietly until it was time to go help Goldie or meet up with Tuwana. On the morning after his second graveyard, I discovered I was down to my last clean pair of underpants. I waited until I heard Daddy snoring, then sorted the dirty clothes from the bathroom hamper.

Mama had taught me about whites and darks and colored clothes and how much soap to use when I was eight or nine years old, young enough that I had to stand on an overturned bucket to clothespin the wet things on the line. I didn't need the bucket anymore. After stuffing a load of whites in the washer on the back porch, I turned the dial for the water and got out the Tide. "One level cup per load," Mama had told me. The soap box was empty, just a few grains in the bottom. I looked around for another box, but didn't find one. I got the Palmolive dish soap that Mama liked because it made her hands soft, measured out a cup of the liquid, and poured it in. Then I left for Tuwana's.

She had on new purple shorts and a lavender-checked halter top and twirled around so I could get the whole effect.

"I'm waiting for PJ to get here so we can practice our cheers."

"PJ?"

"Yeah, I talked her into trying out since you don't want to."

"Sounds fun. I've been thinking about something else though. Since you want to know more about Cly, maybe we could write an article about him for our newspaper."

"That's a little juvenile, don't you think?" Tuwana bent over and touched her toes.

"We need new ideas for the paper. Think about it. Cly appears out of nowhere for some reason we don't yet know. That would grab people's attention."

"It's not that. The whole paper is juvenile. We're not in grade school now." She plopped into the green glider on her front lawn and picked up her *Teen* magazine, flipping the pages as she used her foot to scritch the glider back and forth.

"Are you saying you don't want to do the paper anymore?"

"You got it. I'd rather work on my cheers. With PJ." She stood up and stretched her arms over her head, leaning to one side and then the other.

"You and PJ, huh?"

What was so special about PJ? Aside from being a little plump— like her mother, Mrs. Ford—she was nice, but up until now Tuwana had never paid her a speck of attention. Besides, Tuwana and I had been best friends since first grade. On the first day of school when I headed down the aisle of the bus, a girl with yellow pigtails and no front teeth grabbed my arm. "Whatcha think you're doing? Only the big kids get the back seats. My mother says you and me gotta sit up front so we can't hear the teenagers talking dirty."

She yanked me down beside her. "I'm Tuwana Johnson, and we can't even sit over the tire humps until junior high." She giggled, the same giggle she still had.

Was it the newspaper or was it me she didn't want anything to do with? Before I could ask her, PJ jogged up, panting and wiping sweat off her forehead.

"You'll never guess who I saw! Doobie and that new kid from California. Buzzing around on Doobie's Vespa. Two creeps together." She looked over her shoulder like maybe they had followed her.

"Cly and Doobie?" Tuwana wrinkled her nose. "Doobie's the biggest nerd in six counties. Why would Cly be hanging around him?"

"I just report the facts. However, they did mention playing basketball down at the playground in case you're interested."

Tuwana jumped at the idea. "Let's go." She looked at me. "You coming?"

Why not? All I had to do was laundry.

When we arrived at the court, sweat glistened on the shirtless backs of Cly and Doobie, who were playing one-on-one. Cly reminded me of a bulldog, and Doobie looked like part monkey with his stringy arms and legs.

"You birds want to play?" Doobie yelled, then leaned over to catch his breath.

"Cheerleading's more my sport. Mine and PJ's." Tuwana grinned at Cly.

"Yeah, Doobie said you dolls have some fancy clinic where you're going to learn how to rattle your pom-poms." Cly grinned in a lopsided way. No sneer.

"For Doobie's information"—Tuwana had an edge in her voice—"it's a school to learn proper techniques and poise."

"Didn't mean to razz your berries, Tu-tu." Doobie snapped his fingers.

Trying to act cool like Cly?

"So, Cly, you're liking it here?" I threw that out, still thinking about writing a newspaper article about him.

"What's not to like? The drill sergeant and I have come to a truce. I do all the jobs Norm lines up for me; then I get time off for good behavior." His eyes crinkled at the corners when he smiled.

"So tell us about California." Tuwana batted her eyes and stepped close to Cly. "I bet you see movie stars all the time, right?"

"Let them run in my crowd? They're too stuck-up. Me and my buddies, we make our own fun."

I wasn't sure I wanted to know what that was, but Tuwana did. "Like what?"

"Nothing your pretty virgin ears oughta hear." He winked at Doobie.

I picked up the basketball and bounced it a few times. "Beat you in a game of twenty-one."

Tuwana gave me a funny look, but Cly and Doobie both hollered, "You're on."

Cly was better than I expected him to be and beat Doobie and me twice by the time the noon whistle blew. Cly said he had to go see what the sergeant had for him to do. He and Doobie roared off on the Vespa.

"Show-off," Tuwana said as the three of us started home.

"What?" Sometimes Tuwana's thoughts came from midair and straight out her mouth.

"You heard me. Shooting baskets with the boys. Mother says you have to let men think we're the weaker sex."

"It's not like I won. Besides, I think the best way to get to know someone is by being yourself. And it was fun."

"Come on, PJ. We've got cheers to practice." To me she said, "Don't bother coming over tomorrow. Mother is taking me and PJ shopping in Amarillo."

Arm in arm, they pranced off.

I shuffled home, kicking rocks the whole way. Cly seemed different now. Not such a greaser. And fun. Still a mystery, though, about why his dad brought him to Texas.

The minute I got to the back door of our house, the bottom fell out of my stomach. Water seeped under the screen door, trailing down the porch steps. Foamy water with a Palmolive scent. I opened the screen, and all I could see was foam as high as the washer, bubbles popping everywhere, and above that—Daddy's face.

"What the devil happened here, Sis? Run and get some towels. Be careful...."

My feet slipped on the slick floor, and I cracked my knee on the door frame, landing on my behind in a cloud of bubbles. Every time I tried to push myself up, my hands flew out from under me, and I got a soapy taste in my mouth. Daddy disappeared, came back with an armful of towels, and made a dam so the water wouldn't go any farther into the kitchen.

When I finally got to my feet, my knee hurt so bad I couldn't put any weight on it. Daddy propped open the back door and pushed water outside with the broom. Biting my lip to keep from crying, I tried to say I was sorry, but Daddy yelled at me. "Don't just stand there. Wring out those towels and see if you can find some dry ones."

I got to work wringing out the wet towels and found three dry ones in the bathroom to put down in their place. The bubbles only came to my knees now. Mop, wring. Mop, wring. My arms ached from twisting the towels in the sink. We worked and worked until the water and foam were all gone.

Daddy frowned at me. "Care to tell me what happened?"

I explained about needing clean underwear and that we were out of Tide so I used a cup of Palmolive instead. The words choked in my throat as I realized my mistake and told Daddy I was sorry.

"A girl your age ain't got no business running a house. The thing is, a cup of Tide and a cup of dish soap ain't the same thing. Danged if I know why, but them's the facts."

"It's a good thing you woke up when you did or it might've flooded the whole house."

"The phone ringing's what roused me."

"Who was it?"

"Bad news, I'm afraid." He cleared his throat. "Mama's going to be gone longer than we thought. An extra week, the doctor said."

"No! You should go get her now. I know I can make her feel better. I'll stay home and not run off to Tuwana's and..." My shoulders started shaking, and tears stung my eyes. I reached for Daddy and buried my face in his undershirt. He stroked the back of my head with his rough hand. I fought back the tears and looked up at him.

"And another thing. I hurt my knee." A purple lump the size of an egg swelled below my kneecap. My chest got a tight feeling. "It hurts so bad."

The ache didn't come from my knee, but someplace deep inside. Daddy put his arms around me and held me close. Tears built up again, and I couldn't stop crying.

## SEVEN

AFTER ALL THAT CRYING, I decided to quit feeling sorry for myself and just enjoy the summer. I would worry about Mama when she came home. Daddy took me to Piggly Wiggly in Mandeville to get some more Tide, and I threw in a tin of cocoa for the brownies I wanted to make for the Fourth of July picnic. I made a batch every two days, having little conversations in my head with Mama, pretending we lived on a plantation in Georgia, just like in *Gone with the Wind*.

"*Tell me, Mama, do you like pecans in your brownies?*"

"*I love anything you make, as long as you serve it with sweet tea.*"

Mama would nibble the edge from the brownie and laugh like Scarlett, and I would think about us wearing swishy dresses and sitting on the veranda, fanning away the mosquitoes.

I made a new circle on the calendar for July 7, when Mama would now be coming home. Every night I read more of Mama's favorite book and wrote her long letters so she wouldn't have so much to catch up on when she did come home.

Dear Mama,

What a weird day. This morning Daddy said we ought to give Brother Henry a whirl. Irene Flanagan gave an update on her husband's gout, and Brother Henry asked for prayer for the safe delivery of their baby. "The sooner the better," Sister

Doris said, as she sat there shushing Matthew, Mark, and Luke in the row ahead of us. During the singing of "Showers of Blessing," Sister Doris grabbed her back and let out a squawk. Then she waddled down the aisle to the back of the church. Lola Greenwood said her water broke. Luke ran after her, stomping in the puddles.

That was the end of church. Mrs. Greenwood grabbed the little boys, and Brother Henry took off with Sister Doris.

Tuwana called this afternoon to say Sister Doris had a girl. No John-John in keeping with the Gospels like everyone figured. They named the baby Penelope. Tuwana said Penelope was a prophetess in the Old Testament, but I think Tuwana's a little off, don't you?

Tomorrow Tuwana and PJ leave for their cheerleading clinic. They're going to make great cheerleaders.

Love and kisses,

Sammie

Daddy had daylights the week Tuwana and PJ were gone, so I helped Goldie every morning with the parakeets. Above the racket of Lady Aster and the others, she gave me advice about the three new pimples that had popped up on my forehead overnight. "Just a part of growing up, child. Your body's changing. Before you know it you'll be needing a brassiere and will start getting your monthly visits."

Eew! I looked at my chest. Flat. Like a boy's. And I didn't even want to think about what would happen when I got my period. Who would I tell?

Goldie dabbed witch hazel on my face and gave me the bottle to take home. That and a fifty-cent-piece-sized pot of pasty goo. "To hide the damage," she said, and sent me on my way.

At home I read another eighty pages of *Gone with the Wind.*

Things weren't going well for Scarlett. Married to Frank Kennedy and the Civil War going on all over the place. When I took a bathroom break, I decided to use the cover-up cream from Goldie. I leaned in close to the mirror, and when I did, something caught my eye near the baseboard between the toilet and the sink. I got down on my hands and knees and picked up a small white pill. One of Mama's. I held it between my finger and thumb and examined it. One tiny pill lost from the whole bottle. What if Mama had taken this one too? Would one more have been enough to kill her? How had it ended up on the floor? Did Mama have a screaming fit and fly apart? So much that her hands shook and she lost this one pill?

My chest got that squeezed-out-of-air feeling.

The glare of the light over the mirror made me imagine they'd strapped Mama in a chair to interrogate her, like the communists I'd seen on television. Question after question, zapping her with an electric rod if she didn't get the answer right. Was that what shock treatments were?

I couldn't breathe. Air. I needed fresh air. I slung the pill into the toilet and flushed it, watching the water swirl around and *glug-glug-glug* to the bottom, taking the pill with it.

I ran out the door and grabbed my bike, just to get away. My knee still hurt from the day I banged it on the door frame, so I rode slow, just taking it easy. Besides the street running through the middle of camp, a blacktop circled all the houses, passing the playground and community hall. One mile exactly. I made one loop, the wind flying through my hair, then reversed and started the other way. By the time I turned west, the sun angled down overhead, leaving a glare on everything. Two figures stood in Slim Wallace's garden, but I couldn't make out who they were.

One of them, the short one, had a hoe that he kept chopping toward the ground. I heard Mr. Wallace's voice when I inched closer. "You can do it, son. Give it another go." More whacking. Was it Cly with the hoe?

I stopped pedaling and coasted forward slowly. Sure enough. Cly turned around and saw me.

"Hey, Sam." He waved the hoe. "Come see what I did." He and Slim gazed at something in the dirt.

Mr. Wallace bent down with a stick and moved the earth around. When he stood up, he held a small object in his hand and shoved it toward Cly. "Your bragging rights, son."

Cly held up the tail end of a rattlesnake.

Mr. Wallace chuckled. "Bet you ain't ever killed one of these in California, have you?"

"No, sir. 'Bout scared me into next week." He held up the rattle for me to see. To Mr. Wallace he said, "Thanks, that was wicked. And forget what I said earlier...about you being an old coot and gone off your rocker."

"No problem." Mr. Wallace took the hoe. "Reckon I do give that image, talking to Dottie the way I do."

"Who's Dottie?" I asked.

"My wife. Leastwise, she was once upon a time. Sure gets lonely without her. Me and her have some good talks out here in my garden." His neck colored a splotchy red. "Guess I'd better mosey on home. See you young'ens later."

Cly told me the whole story—how Mr. Wallace made him kill the rattlesnake. He pointed to a spot on the ground where a pulpy, bloody mess remained. A few bits of shiny flesh shone through. Gross, like fish guts.

"Musta been four or five feet long. Coiled up like a spring when I started toward him. I coulda been killed, you know." He held up the rattle and shook it. The papery chatter made us both laugh.

"Like crazy, man, that was pure wicked. Wait till I show Doobie. You know for an old guy, Slim's pretty cool."

*     *     *

That night I wrote Mama a letter telling her about Cly coming from California to visit his aunt and uncle, about shooting baskets with Cly, and wasn't it stupendous that he killed a rattlesnake. After I took my bath, I stood in front of the mirror and gazed at myself. Skinny. Straight as a yardstick. I squinted and tried to imagine what I'd look like when I grew up, or at least when I turned thirteen. My eyes played a trick on me. Right there on the front of my chest, a pair of tan lumps about the size of two mosquito bites had raised up. I turned sideways to get a different angle, and sure enough, I had the beginning of breasts. Jeepers. I hoped I wouldn't need a training bra before Mama got home.

## EIGHT

WHILE WAITING FOR MAMA to come home, I laughed and clapped for Tuwana and PJ as they showed off the splits and jumps they learned at cheerleading school. Poise and technique weren't all they picked up. Words like *indubitably, precisely,* and *consequently* rolled off their tongues as easy as the "Two bits, four bits, six bits, a dollar" that echoed through the streets of Graham Camp.

On Father's Day, I wrote a poem for Daddy about fishing at Gopher's Pond and worms and lantern lights. Brother Henry gave me the idea in his sermon that day. "We honor God by honoring our parents." Daddy's lips quivered when he read it out loud. He Scotch-taped it to the Frigidaire and made us frog-in-the-hole eggs for supper.

The days flew by, hot and windy, blowing on toward July 7. When I wasn't helping Goldie or reading *Gone with the Wind,* I practiced making brownies for the Fourth of July picnic and wrote my daily letter to Mama. The one thing I tried not to do was spend too much time thinking about her shock treatments. Or what she would be like when she got home. Every night I prayed for a miracle—that the Mama I knew before Sylvia died would somehow be the one who came home.

Two days before the Fourth, all the older kids went to the

community hall to clean up for the celebration. You know, sweeping, mowing the grass, setting up the tables.

By the time we finished and stepped outside, the air felt like it was five hundred degrees. All the boys had gone, so Tuwana asked PJ and me to come over.

"I simply can't wait until the picnic," Tuwana said. "An entire day for fun. I'm hoping Cly will sit next to me."

PJ gnawed on a fingernail. "You ask me, you need to get your mind off Cly. Mom says he's nothing but T-R-O-U-B-L-E, same as his uncle."

"What's that supposed to mean?" Tuwana stopped in the middle of the street.

"Norm's got a temper. Mom says he's always mouthing off down at the plant."

I came to Tuwana's defense. "Just because Norm's that way doesn't mean Cly is."

"Yeah, well, think about this. Cly's dad got arrested one time for assault and got out of going to jail on a technicality. I think it's bad blood, if you know what I mean, Jelly Bean."

Tuwana's eyes lit up, and I thought she might sock PJ and knock off her glasses. Instead she said, "You're just jealous because the only one who will look at you is Doobie."

"Doobie's not as bad as you think. Besides, I just speak the truth as I see it." Her splotched face glistened with perspiration. "I'm going home. This heat's giving me a headache." She squinched her eyes and wiggled her fingers at us. "Toodles."

Tuwana and I trudged on toward her house in silence. To tell the truth, it was too hot to talk or even do much thinking.

Tuwana's mother sat in the green glider, a tall iced drink in her hand when we walked up. She had on a crisp yellow dress with cap sleeves and cheery pink lipstick.

"Hello, girls. Looks like you could use some lemonade."

"Absolutely." Tuwana frowned at her mother. "Why are you so dressed up?"

"Oh, you know. This heat's had me in the most dreadful state lately. Cross and grumpy with your daddy."

I knew that to be true as I'd heard them arguing a couple of evenings before when Tuwana and I sat in the very glider Mrs. Johnson now occupied. Something about a blowout on their Studebaker and if Benny Ray had an ounce of ambition, he would go into his father's insurance business and not make his family suffer living in such a dreadful place as Graham Camp.

When I asked Tuwana what was wrong with Graham Camp, she told me her mother thought it was dull and boring and didn't give us any cultural opportunities. "In case you haven't noticed, we're fifty miles from anywhere decent to go shopping or even to the picture show."

Now Mrs. Johnson let out a tinkling little laugh. "I thought I'd show him I'm still the sweet thing he married. You know the old saying: Timing is everything in dealing with a man."

"Timing for what?" Tuwana wanted to know.

"A little birdie told me your daddy was getting a promotion, which certainly will include a raise. Just the thing I've been waiting for, the chance to bring up the subject of new living room furniture. I've heard Danish provincial is the latest rage." She had a faraway look in her eyes.

"A little birdie or Mrs. Ford?"

Mrs. Johnson smiled and sipped her drink, leaving a pink smudge on the rim of the glass.

"Where is Daddy, anyway?"

"Gone to get new tires for the Studebaker. I'm making his favorite supper—grilled cheese on slabs of Texas toast—to show him I'm not mad anymore."

Tara and Tommie Sue sat in the elm shade on the sidewalk play-ing jacks, arguing over what came next.

"Eggs in the basket come next, not pigs in the pen," Tommie Sue whined.

"It's up to the one who's ahead, which is me...." Tara's eyes grew round. Then she screamed at the top of her lungs.

"Oh my gracious." Mrs. Johnson's face turned as pasty as a bottle of Elmer's glue. "How dare he?"

I looked around to see what had caused Tara to scream.

Then I saw it. A car glided to a stop right in front of us. A shade lighter than the summer sky, with scooped-out sides from the middle of the back door clear to the taillights in a dazzling darker blue. Shimmering. Metallic looking. The roof matched the side slashes. Silver trim sparkled in the sun. But the most amazing thing was the driver—Benny Ray Johnson.

My heart pounded. Tuwana's dad hadn't gotten new tires for the Studebaker. He'd bought a whole new car. I couldn't take my eyes off it.

"Daddy!" the girls shrilled, and swarmed the driver's side window. "Is it ours? Is it a Thunderbird? A Cadillac? Can we keep it?"

Mr. Johnson smiled, big beaver teeth shining. He rested his arm on the door where the window had been rolled down, and his muscular, hairy arm had a red heart tattoo with an arrow shooting through it.

"Yes, it's ours." His voice boomed. "Climb in. We're going for a spin." He waved in the direction of the house. "Sammie, Alice, come on. There's room for everyone. Bet I could fit half the block in here."

I raced toward the car, waiting to see where Mrs. Johnson would sit. When I looked back, she stood planted on the lawn, arms crossed. Her nostrils flared on a face that was now the color of strawberry jam.

I flinched and crawled into the back as Mr. Johnson hollered at Alice again. She stomped to the house and slammed the door behind her.

"What's wrong with Mother?" Tuwana asked, settling into the front passenger seat.

"Too much excitement, I reckon," her father said. "Maybe she's never seen an Edsel before. I know the feeling. Knocked my socks off when I first saw it. The car of the future, you know." He patted the dash.

"What does this do?" Tara pointed to a lever above the armrest.

"Electric windows. And up here"—he pointed to a circle of buttons in the center of the steering wheel—"Teletouch drive. Don't even have to take my hands from the wheel to put her into drive or reverse. Just push a button and we're off."

Mr. Johnson cruised along as faces peeked out their screen doors, gawking. He waved and beeped the horn as if it were the Mandeville Pioneer Day Parade. The breeze caught my hair, and I inhaled the smell of the new, cushy interior.

"Oh, Daddy, this is fabulos-o! All my friends will be sooooo impressed. I bet they don't even have cars like this in California. When can we take them for a ride?" Translation: *Cly won't be able to resist me now.*

"Anytime, Princess. Now watch this." He pointed out the power steering feature by using only his pinky finger on the wheel. We passed Bailey's store and the Hilltop Church, where he honked at Brother Henry mowing the parsonage lawn.

The sharp smell of sagebrush rushed in the open windows. Mr. Johnson bellowed "Deep in the Heart of Texas" in a low, throaty voice. I felt swept away to a time long ago when Mama and Daddy and I had taken a drive in the country.

The wind had whipped through the open windows that day

as I tapped my new white cowboy boots on the red pickup's cubbyhole and Daddy sang, "Git along ye little dogies, git along, git along...."

Mama sipped Grapette from a bottle. Her hair, the exact shade of the Indian paintbrush blooming in the bar ditches, whirled around her head. She offered me a swig of the pop, its warm fizz wetting my dry throat. Oil-pump jacks bobbed their grasshopper-looking heads, sucking at the ground. Sunlight slashed through the clouds, aiming straight at us. With Daddy's singing, Mama's laughing, and my boots tapping, we skimmed along, just the three of us under a Texas sky.

*That's how today feels.* In my heart, I knew it was a sign Mama would be all right.

## NINE

We HAD A THUNDERSTORM—a toad strangler according to Daddy—the day before the Fourth, so everyone let out a big sigh of relief when the weather turned clear for the picnic. The Johnsons' new Edsel, though, created more excitement than the celebration. Tuwana's dad took anyone who wanted for a ride. Kids lined up like they were waiting for the merry-go-round at the carnival. No charge, of course.

Tuwana had called me that morning and told me her mother refused to look at the Edsel and hadn't spoken to her dad since he brought the car home. I could tell Mrs. Johnson was hopping mad when I dropped off my brownies at the food table. She and Harriet Ford had their heads together talking.

"I'm furious, I'm here to tell you." Mrs. Johnson waved a spoon around in the air and took my brownies. "Thank you, Sammie. You didn't have to bring anything, you know, with your mother gone and all."

"It's okay, Mrs. Johnson. This is my mother's recipe, and I know she's sorry she couldn't be here for the picnic this year. She's coming home on Monday."

Mrs. Johnson went back to talking to Mrs. Ford. "You'd think he would consult me since I'm the one who has to sacrifice and get all the bills paid. Now he's the hero of the hour, taking everyone and his dog for rides, burning up heaven only knows how many tanks of gas."

Mrs. Ford stabbed a knife into my brownies, cutting them into squares, and said, "Mercy, Alice. You have to admit, your Studebaker had seen better days."

I hurried off and ran straight into Cly.

"Hey, Sam, where you been all day? You missed the basketball shoot-out."

"Sorry. I had to make brownies."

"You okay?"

"Of course, why wouldn't I be?"

"Beats me. You want to go shoot some baskets now?"

Before I could answer, someone rang a cowbell announcing the food was ready. Tuwana and PJ ran up, Tuwana pulling on Cly's arm and dragging him into the food line. We all piled our plates with fried chicken, potato salad, and pickled okra. Cly made a face like he'd sucked a lemon when he tried the okra.

After eating and playing games, like gunnysack races and the egg-on-a-spoon relay, everyone brought out their fireworks and grown-ups supervised their kids, letting them shoot off Roman candles, Black Cats, and cardboard cones that fizzed into fountains. When I closed my eyes, the glare of the sparklers danced like shooting stars behind my eyelids.

"Anybody want to ride in the Edsel?" Tuwana tugged on Cly's arm, but he told her to go ahead. She gave him a frowny face.

When I ran to ask Daddy if I could go, I heard Doobie holler, "Dibs on the window."

Daddy told me to have fun, that he was heading home, so I ran back to the Edsel.

"Sam, over here." Cly pulled me into the backseat square on his lap.

"Everybody in?" Mr. Johnson gunned the engine.

Tuwana scowled at me from the front, squashed between Davie Summers and Mitzi Greenwood. "Do you wanna trade places? There's more room for your long legs up here."

"It's okay," I said, not wanting to delay the ride.

Tuwana crossed her arms and stared out the windshield.

Mr. Johnson pushed a button, and we eased onto the road.

"See this here bar above the radio?" Mr. Johnson pointed out the spot to watch. "Gives you the strongest signal available."

Tapping Mr. Johnson on the shoulder, Doobie said, "Let's see what this baby'll do."

Gravel spun from under the tires as the Edsel peeled out. On the open highway, Mr. Johnson floored it and said, "Keep your eyes on the speedometer."

Necks craned and bodies shifted trying to see the magical spot. A red glow showed up on the half-moon dial when the needle reached 70.

"Speed warning light," Mr. Johnson said. "Safety feature for any of you heavy-footed types."

"You gonna let us drive it?" Davie asked.

"Yeah, when the moon turns to green cheese, I am." He threw back his head and laughed. He slowed down, hung his head out the window looking for cars, then spun the Edsel around on the highway and headed back to the community hall.

"Can you drop me off at my house?" I asked.

"Right-o."

I thanked Tuwana's dad for the ride and ducked out the door. Cly hopped out behind me. "I'll walk home from here, Mr. Johnson. Bossin' car, man."

"You live four streets over," I said as the car pulled away.

"Yeah...well, I wanted to make sure you get home safely."

"What could be safer than Graham Camp? Only thing might

get me is a fang-toothed coyote coming out of the canyon looking for a snack."

"For an ankle-biter, you're pretty funny."

"I don't get it."

"For a kid, you're all right. That's all." Cly started up the sidewalk after me, hands jammed into his Levi's pockets.

The air suddenly felt thicker, the sky blacker. The sidewalk stretched out in front of me a mile long, and my breathing had turned weird, sort of shallow and fluttery. Why was Cly walking with me? Tuwana would have a conniption.

I wiped my sweaty palms on my shorts, then clenched them into fists. Puffing out my cheeks, I let out a slow breath. Cly walked close enough I could feel his shirt brushing my arm.

"A kid? So that's what you think?" I opened my mouth, and that's what came out.

Just a few more steps to the porch. The fixture beside the door made a yellow circle of light that seemed to say *hurry, hurry*.

"I'm home. Safe and sound. You can go now." My voice had a scritchy sound.

"Just one thing...I've been wondering....Everything cool with you here at home?"

"Sure. Why wouldn't it be?" What was this all about? Earlier today he'd asked almost the very same thing.

"Doobie told me about your mom being gone. I thought maybe...Well, I just hoped things were righteous, ya know."

"Doobie? What does he know? My mother's doing fine. As a matter of fact, she'll be back on Monday. Good as new. Besides, I don't think it's *cool* for Doobie to be talking about something he knows nothing about." Just because his mom had gone to the same hospital as Mama didn't mean he knew beans about our situation.

"I'm all ears if you want to talk about it."

"I'm fine. My mother's fine. And besides, I heard you had plenty of your own problems to deal with. I don't think you need to be butting into mine." My mouth had taken on a mind of its own. I didn't know exactly what Cly's problems were, but they weren't the same as mine. Not even close.

"Where'd you hear that?" His chin lifted a notch, and a dark look crossed his face.

"Never mind. Just forget I said anything." I climbed to the top step.

"Wait." Cly grabbed my arm and pulled me around. "What did you hear?"

"Sammie, you by yourself?" Daddy said from the other side of the screen. "Thought I heard voices out here."

"Yes, Daddy...I mean, no, I'm not by myself. Cly walked me up the sidewalk. He's going home now."

I yanked my arm away from Cly's grip and marched into the house.

Daddy sat in his rocker, watching the weather on the television. I wondered if he'd heard my conversation with Cly. I hoped not. And another thing. I wished Cly had never walked me home and that Edsels hadn't been invented. When the weatherman finished, Daddy went to the kitchen and filled his thermos with coffee and made a sandwich for his lunch box.

"I'll be on graveyards for two more nights. Guess you'll be going over to the community hall to clean up tomorrow."

I nodded. He gave me a peck on the cheek, picked up his battered hard hat, and left for his shift at the plant. After taking a bath, I tried reading *Gone with the Wind,* but the words blurred together. All I could think about was why Cly asked me so many questions. I concentrated on the words in the book, but I was too sleepy to make any sense of them. I turned out the light and thought about Mama. Only two more days and she'd be home. The last thing I remembered before falling asleep was wondering if a person was allowed to eat fried chicken when receiving shock treatments.

The next morning Tuwana lit into me the minute I showed up for the cleanup. "What? You didn't bring Cly along so you could kootchy-koo while we sweep the floors?"

"What?" I stepped away from her.

"Don't act so dumb, like you don't know what I'm talking about," she hissed.

"If you're talking about when Cly walked home from my house, I didn't have anything to do with that."

"Yeah, and sitting on his lap in the Edsel wasn't your idea either, I suppose." She crossed her arms and slitted her eyes at me.

"For Pete's sake, Tuwana, I don't know how you come up with these harebrained ideas. You're the one with the big crush. Not me."

"You say that, but I know you ride your bike past his house all the time, show off on the basketball court...."

"Think whatever you want. Trust me. I'm not trying to steal your boyfriend. Now maybe we ought to get busy." I picked up a wooden folding chair and stacked it near the wall.

Thankfully Cly didn't show for the cleanup. Every time the door opened, I looked up, half wanting it to be him, half scared to death. Sometimes I could still feel his hands around my waist as we'd sped along in the Edsel. *Is this what a crush feels like?* I didn't feel all swoony or anything, so I guessed not.

I kept my distance from Tuwana and worked outside, picking up stray paper plates and burned-up sparklers from the night before. When we finished, I walked home alone and spent the afternoon reading the last fifty pages of *Gone with the Wind* while Daddy took a nap before his graveyard shift.

What did Mama love so much about this book? The adventurous

Scarlett? The rascal Rhett? Maybe when Scarlett's little girl, Bonnie, died, it reminded her of Sylvia. I personally didn't think that would be a good thing. Still, I couldn't wait to see her and tell her I'd read her favorite book, the whole thing.

I'd just finished when Daddy woke up and asked me to come outside with him. He lowered himself onto the porch step and lit a Camel.

"I had an interesting conversation down at the plant last night." He sounded odd.

"What was that?"

"Norm MacLemore told me you'd been spending a lot of time with his nephew."

An up-and-down roller-coaster feeling started in my stomach.

"Not really. He hangs around with all of us, actually." What was going on?

"What's he like? The nephew."

"Well, at first..." I took a deep breath. "When he first came he acted different, talked like they do in California, I guess. But now he seems like everyone else. Riding Doobie's motor scooter. Playing basketball. Just regular stuff."

"Norm thinks I oughta keep a better eye on you. Says his nephew's been in trouble at his school. He doesn't want anything to happen here."

"Trouble? What trouble?" Tiny prickles danced up my spine.

"Skipping school. Running with a bad crowd, from what I gathered."

"He seems all right to me."

"I saw him grab your arm last night on the porch. Now, I ain't saying he was up to no good, but you're only twelve. The nephew's fourteen. Probably be best for all concerned if you stayed away from him."

"You mean I can't even pick my own friends?"

"Not if it's the MacLemore kid." He stubbed out the cigarette butt in the Folgers can. "It's times like this I wish your aunt Vadine had come to stay while Mama's gone. You're too young to be on your own."

"That's not fair. I haven't done anything. Mr. MacLemore got it all wrong."

"Life's not always fair. I've told you that. It wasn't fair when your sister, Sylvia, died, and that's what's kept your mama worked up all these years. Thing is, we don't know anything about this kid, and you adding to Mama's problems when she gets back wouldn't do. Not at all." He got up and went into the house.

End of conversation. Great. Tuwana hated me. I could never see Cly again. Daddy didn't trust me. All this time, I'd thought we were doing all right. What had I done wrong?

The most disturbing thing, though, was the idea Mama might still have problems when she got back. Half the summer wasted, and for what? Angry tears stung my eyes, but I didn't know if they were for Mama or for me.

[ TEN ]

ON MONDAY, DADDY LEFT before sunup to get Mama. He apologized about leaving me home. "Rules are rules. No visitors in the hospital under fourteen." I didn't mind. I had this idea of decorating the house for Mama. Daddy's Old Spice filled the house as I hung chains made with construction paper. I strung a *Welcome Home* sign in big cutout letters over the kitchen doorway.

When I finished, I went over to Goldie's.

"Exciting day for you," Goldie said. "Nervous?"

"A little. What do you think Mama will be like?"

"Probably anxious, like you. Maybe embarrassed." Goldie clicked and banged the feeding tins for the parakeets while I filled the watering bowls.

"I hadn't thought about that." I unwired the latch to the outdoor flight and shooed out the birds from the top two rows. Goldie had shown me how to keep the birds separated into the four different levels divided by chicken wire. They splashed and flew around, chirping like it was Christmas or something.

"Your mother's been through a lot. You may have to give her some time for the routine to return." Goldie helped me whoosh the next batch of parakeets out. "It's not like my loves here, always flapping and eager to enter the fray. Let your mama get her wings back."

With the birds out, we scoured their boxes (Monday the boxes, Tuesday the floor, every day its own job), and then we fixed macaroni and cheese for lunch.

"Let's cut a few of George's roses for your mama." Goldie dug in the cupboard and pulled out a tall, flared vase. Wearing canvas gloves, she snipped a handful of thorny stems from the side yard and arranged them.

"Fill it with water and add a teaspoon of sugar when you get home. And give your mama my love."

Old Spice still lingered in the house, but fainter now with the roses I'd brought.

A long soak in the tub got rid of the aviary stink, and I put on my best pair of Bermuda shorts and a cotton eyelet blouse I'd ironed the day before and waited for Daddy to bring Mama home.

On about my millionth trip to peek out the window to see if they were coming, the Chevy pulled up in front of the house and Mama got out. My heart skipped a beat. I ran out the door and straight to her. She hugged me so tight I thought I would faint. Then she held me at arm's length and looked me over, her blue eyes as sparkly as sapphires. "Just look at you, all tanned and smart looking. Mercy sakes, I've missed you." She drew me in again, close to her. I closed my eyes and inhaled. Mama smelled of Ivory soap and something I couldn't place. A mixture of disinfectant and the way the house smells after we've had the flu. Hospital smells, like when Grandma Grace died.

Daddy carried Mama's brown suitcase, and we all went into the house.

"Well, now..." Daddy winked at me and then Mama. "Here we are."

"Look at that, will you?" Mama pointed to the welcome sign. "Oh, and paper chains. Just like a party." A party for just the three of us, but it felt right. And what's a party without presents? I ran into my room for the coming-home present I'd bought for Mama at Willy's store.

"I have something for you." I handed it to her. "Lilac soap. Imported from Paris, Willy said."

Mama held it in her pale fingers as if it were fine china, worked the tissue wrapper off, and sniffed it. When she tossed her head, red and gold curls spun off in spirals. "Lilac. Mmmm. Luscious. I'll use it tonight in the bath. What a treat. A whole month with only a drippy shower. Funny, I spent more time longing for a bath than I did eating. Thank you, sweetie."

And that's the way it went. Not at all like Goldie said, easing Mama back into her old life. She changed from her gingham shirtwaist into shorts and one of Daddy's old work shirts. She padded around barefoot, stopping to touch everyday items as if she had just laid eyes on them for the first time.

Daddy fried sausage patties and whipped up pancake batter. On the griddle, Mama dropped teaspoons of batter that came off no bigger than silver dollars, golden with crisp brown edges. She moved the roses to the enamel table on the back porch, where we ate supper.

No one mentioned the past four weeks, and for once, I didn't care about the hospital and what went on there. Mama had come home just like in the Tide commercial—new and improved.

We sat on the front porch until way after dark, listening to the crickets and Mama's tinkling laugh. Once in a while the smoke from Daddy's cigarette would curl up like skywriting headed for the Milky Way. Mama and I traced the Big Dipper with our fingers.

Daddy slipped his arm around Mama's shoulders and nuzzled her neck. "You know, I'm beat. I think it's time my girls and I got some beauty sleep."

Curled on my side clutching Pedro, I listened to the roar of bathwater filling the tub. In all the excitement, I'd forgotten to tell Mama about reading *Gone with the Wind*. At least I'd have tomorrow and a thousand tomorrows to share it with her. The last sound in my ears was the *glug-glug-glug* of the water going down the drain and Mama's soft giggle.

The next morning we sat on the couch in our pajamas, crosslegged, sipping coffee—Mama's black and mine the color of soft caramels since I'd put more milk than coffee in it.

"My roommate was Marilyn Monroe....Leastwise, she told everyone that. Big, pouty red lips and a penciled-on beauty mark." Mama's face glowed as she described the various people she'd met in the hospital.

"Oh, and Rose, poor thing. Piled on all her clothes, just layers and layers of sweaters, blouses, heaven only knows how many pairs of underwear—every stitch she owned—all at once. The attendants would say, 'It's hot today, Rose. Take off your sweater.' She would take every stitch off and rearrange it all, ending up with her bra and panties on top, and say, 'Happy now? I'm plumb down to my undies.'"

Mama made it sound like she'd been off on an adventure, a voyage into the weird and wacky. I kept waiting for her to slip me a tidbit about what torture they'd performed on her, but she just sipped her coffee and said, "Let me tell you about our calisthenics instructor...."

She uncurled her legs and reached for her cup. "You just can't imagine the awful taste of institutional coffee. Any thicker and it would've been motor oil." She stood up and stretched, taking her cup to the kitchen for a refill. Over her shoulder she said, "Well, now you know all about my summer. Tell me about yours."

"You'll never guess what Benny Ray Johnson bought. A new Edsel. It's dreamy and fast and he loves taking everybody riding in it."

"An Edsel, huh? Don't believe I've ever seen one of those. What else did you do?"

And next thing I knew I was telling her about the Fourth of July and Cly walking up the steps with me. How it made Tuwana get all in a snit and then Norm MacLemore talking to Daddy.

"Daddy told me I had to stay away from Cly, but he's nice, Mama, he really is." I gushed like an oil well, spewing it all out. I stopped for a breath, and a bell went off in my head. *This is my mother I'm talking to. My own mother who does care about me.* Goldie's words came back to me: "Let her get her wings back." All of a sudden I felt shy, tongue-tied, like maybe I shouldn't dump everything on her at once. A gap slipped into the air.

Mama sipped her coffee, waiting for me to continue. A tiny sigh escaped her lips.

"You'll never guess what else I did," I finally said.

"Oh my, I guess I wouldn't."

"I read *Gone with the Wind* cover to cover." I waited for Mama to pounce on that and start divulging her favorite parts, but a funny look had settled on her face, like an eraser had wiped over it and left a chalky blank slate.

"How wonderful," she said, her tone flat.

Racking my brain trying to think what to say next, I jumped when someone knocked on the door. I peeked around the curtains and saw Tuwana standing there holding something. I opened the door for her.

"Mother thought you might like this." She shoved a pie into my hands. "Peanut butter icebox pie."

"Thanks. Come on in and see Mama."

She stepped inside.

"Mama, look what Mrs. Johnson..." Mama had disappeared. The door to her room was closed.

"Mama and I were having coffee in our pj's." I shrugged at Tuwana. "She's probably getting dressed."

Tuwana stayed by the front door, looking off at a fly on the ceiling or something.

"Thank you for the pie."

"You're welcome."

"Peanut butter. That's your mom's special recipe, isn't it?"

She shrugged.

"Tuwana, are you all right?"

"I'd be a lot better if you would accept my apology for what I said the other day."

"Apology? When was that?"

"Now, you big doofus. I'm apologizing. I'm sorry for what I said...about you trying to steal Cly away."

"Well, then...apology accepted." I wrinkled my nose at Tuwana. "*Now* will you sit down?"

"PJ thinks Cly is playing hard to get, trying to make me jealous."

"I hadn't thought of that."

I watched Mama's door, thinking she would come out any minute. Tuwana flopped into Daddy's platform rocker and after a bit mouthed the words, "How is she?" and pointed to Mama's bedroom.

"Fine. Just fine." I took the coffee cups to the kitchen and put the pie on the counter.

"How's your cheerleading?" I asked, filling up the space of time waiting for Mama to come out.

"PJ's got shin splints or something. Lays around watching her soaps all day."

"Good ol' PJ. I think I'll go check on Mama. See if she wants some pie."

Mama sat on her vanity stool fastening tortoiseshell clips in her hair. She had on bright coral lipstick but no powder, so her freckles shone like tiny constellations on her face.

"Tuwana still here?"

"Yeah, I wondered if you were coming out to see her?"

"Sure am." She spritzed on some lilac water, stood up, and followed me into the front room.

Mama chattered away with Tuwana, talking about how grown-up she looked with her new poodle haircut, and I could tell Tuwana was surprised at Mama's perkiness.

"Let's have a slice of whatever your mother sent." Mama whooshed into the kitchen.

"No thanks," Tuwana said. "Mother made another one for our supper."

"How is your mother?" Mama took down the plates and put one slice on a plate for her and another for me.

"Oh, she's much better now since she got over that fit with Daddy. You know, buying the Edsel without telling her. What she really wanted was new living room furniture."

Mama's magic made me first, and now Tuwana, spit out everything from our summer. It scared me in a tingling sort of way. I loved the new Mama.

Mama patted Tuwana on the arm and said, "Sounds exciting, your getting an Edsel. Sammie told me all about it. I can't wait to see it." She ate a bite of the pie.

Tuwana hadn't finished though.

"After she told Daddy about the furniture, he stomped into the bedroom and came out waving an envelope, a big old grin on his face. 'Alice, come here. I've been waiting for just the right moment for this.' He pulled a wad of bills from the envelope and said, 'The

Ford dealer had one of them special deals—cash for your trade-in if you bought a new Edsel. Here it is—cold, hard cash. And that got me thinking—wouldn't it be nice for Alice and my princesses to get some new furniture?' He wrapped his arms around Mother, and now he's taking her to Amarillo next week to pick out what she wants."

"How lovely." Mama had a strained look on her face. "Why don't you girls go out and do whatever it is you've missed the last week. Tell your mother the pie was delicious. I'm going to rest awhile."

I threw on some shorts and a halter top and snagged a quarter off my dresser. Mama had already disappeared into her room, so I skipped out the door, telling Tuwana I'd buy her a Coke at Willy's store. Perfect. Everything had turned out perfect. For us. For Tuwana.

When we started up the grocer's wooden steps, the entrance bell jangled, and Cly MacLemore stepped out, swigging a root beer.

## ELEVEN

Tuwana gushed, "Oh, Cly, fancy meeting you here."

"Yo, Tu-tu. Hey, Sam, where ya been keeping yourself?"
He smiled under a baseball cap and black-framed sunglasses.

"Around. Here and there." Did this qualify as seeing Cly?
Surely Daddy had figured out I'd run into Cly sometime. The
camp consisted of five whole streets, for Pete's sake. Still...just to
be safe, I started into the store.

"Hey, what's your rush?" Cly asked.

"No rush. Just came for a Coke. Nice seeing you." A tinny
bell jangled when I entered the store. It felt like entering a cave.
Two measly lights dangled from the ceiling. Willy leaned over the
candy counter, his smooth, shiny head bobbing as he counted to
himself, "Four Snickers, six Valomilks, five Slo Pokes."

I let my eyes adjust to the darkness and piddled around among
the narrow rows. Six aisles times two made twelve rows. Four
shelves each. Forty-eight wooden planks packed with vegetable
cans, sardines, Epsom salts, dog chow, Windex, magazines. I studied items until I had practically the whole store memorized by the
time Tuwana came in.

"Hurry up. Let's get our drinks. Cly's waiting. Wants us to
shoot baskets. I know how you love to play basketball." She put her
hand on my elbow, steering me back to the Coke cooler.

"Actually, I thought I'd write an article about Willy for the *Dandelion Times*."

Tuwana looked at me as if I'd lost my mind. "I thought we'd quit doing that ding-dong paper."

"Maybe you have. Not me."

"What's gotten into you? I, for one, would prefer to play basketball than hang around here."

"You go on ahead. I'll catch up later."

"What's wrong? Are you afraid I'll get mad if you flirt with Cly?"

"No, I'm not afraid you'll get mad." I told her I didn't feel like playing basketball, but that she should go on and have fun. I didn't tell her about the pounding in my chest when I saw Cly pop out the door. Or about that business with Daddy.

Tuwana pranced off.

"Say, Willy, what would you think about me writing an article about you and the grocery business for my newspaper?"

He puffed out his chest. "That would be quite an honor. Give me a couple minutes to finish this inventory."

I picked up a Big Chief tablet from aisle two for taking notes and went to the cash register.

Willy took the change I'd plunked on the counter and said, "Now, what was it you wanted to know?"


I went straight home when I got through interviewing Willy. Our own vegetable and fruit cocktail cans, the cocoa tin, boxes of macaroni, practically everything from our cupboard covered the kitchen counter. Mama stood on a chair emptying the top shelf.

"Cleaning out the cabinets, Mama?"

"Yes...no, but it's got to be in here somewhere. Did you and Daddy move things around?" Her eyebrows puckered together.

"Nope, though they might have jumbled up when we hunted for the ranch beans or the canned tuna."

"It's Patch. I haven't seen him since we got home. Went to the back door and yelled for him. I thought if I put some Alpo out, he might come." She stood on tiptoe, reaching as far back as she could. "The problem is I can't find any of his food."

"Mama, are you okay?"

"Certainly. Never better." She stepped off the chair and rummaged through all the things on the counter, checking each label.

My stomach went queasy. She looked okay. Lots of energy. *But, Patch?*

"Mama, are you talking about our terrier, Patch?"

"Good heavens, what other Patch would I be talking about? How many dogs named Patch do you know?"

"Uh, none. There could never be another Patch."

"Well, he's out of food. Would you run down to Willy's and get some?"

"Mama." I touched my fingers lightly on her arm. "Don't you remember Patch got hit by the school bus when I was in third grade? He followed me out of the house, and when…" I took a deep breath. "When the bus started rolling, he got under the tire. How could you forget that?" A lump formed in my throat.

"Well, that explains it then." Her face went blank and smooth as if a rag had washed over it.

"How could you forget about Patch?"

"I didn't forget about him. I wouldn't be looking for his food if I had forgotten him, now would I?"

"That's not what I mean." I didn't know what I meant, but then I couldn't explain what had just happened either. I moved over to the chair and said, "Here, Mama, let's put things back."

Why hadn't I stayed home with her? Her first day back and all. How could I have run off like that?

Mama handed me the cans to put back and laughed in her regular way when I told her about my interview with Willy. He'd come from Minnesota to open up the store here at Graham Camp. His cousins had a farm near here, and when he and his wife had come to visit they liked it.

"Graham Camp is a nice place," Mama said. "Your daddy and I have always thought it was a wonderful place for you to grow up."

When a knock came on the door, Mama went to answer it, her steps light and springy.

"Yes?"

I expected it would be Tuwana, but...

"You must be Sam's mom. I'm Cly MacLemore, Norm and Eva's nephew."

"How nice to meet you. Come in, young man."

I stepped into the front room, my stomach heaving triple somersaults.

"Hi, Sam." Cly took off his baseball cap, and underneath it he had a new flattop haircut.

"Nice hair."

"Yeah, got Slim to do that."

"Slim?" Mama asked, looking Cly over.

"Yeah, old man Wallace, across the street from my uncle. He's pretty hip for an old guy. Which is one reason I came over. He's been teaching me the finer points of backgammon. Whips me every time. And, well, bein' Sam's such a brain and all, I thought maybe she could learn too so I'd have someone to practice on."

Was this the same Cly? What kind of magic did Mama have that he just opened up his mouth so whole paragraphs poured out? Just like with Tuwana and me.

"Slim gets home about five," Cly said. "You could come after supper for a lesson." He gripped his cap in both hands, bending the bill back and forth, standing on one foot and then shifting his weight to the other.

"How nice." Mama apparently didn't know about Daddy forbidding me to see Cly. I swiped my sweaty palms on my shorts.

"Tell me, Cly, where are you from?" Mama said.

"LA mostly."

"California? Oh my, you're a long way from home. What do your parents do?"

"Dad's in construction." The way he kept folding the bill back and forth, I figured a permanent crease had formed. It was nice of Mama to ask Cly all those questions even though I'd already told her all about him in my letters.

"I'm sure they miss you. I know I sure missed my Sammie while I was away." For a minute I thought she might run right into a spiel about Marilyn Monroe and the layered lady, but she just tilted her mouth into a grin and said to me, "I think I'll take a bath before your dad gets home. You two can chat."

"Wanna sit down?" Alone with Cly for the second time, I got the same butterfly-wing-flapping I'd felt that night on the sidewalk.

"That's okay, I oughta get going. See if old Norm's got anything for me to do."

"You're doing okay with your uncle then?"

"I'm trying. He ain't the easiest fellow to please, but Aunt Eva's a bossin' cook."

"About tonight. I don't think..." I could hear Mama's bathwater running.

"Your mom seemed cool with it."

"It's not that....Well, it sort of is. I need to stay home with Mama, with her just getting back and all."

"Jeepers, she ain't a baby."

"Look, Cly, I like you. Honest, I do. It's just that..." A spider no bigger than a grain of rice shinnied up an invisible thread near the ceiling. I watched it instead of looking at Cly. "It would be easier if you just sat down." I pointed to Daddy's chair.

He sat down, and I perched on the edge of the couch.

"Well, you see, it's like this. Tuwana's crazy about you. I'm sure you've noticed the way she goes into orbit the minute you're around. She's been my best friend since first grade, and if I hang around you, she gets upset."

"Tu-tu? She's a show-off. Everybody thinks so. So Miss Paper Shaker decides who you can and can't be friends with?"

"No, we have lots of different friends at school, but here at Graham Camp, we've just always stuck together."

"Well, then, we'll invite Tu-tu along to Slim's."

Tuwana visiting Mr. Wallace? Not in my lifetime. I checked on the spider.

"Another thing. Daddy says I can't hang around you." *There. I said it.* I waited, watching Cly's face. He scrunched his eyebrows together, and then his jaw tightened.

"And what reason did your old man give?"

"Don't call him that. I don't like it. I'm trying to be as honest as I can. It's because of your uncle."

Cly straightened up, surprised, I could tell.

"Norm?"

"Yes, it's like I tried to tell you the other night. People say you had problems at your old school, skipping or something. Your uncle told Daddy about it, and Daddy said I couldn't be around you."

Cly's breath hissed out through his teeth. "Norm's always having a cow about something. It's bad enough getting shipped to Nowheresville. But you and me. Well...I thought we were pretty tight, you know? Guess I was wrong."

I squeezed my eyes shut, trying to think of something, anything to say.

Cly stood up and walked to the door. I heard the bathtub draining and the back door slam at the same time. Daddy breezed in, bringing the scent of petroleum on his work clothes.

Everything swirled together. The plant smells mixed with Mama's lilac soap from the bathroom. Cly standing with his cap in his hand.

Cly twisted the front doorknob and said, "I was just leaving, Mr. Tucker."

My insides felt scrambled.

## [ TWELVE ]

A T SUPPER MAMA CHATTERED nonstop while we ate salmon patties and macaroni and cheese.

"I thought the MacLemores' nephew was nice. Very polite." Mama waved her fork around while she talked.

"First impressions ain't always what they appear. Norm's not much of a specimen himself. Reckon the nephew's made from the same cloth. I'll have another salmon patty, sugar." Daddy held out his plate to Mama.

"I don't know. You seemed to think I was all right the first time we met." She gave Daddy a wink.

"Different deal entirely. It's Sis here we got to concern ourselves with."

"I suppose you're right." Mama reached over and touched me on the arm. "Sammie, you've got all the time in the world for boys."

"He just wanted to teach me backgammon. It's not that big a deal." And that wasn't the point. Daddy didn't trust me to pick my own friends. My stomach churned, but before I had time to think about it, Mama skipped off in a whole other direction.

"I've been thinking...." Mama took a sip of iced tea. "We ought to get another dog. A puppy. I've missed our Patch, haven't you?"

"What made you think of old Patch?" Daddy's fork stopped in midair.

"Nothing, really. Just thinking."

The macaroni in my mouth swelled up with my chewing. I concentrated on working it around. Would she tell Daddy she hadn't even remembered Patch died?

"Maybe we'll look into it after our vacation. What do you think, Sis? Would you like a new mutt?"

"I guess." I managed to swallow as I considered it. "Yeah, I think I would."

Mama made an O with her mouth. "What vacation? When did you decide this?"

"Today. A spot came open on the vacation list for next week. Since you're doing better, I thought we'd go to Red River for a few days. Rent a cabin, do some fishing…"

"Oh, Daddy, that'd be great!" Getting off the subject of Cly and Patch suited me fine. "Don't bother with the dishes, Mama. I'll do them."

"That's my girl." Daddy slipped his arm around Mama's waist. In the front room I heard them rustling the map and planning the trip. Every once in a while Mama laughed, and I imagined them cuddled on the couch with Mama's head resting on Daddy's shoulder.

A puppy? Small dog or big? Fuzzy or slick-haired? The only image that came to mind was Patch, squashed flat under the bus.

I took my sweet time drying the dishes and putting them away. Just as I finished, Mama said, "I think a nice bubble bath would feel good."

Four whole hours had passed since her last one.


"Half cocker and half fence-jumper," the scruffy boy at the roadside filling station said as he showed us the cardboard box full of puppies. "Pa says we gotta get rid of 'em or he'll shoot 'em." The boy's brown eyes pleaded with us as Mama and I looked them over.

"Glad to help you out," Daddy said when Mama and I both started to pick up the same black ball of fluff.

"That'n's a female." The boy pointed to Crayola lettering on the side of the box. "Free. They's all free."

"We'll take her." Daddy handed the boy two one-dollar bills.

We named her Scarlett, what else? Glossy black fur and shiny, button eyes. Getting her was the best part of the whole vacation.

Not that we didn't have a good time. Daddy fished while Mama and I picked wildflowers. One night we drove over to Taos for the Indian dances, and I loved the *bum-bum-bum* of the drums as I watched the twirling, high-stepping natives in their war paint. Daddy kept his arms tight around Mama, whose hair swirled around her head like the flames of the dancers' campfire.

Mama seemed like a whole different person from the Mama I'd known since Sylvia died. Happy-go-lucky. Laughing with me. Whispering secrets. But other things popped up too, just out of the blue.

"Remember when I dressed up like an Indian princess for Halloween?" I said to Mama the morning after the Taos trip.

She nodded and smiled, but her eyes looked like the glass eyes in my old Betsy McCall doll. I could tell she had no idea what I was talking about. Instead she pointed to a clump of wild daisies. "Oh look, what is that?" A green dragonfly with wiry-veined wings buzzed up and down.

One night, after frying the rainbow trout Daddy caught, we sat on the cracker-box porch in front of our cabin. Fireflies blinked in the bushes. Mama sat on the step with her knees tucked up close to her chin.

"Grandma Grace loves rainbow trout. Wouldn't it be nice if we could take her a mess of them? Just the thing to cheer her up."

Daddy, who'd been whittling on a cedar stick, quit whittling. The sound of the creek tumbled in our ears, and we sat there, not answering, not knowing exactly what she meant.

After an eternity, Daddy said, "Nothing beats a skillet full of fresh trout."

"They do smell up the place though," Mama said. She stood up and stretched. "Think I'll go soak in the tub before bedtime." She went inside, leaving Daddy and me alone.

"Daddy, have you noticed how Mama forgets stuff?" I kept my eyes straight ahead, watching for fireflies, and afraid to look Daddy in the face.

"She's doing all right, seems to me."

"Yeah, mostly. It's just every once in a while, she says things. Like Grandma Grace just now. She's been dead for ages."

"To be expected, I suppose. Temporary, the doctors said."

"You *knew* she would be like this?" My chest felt as if I'd been stabbed. "She's my mother. Don't you think you should have told me?" Maybe there were other things I needed to be on the look-out for.

Daddy didn't answer, just sat there and whittled in the moon-light, the soft scrape of his knife against the stick in his hand.

"When did you take up whittling?"

"Oh, 'bout an hour ago. Ran out of Camels. Thought I'd give it up." He held the wood up and eyed it. "Smoking, that is. Gives your mama a headache."

"You could've told me what to expect—Mama's forgetting things," I said.

"She remembered Patch."

"She didn't remember he died. Tried to call him and turned the kitchen upside down looking for his food."

"Ummm, guess I didn't catch that." He folded the knife and slid it into his pocket.

"And another thing—you noticed how she spends half her time taking bubble baths? Three, four times a day. Did the doctor say that would pass too?"

"Can't say. I know she missed 'em while she was gone."

"Still..." I tried to gather the words in my head, but none came. What I wanted to say was, *What about Sylvia? Did she forget all about her too?*

"It's getting late. Maybe we ought to turn in." Daddy stood up and held the screen door open. "Coming?"

The next morning we left, and about halfway home we saw the boy with the puppies. By the time we pulled into Graham Camp, it seemed like Scarlett had been part of our family forever. Fuzzy and cute, bouncing along behind me everywhere I went. Mama and I both loved her to pieces.


"You ever seen such a mess of feathers?" Goldie scooped a handful of green fluff from a cubicle. More fuzz swirled in the air. "This infernal heat started them molting earlier than usual. Now it'll be feathers, feathers, feathers for another month, maybe two." She slung her down-covered hand into the wastebasket. Silver threads shone in her cinnamon-colored hair. It looked like she'd turned a bowl upside down on her head and given herself a new haircut. Straight bangs, straight all around her head, level with her earlobes. No nonsense, that was Goldie all right.

A feather drifted by, settling between two wires of the just-cleaned cage. I pulled it out and sat on the wooden stool twirling the feather, examining it.

"A clean bird is a happy bird." Goldie handed over two ceramic bowls. "Fill these with water and let the ones over here take their baths."

Just like Mama and her bubbles.

Some of the birds stepped timidly into the water, plucking softly at their feathers. Not Lady Aster. She dove in, splashed, and shook her whole body.

"The queen bee, that one is, my Lady Aster." Goldie laughed a throaty cackle.

"Goldie, did you ever want to have children?"

"I've got my babies here. That's enough."

"Well, before you started your aviary, did you want real children?"

"The Lord gives; the Lord takes away." She turned her back and stuck her arm far into one of the boxes.

"You sound like Brother Henry. What do you mean, the Lord gives and takes?"

Goldie pulled out a fistful of feathers. A softness had settled on her face, and her eyes looked sad.

"I had a boy once. He drowned when he was fourteen."

The air fuzzed around me, thick with molting fluff and Goldie's words.

"I didn't know." I jumped off the stool and held out the feed sack for Goldie to shake the feathers she'd gathered. "How long before you . . . well, got over it?" It didn't come out sounding right, not the way I meant somehow.

"I don't know. I'm still waiting."

"But you're so jolly, always carrying on with Lady Aster and the others."

"That's George's doing. Moved me to Graham Camp a while after it happened. Folks here just took me in, inviting us over for bridge and picnics. One day George announced I needed a hobby. Bein's I always had a canary or a parakeet or two, that's what I settled on. Next thing I knew, George started hammering and stringing up wire, looking in a book for instructions. Slim and

Benny Ray and Deacon Greenwood, they all stopped by to help. Now I've got these babies."

"I'm sorry about your boy. Just think, if you hadn't...well...if you hadn't got the aviary, I wouldn't be over here half the summer pestering you."

"It's a mystery all right, the way the Almighty works." She wiped her hands on a damp rag from the pine table. "Now, tell me about this mutt you got."

## THIRTEEN

ONE MORNING MAMA AND I made chocolate no-bake cookies and watched three game shows in a row on television. That's the way it was. I stayed home with Mama when Daddy worked and helped Goldie or ran around the neighborhood when he was home. Every day I thought Mama seemed to be getting better as far as her memory went. When the Montgomery Ward catalog came in the mail, we sat on the couch and circled our favorite outfits. I got up the nerve to tell her I needed a training bra, and she measured around my chest with the cloth tape and studied the size charts. She let me fill in the order blank from the middle of the catalog, getting me set up for junior high. It was the happiest time I could ever remember. Ever.

Later, while she and Daddy watched a *Gunsmoke* rerun, I took Scarlett for a walk and ended up at Tuwana's. Their front door stood propped open while Mr. Johnson hauled an end table out.

"Tomorrow's the big day." Mrs. Johnson's cheeks flushed a rosy color. "The furniture will be delivered around noon. I don't suppose your mother would like any of this old stuff?" She swooped her hand across the room.

"I don't think so, but thanks for asking."

"Can't say I blame her. Early orange crate. That's what it is." She laughed and told Tara to get off the sofa. "Your daddy needs to move it to the garage." Tuwana and I offered to help him carry it. Good thing. It weighed a ton.

"Shoulda called you girls' boyfriends to help with this heavy stuff," Mr. Johnson said as we dropped our end on the sidewalk. We pushed it along, gouging ruts in the grass where the legs dug in.

"What boyfriends?" Tuwana asked, hands on her hips.

"Ol' Norm's nephew, for one. California, was it?"

"Daddy, I wouldn't want him for a boyfriend if he was the last human on earth. Always holding that rattlesnake rattle up when I'm not looking, scaring the pee-wadding out of me."

I raised my eyebrows at Tuwana. *The last human on earth?*

"My boyfriend lives in town, and that would've been too far to come." She put her hand over her mouth and giggled.

We carried the sofa over the gravel driveway, Tuwana and me on one end, Mr. Johnson on the other, and got it to the garage. My arm muscles quivered like frog legs jumping in a frying pan when we set it down.

"I never can keep up with all your shenanigans. You girls did all right. Let's catch our breath before we go back in the house." He walked over to the side of the garage and lit a cigarette while Tuwana and I settled on the glider.

"You didn't tell me you had a new boyfriend." I looked at Tuwana's profile in the moonlight. In my side vision, the end of Mr. Johnson's cigarette glowed red as he mopped the back of his arm across his forehead.

Tuwana dangled her foot to the ground and scritched the glider faster, back and forth, back and forth. "I forgot."

"You wouldn't forget that. Who is it?"

"An eighth grader. He's not exactly my boyfriend, but I think he will be."

Faster and faster went the glider. *Scritch. Scritch. Scritch.*

"So, you gonna tell me who or do I have to guess every boy in eighth grade?"

"Mike Alexander."

"Mike, the football captain?" I planted my foot on the ground, bringing the glider to a halt.

"He's not *just* the football captain. He's on the student council *and* the honor roll. My heart just does flip-flops when I see him. You know, at the football field in town when PJ and I go to cheerleading practice. Surprised?" She cocked her head and batted her eyelashes.

"What about Cly?" The question burned within me. It was dumb, I know, but I still thought about him and wanted to be his friend.

"He was just a temporary diversion, only here for the summer. Besides, he acts just like all the other camp clowns if you ask me, which I know you didn't, but...well, there you have it. Mike carried my pom-poms to the car when Mother picked me up this afternoon. Can you believe it? This is what it's like to finally be in love."

"In love? You mean like puppy love?"

"No, I can feel it. My skin just goes all goose-bumpy when I think about him." She did a little shiver.

"You're smitten all right." I stood up from the glider. "Time for me to go. I'll go in and get Scarlett."

Tara and Tommie Sue had put doll clothes on Scarlett—a lacy pink dress and a bonnet. They giggled and smothered her in kisses before handing her to me.

"Oh, Sammie," Mrs. Johnson said as I wriggled Scarlett out of the dress. "I'm having a coffee on Friday morning for the ladies in camp. I want to share our home with everyone. Tell your mother I hope the two of you can make it. Ten o'clock."

"Thanks. I'll tell her."

Gathering Scarlett in my arms, I took the long way around, sticking with the camp streets, laid out like long black tongues in the moonlight. A party would be fun for Mama. Give her a chance to "try her wings," as Goldie would say. The only time she went out was church on Sundays. Swoosh in. Swoosh out. No chitchat. My steps felt light as I drifted home. I might even talk Daddy into letting me learn backgammon with Cly. Now that Tuwana didn't want him.

A moist lilac scent floated through the front room when I entered the house. *Mama and her bubble baths.*

I found Daddy at the kitchen table eating a no-bake cookie and slid into the chair opposite him.

"These ain't bad. Want one?" He shoved the plate across to me.

"No thanks. I wanted to ask you a question." Might as well plunge right in. "Remember a while back when you told me I couldn't be around Cly?"

"The MacLemore kid?" Daddy gave me a sideways glance.

*Act nonchalant.* "Yeah. Cly wants to teach me how to play backgammon so we can outwit Mr. Wallace."

"Slim'd be hard to beat. Shrewd, I'd imagine." He picked up his plate and put it in the sink.

"It's like this." My heart pumped ninety miles an hour. "Tuwana and PJ are busy all the time practicing their cheers, and Cly will only be here a couple more weeks, so I thought if you didn't care, maybe I could learn. I might even teach you like you taught me to gut a catfish."

Daddy rummaged in the cabinet, looking for something. "Do you know if we've got any toothpicks?" he asked.

"Other side, bottom shelf."

He opened the door and found the toothpicks we kept in a shot glass. He worked on a couple of spots and said, "I don't know. Norm's a hothead. Figgered his nephew would be too. Thing is, I don't want you getting into a situation you can't handle. Gotta protect my girl, you know." He ruffled my hair. The toothpick bobbled up and down in his mouth the way his Camels used to.

"Don't you trust me?"

"It's not that. It's other people you gotta watch out for. You're too young to have much experience with that." He sat back down and crossed his legs. "I'll think on it and let you know."

"But Cly will only be here two more weeks. Maybe less."

"I said I'd think on it."

"Think on what?" Mama breezed in, clean smelling, her mouth tilted up at the corners.

"Sis here wants to learn some game from that kid from California. Over at Slim's."

"Good grief, Joe. Let her go. You're fussier than an old mother hen. She needs to be out having fun. Besides, you can trust Sammie. Has she ever once done anything to cause you any doubt?" Mama picked up a cookie and nibbled the coconut from the edges.

"That's my job—taking care of my girls. I know when I'm whipped though...you two ganging up on me." He rubbed a whiskery place on his chin. "I suppose you can go. Just a round or two."

"Thank you, Daddy. Cly's a good kid. You'll see." I hugged him and snagged the last cookie from the plate.

The ladies of Graham Camp streamed into Mrs. Johnson's party. Tuwana dipped lime sherbet punch into cut-glass cups while her sisters served cream-cheese sandwiches with olives toothpicked to the top and lemon squares dusted with powdered sugar. Very festive.

The furniture—Danish provincial, Mrs. Johnson said—was an aquamarine color. It filled up the front room, squeezed into every inch of space. The curved arms of the sofa butted up against the end table on the long outside wall with the chairs angled in on either end. You had to turn sideways to make it past the cocktail table planted like an island in the center of it all. Tuwana's mother flittered around, beaming at all the compliments.

"Marvelous color, Alice."

"You're a lucky lady, getting a new Edsel and this divine furniture all in the same summer. Tell us your secret. How'd you get Benny Ray sugared up for all this?"

Mrs. Johnson lifted her shoulders. "Oh, get outta here. You know men. Just gotta get your timing right." She patted her hand on the back of the sofa and turned to Mama, who'd found a spot in one corner of the sofa. "Rita, it's lovely to see you. New dress?"

"This?" Mama sipped from her cup, and from across the room, she looked like a strawberry sundae in her pink sundress. "Gracious no. I've had it for ages." When she smiled, her whole face lit up. Mama was getting along fine.

I found Tuwana in the kitchen filling the punch bowl and talking to PJ.

"I knew he was trouble from the beginning." PJ's eyes twinkled behind her rhinestone glasses.

"How creepish. Where do you think he went?"

"Hi, guys." If they heard me come up, they didn't act like it. "Where did who go?"

"Cly, that's who." Tuwana had her know-it-all look. "Took off from his aunt and uncle's house yesterday. No by-your-leave or nothing."

"Norm went to the plant office this morning, asked my mom if she'd seen him." PJ helped herself to a sandwich. "Called him an ungrateful little so-and-so and some other stuff I can't repeat.

Mom wanted me to ask around with some of the kids. I thought about Doobie, but his mom's nerve treatment from last year didn't take, and he went with his dad to put her back in the hospital."

"You mean...Cly's...gone?"

"Flew the coop. Probably had a fight with his uncle." PJ shrugged.

My stomach gurgled. "Cly said he'd been getting along okay with Norm. Something must've happened." Something no one knew about. Whatever it was, I couldn't imagine. Just then a new batch of noises came from the front room.

*Oohs* and *aahs* drifted toward me. Standing on tiptoe, I saw Sister Doris, Brother Henry's wife, and her whole brood—baby Penelope in her arms, Matthew, Mark, and Luke scrunched around her at the edge of the furniture.

"Sorry about bringing the whole gang," Sister Doris said. "Henry got a call, so here we are." Luke pulled on his mother's saggy dress, one I'd seen her wear dozens of times, a tent outfit that hung from her shoulders and hid the plump parts. "What is it, Lukie?" She bent down and cupped his face in her hand. He whispered something to her. "All right, dear, just a moment."

Sister Doris handed Penelope to Poppy Brady, who was wedged on the sofa between Mama and Mrs. Zyskowski. "Potty training," Doris whispered, and guided Luke toward the bathroom.

Poppy didn't have any children. She was just barely married to Fritz, not more than a few months. She stiffened like she'd been handed a lizard instead of a baby. Penelope started wailing. Poppy held the baby up under the arms, leaving her plump sausage legs dangling in the air.

"It's okay," Mama said. "I'll take her." She held out her hands and curled the baby close to her breast, cooing softly as their eyes met. Penelope settled right down, and Poppy announced it was time for her soap opera and whooshed out the door.

I slipped into Poppy's spot. "Cute, isn't she?" I ran my finger over a dimpled fist clutching Mama's finger. Mama made baby sounds and snuggled Sister Doris's baby even closer.

"Such a sweet girl, my precious cream puff." Mama's lips brushed Penelope's milky white forehead. The baby whimpered, a kitten kind of mewing sound. "There now, no need to fuss, my darling Sylvia. Mama's here. Shhh. Everything's fine."

*What did Mama say? Sylvia? Surely it just slipped out.* Peeking around, I hoped no one else noticed. Everyone chatted nonstop, going on about how the summer had flown by and school would be starting in two shakes of a lamb's tail.

Penelope yawned and stretched one leg out. Mama shifted a bit, never taking her eyes from the baby. Another whimper, then Penelope wiggled and fussed louder. Mama picked her up and held her on her shoulder, but the pink bottoms of Penelope's feet pumped against Mama.

"Don't cry, Sylvia. We'll fix you up. Mama's got you." She spoke louder this time, and the whole room got quiet. Except for Penelope's screaming.

"Tara, Tommie Sue, please see if the ladies would like another sandwich." Mrs. Johnson busied herself picking up empty punch cups and stray toothpicks from the cocktail table.

"Penelope, that's the baby's name. Remember I wrote you a letter about her." I didn't even know if Mama heard me the way she kept talking to *Sylvia*, cooing and making shushing noises, kissing her neck, jiggling her up and down. My skin crawled with chill bumps.

By now Sister Doris had finished taking Luke to the bathroom and sat in the armchair nearest Mama's end of the sofa. Doris smiled and acted as if it were the most natural thing in the world for Mama to be holding her baby and calling her another name. I made a motion to Doris, pointing to Penelope, trying to see if she wanted to take the baby back. She shook her head no and looked at Mama with soft brown eyes. Her sturdy hand moved to Mama's knee, and she patted it softly.

When Penelope screamed loud enough to hear two houses away, Mama stood and paced around the cocktail table, soft, rocking steps trying to calm the baby, but it didn't help. After a while Sister Doris stood also and gently cupped Penelope's bottom in her hand and took her from Mama.

"Must be hungry. My, this girl likes to eat."

Mama blinked a time or two, then flicked her hair away from her face and said, "You know, Alice, I would love another of those lemon bars. And when you have time I'd like the recipe."

Tuwana raised her eyebrows like maybe Mama's nerve treatment didn't take either. She didn't say it though, and right then my heart swelled with gratitude for Tuwana.

Mama stood poised with a lemon square. When she raised the sweet to her mouth, dots of powdered sugar swirled like the teensiest snowflakes. Floating, twirling, like the inside of my head spinning with thoughts of Sister Doris and Penelope, Mama and Sylvia, Cly and his uncle Norm. I sat glued to Mrs. Johnson's new couch with the smell of furniture polish and baby powder and the clatter of forks and punch cups and didn't know what to do. I clenched my fists and closed my eyes, hoping when I opened them everything would be all right.

My insides felt like the day when Mama swallowed the pills. Something was bad wrong, but I didn't know what. When I opened my eyes, Mama stared in my direction, a strange look on her face. Detached. Vacant.

## FOURTEEN

Mama didn't mention baby Penelope when we left the party, but the minute we got home she took a bubble bath. At supper she told Daddy all about Alice Johnson's furniture and how much she enjoyed visiting with the ladies. I sat there thinking that Mama's shock treatments had done something to her brain so when unpleasant things slipped out, they got erased, never to be remembered again. I couldn't figure out anything else it could be.

And what about Doobie's mom, Mabel Thornton? What did it mean that her nerve treatment didn't take? Did you have to go back and get a booster once in a while or what? Maybe Doobie acted like such a doofus because he worried about his mother the same way I did mine. All this time I thought he just orbited another planet, like Saturn or something.

When Scarlett scratched at the front door, I followed her out and sat on the front porch while she did her business. She romped and rolled over and over in the grass. Her front paws bounced back and forth, begging me to play chase.

"Oh, all right. I'll take you for a walk."

Another thing. Cly. Why did he leave? What happened between him and Norm? Maybe his dad called and wanted him to come back early.

I let Scarlett lead the way while we walked. She raced up the middle of camp. When she chased a cat, I followed. The next thing I knew, we were in Mr. Wallace's yard. Across the street, the Mac-Lemores' drapes were drawn, the front door closed. I was pulling on Scarlett's leash to take her back home when Mr. Wallace drove up in his truck.

"Evening, Sammie. Out for a walk?"

"Sorta." Mr. Wallace might know something. He and Cly got along. I took a deep breath. "Actually, I was wondering about Cly. I heard he might be leaving."

He gathered his lunch box and started toward the house, motioning for me to follow.

"Maybe you oughta ask him yourself. He's keeping me company awhile."

"Here? At your house?"

He nodded and pushed open the front door. "Say, young man, you got a visitor."

Cly's ears reddened when he saw me. Scarlett raced ahead of me into Mr. Wallace's front room and sniffed Cly's leg.

"Sam. What're you doing here?"

"What's it look like? I came to learn how to play backgammon." Where that came from was beyond me.

Mr. Wallace's leathery face, lined like a faded road map, broke out in a grin. "Well, son, aren't you gonna ask your guest to sit down?"

"Uh...sure. Have a seat." Cly pointed to the couch.

Now I felt stupid. *What do you think you're doing?* Scarlett jumped on my lap and licked my face. "I guess you want to know why I came."

"To learn backgammon, you said." Cly stood with his hands jammed in his pockets.

"That's just part of it. Earlier today, I heard you'd left, gone back to California...."

A look passed between the two, something I didn't understand.

"Not exactly..."

Mr. Wallace cleared his throat. "Think I'll go check on the garden. Give you two time to talk."

The house had an old-fashioned feel to it. Furniture with worn spots, a braided rug over the pine floor in the front room, a floor lamp beside a spindled rocking chair. A painting of the Last Supper hung on the wall. Angled between the couch and the rocker, a small coffee table had a game board on one end and a Bible, whose cover had a dull, worn-out look, on the other.

"This where you play backgammon?" I pointed to the table, feeling even more stupid since it was so obvious.

"Yeah." Cly lowered himself into the rocker with his legs stretched out in front.

"So what did you mean *not exactly*?"

"It's a long story." He looked at the rug like the braided coils might give him the answer.

"I'm listening."

"California's not all I made it out to be. My old man..." He stopped and looked at me. "Sorry, I know you don't like that expression. My *father* got himself arrested two days ago. Armed robbery this time. And assaulting a cop. Probably drunk too."

"How awful."

"When Norm got the call, he got bent, cussing, and all that. He yelled about where did that leave me, said he had half a mind to ship me back to California and let the state deal with me. Aunt Eva started crying and said I was staying put, right here." A thin line of sweat bubbled above Cly's lip.

"That was a nice thing for her to say."

"Get real. I know when I'm not wanted. It's bad enough getting knocked around by your old man." He didn't bother correcting himself this time. "I decided not to stick around and get the shaft by old Norm too."

"So how'd you end up over here with Mr. Wallace?"

"He saw me thumbing a ride on the Mandeville highway. He said I oughta consider my options and brought me back here."

"Your aunt Eva wants you to stay. That's something."

"Yeah, she kept going on about how much I'd like school in Mandeville, but jeepers, how would she know?"

"What about your mother? Couldn't you go live with her?"

His eyes bugged out like I'd just asked him if he wanted to eat a plate full of worms. "My mom split when I was two years old. We ain't seen her since."

"Oh." I couldn't think what else to say.

Just then Mr. Wallace came in, and Cly jerked his head toward him. "Slim's letting me stay here till I figure out something about Norm."

Mr. Wallace knocked the dust off his work pants and hung his cap by the front door. "Norm's not all bad. He just ain't had the pleasure of raising a kid."

"Some blast."

"We'll see." Mr. Wallace washed his hands in the kitchen and hollered. "I thought you two were gonna play backgammon."

Cly pulled out the board and showed me how to set up and the basic moves, how to block points and cast off when we'd worked our men around the board. By the second game, I'd gotten the hang of it and beat Cly by two. Scarlett started prancing around, so I scooped her up and thanked Cly for the lesson.

"Anytime, cat."

When he opened the door for me, I saw him look across the street at his uncle's house, but I could tell he didn't want me to see him looking, so I turned to Slim. "Thanks, Mr. Wallace."

"Just call me Slim. That'll do." He gave me a nod. I felt bad for

Cly, but Slim seemed awful nice—nothing like Tuwana always went on about. I couldn't wait to call and tell her Cly might be going to Mandeville to school.

The phone was ringing when I got home. Daddy answered and handed me the receiver. Tuwana plunged right in on the other end. "PJ had her facts all screwed up. Cly didn't run off to California. It's worse. He's staying with Slim Wallace."

"Really?" I decided to hear what wild story Tuwana had now.

"Yes, really. He had a fight with his uncle, but Slim stepped in and took over. Norm's all broken up about it. Now there's no telling how things will turn out."

"Slim's not so bad."

"Mother says nothing good will come of it. What with his reputation and all."

"Tuwana, you are the only one I know who thinks Slim has this dark, criminal background. Not one shred of evidence exists to support your theory. He's helping Cly patch things up with his uncle. Furthermore, Cly's staying at Graham Camp and going to school in Mandeville this year."

"Oh really? And how would you know this?"

"I have my sources." It came out snottier sounding than I intended, so I added, "Actually Cly told me himself."

Tuwana snorted into the phone. "Cly MacLemore? Going to Mandeville school? Trust me, Texas is not ready for Cly Mac-Lemore."

"Well, they'd better get that way. I think he'll be in Doobie's class."

"Speaking of which, PJ didn't get that story straight either."

"How's that?"

"Doobie's mother."

The hair on my neck prickled.

"When Mrs. Thornton called the plant office screaming and

carrying on about needing her husband to get her to the hospital, she didn't have a nervous breakdown collapse."

"Relapse, Tuwana. The word is *relapse*."

"Whatever. She had kidney stones, and Mr. Thornton called back later and said he wouldn't be to work until the neurologist figured out how to get them to pass."

"Urologist. That's what a kidney doctor is called." I knew because I'd had a bad kidney infection in third grade and had to go to a specialist...a urologist.

"Stop correcting everything I say. You'd think you were a walking encyclopedia. Here I am, telling you what's going on, and what do I get? Vocabulary lessons. Next time I won't bother calling you at all."

"I apologize. I just wish for once you'd get your facts straight."

Tuwana slammed the receiver in my ear.

The next day and the day after, I tried to call Tuwana to apologize for being a snit, but she was always out. Or told her sisters to say she was out.

Then out of the blue, she was on the phone, jabbering as if nothing had happened, hysterical about cheerleading tryouts and whether or not to wear mascara to school. More than once she recited a list of the teachers who gave detentions for any no-good reason. Her nervous talk didn't do anything to erase my fears about leaving Mama alone when school started.

Cly, on the other hand, didn't seem the least bit concerned about school. He told me his uncle apologized and wanted him to try out for the Mandeville basketball team. Shrugging like it was no big deal, Cly said he couldn't wait. He'd moved back in with Norm and Eva, but we still met at Slim's, who seemed like the grandpa I never had. His slate-colored eyes crinkled up when

I outsmarted Cly, and he was nowhere near the murderer Tuwana still proclaimed him to be.

Mostly, though, those dying days of summer, I stuck close to Mama. I watched her when she thought I wasn't looking, trying to pinpoint little signs of her memory slipping. But honestly, she just sailed through each day, pretty as you please, chatting about this and that, sipping her coffee and leaving pink lipstick smudges around the edges of the cup.

No matter how hard I tried not to think about it, every day brought the first day of junior high nearer, and with each new day my stomach gnawed deeper. A terrible empty feeling like fingers clawing their way to my backbone. When I mentioned it to Mama, she said, "It's the excitement of junior high. Changing classes, having a locker for the first time, just a whole new part of your life."

Then she gave me a teaspoonful of Pepto-Bismol and showed me how to clip the new sponge rollers around my hair.

## [ FIFTEEN ]

SITTING OVER THE TIRE humps wasn't all it was cracked up to be. The only way to get any leg room was to turn sideways so my new penny loafers stuck out in the aisle. Tuwana put one knee in the seat we shared and turned around. "Y'all have to yell and clap for PJ and me at the tryouts. Crowd enthusiasm counts as one-fourth of the total points."

"You bet, Tu-tu," Doobie said.

Tuwana scrunched her eyes at Doobie, and I could see she'd gone with the full makeup treatment—blue eye shadow, black liner, and the new Maybelline mascara she'd bought down at Willy's.

Cly sat next to Doobie, his feet turned to the aisle to make room for Doobie's orangutan legs. He had his gym shoes—new Converse high-tops—on his lap. They were a peace offering from Norm and Eva, he said. Along with a new basketball since he was trying out for the school team. Cly's flattop haircut shone and smelled of Vitalis.

I edged my foot over to his and nudged it. "You nervous?"

"Nah, I got this gig made in the shade."

"Oh sure. You talk like that in Texas, they'll boot you all the way back to California."

"Hey, I'm tight with Doob here. He'll show me the ropes."

"That's a scary thought."

Before we knew it, the bus passed the Mandeville, Population

1,639 sign and rolled to a stop behind the school. As we piled out, Cly whispered behind me, "Cool haircut, Sam."

"Thanks. It's called a pageboy. Good luck on your first day." I waved as he followed Doobie toward the high school entrance.

The junior high had to report to the auditorium, where a proctor passed out stapled packets.

"Sammie, over here!" Gina Hardy jumped up and down, waving her arms and pointing to the seat she'd saved me. "Tell me about your mother." We sat down. "I heard she had a nervous breakdown."

"Oh that. She had some problems, but she's all over it."

"You never get over nerve problems."

I smiled. "Some people do, I guess." I liked Gina. Friendly. Bookish, like me. Taller than all the boys in our class, like me. My best town friend.

A microphone screeched from the stage. "Testing. Testing. Find your seats, please."

"It's Howdy Doody time," Gina whispered behind her hand.

Carrot-colored hair and buckteeth got Mr. Howard, the principal, his nickname. It fit him to a T. His voice boomed into the microphone, "For you who are seventh graders, you've passed the diapering, baby-coddling stage. Things work different from now on. We have high expectations, and you will be held accountable. The packet we handed you is your instruction bible for the next nine months. Guard it with your life." His eyes bore down, searing deep into ours. A blistering sermon followed, citing all the deadly sins like smoking in the parking lot, monkey business in the halls, and a long list of don'ts for the dress code. Brother Henry could have gotten a few pointers on pulpit pounding and driving home the wages of sin from Mr. Howard.

"It's all a big show," Gina whispered. "He just does it to scare the bejeebies out of us."

"He certainly got my attention." I thumbed through the instruction packet.

During the bathroom break, we talked about the extracurriculars we wanted. School newspaper for me. Typing for Gina. Thankfully, she didn't bring up the subject of Mama again.

"I'm having a slumber party Friday night after the football game. Can you come?" We found our way to our lockers and then homeroom (second page in the bible packet), both of us glad we had classes together.

"Sounds like fun. I'll let you know."

Both the junior high and high school came to watch the cheerleading tryouts right before lunch. While the girls did their jumps and cheers, I heard Doobie and Cly in the section behind me: "Tu-tu! PJ! Tu-tu! PJ!"

I turned my head and saw Cly with freshman girls on either side of him. Very friendly freshman girls. I whipped my head back around to the action on the floor. A flush crept up my neck, and I swallowed the lump in my throat. I should have been happy Cly was getting along great. Too great, it seemed. Why hadn't I thought about all the girls who would be swooning over the new kid from California? My stomach cartwheeled like Tuwana on the gym floor.

Tuwana finished her jumps in the individual competition and ran up into the stands to sit by me, still carrying her pom-poms.

"How'd I do? Do you think I have a chance?" Her breaths came in short spurts, and her eyes twinkled like blue sparklers.

"The best I've ever seen!" I meant it from the bottom of my heart. If anyone deserved to be a cheerleader, it was Tuwana.

We had to wait until the last hour of the day to find out the cheerleading results. Back in the auditorium, extracurricular sponsors sat at tables with cardboard signs for the various options—yearbook, drama, newspaper, art, etc. Mr. "Howdy Doody" Howard gave us our instructions about signing up before announcing the 1958–59 cheerleaders. Ten girls had tried out for four positions. I held my breath as each name was called. Darsha West. PJ Ford. Linda Kay Howard. Patty Gruver.

My heart sank. There had to be a mistake. He hadn't called Tuwana's name. Claps and cheers broke out, but all I could think was *poor Tuwana*. All those hours of practice down the tubes—her summer a complete waste. As soon as we were dismissed, I stood on tiptoes, scanning the auditorium. She had disappeared. I looked up and down the aisles, at the various tables where groups of students huddled, waiting to sign up. Finally I dashed to the bathroom and found her slumped on the floor, her back against the gray tile.

"You *were* one of the best," I said when she looked up, streaks of black mascara running down her cheeks.

"You know what stinks? Miss Howdy Doody."

"Linda Kay, the principal's daughter?"

"She can't even do the splits, not with those thighs. And another thing—PJ. She only tried out 'cuz I made her. She wasn't supposed to beat me. All summer me telling her, 'You can do it,' and then what does she do? She gets to be a cheerleader, and I don't. It's just gross, that's what. I might as well move to another planet or Italy. There's absolutely no possible way I can ever show my face in this school again."

"Don't exaggerate, Tuwana. You have no choice. Next year will be here before you know it, and you'll make it then." I turned the crank on the paper towel machine and yanked off a scratchy brown strip. After wetting it with cold water, I handed it to her. "Here, clean your face. We've got to sign up for extracurriculars."

"I...I...can't face anyone." Her eyes widened. "Mike, oh my gosh. Mike Alexander will never speak to me again. You know football players only want to go out with cheerleaders."

"They may want to, but so what? There are only four

cheerleaders and how many on the football team? Thirty? Maybe more. It doesn't add up."

"You know what I mean."

"Yes, but when I was searching all over the place for you, I checked with Mike, and he was looking for you too. Hurry up or we won't get to sign up for stuff and we'll be stuck in study hall all semester with the goofballs who never do anything."

We went back to the auditorium. I dashed over to the school newspaper table.

"Signing up for the newspaper?" A tall, thin lady smiled at me. Her hair, twisted into a knot, was held in place by two wooden sticks with rhinestone tips sparkling like antennae.

"Yes, if I'm not too late."

"I'm Mrs. Gray."

"Sammie Tucker."

"I'll need a copy of some of your writing—schoolwork, poems, anything you've done in the past. Bring it by Room 12 tomorrow, and I'll make a decision by Friday."

She had a sweet laugh, and her friendliness made me like her right off. Now, more than ever, I wanted to write for the news-paper.

I hurried off to catch the bus. I couldn't wait to get home and tell Mama about Howdy Doody and Mrs. Gray and Gina Hardy's slumber party. I climbed the steps and turned to find my seat over the tire hump.


"I'm home, Mama!" Scarlett bounced up and down doing her basketball impersonation the moment I stepped into the house. Dropping my books into the rocker, I scooped her up and buried my face in her fur. Through the puppy slobbers, I didn't notice the mess in the front room at first. Magazines and books from the squatty bookcase littered the floor and teetered in a lopsided pile in front of the television. Then Mama came from the bedroom, her eyes wide and wild-looking. Her whole body trembled, shaky and ruffled.

*Nervous breakdown* flashed in my head.

My body froze, but in my heart I prayed, *No, God, please don't let this happen!*

## SIXTEEN

"MAMA, WHAT IS IT?" Her eyes flashed when I stepped toward her. *Does she even know me?*

"I've looked everywhere, and I can't find them." She aimed the comment at the room in general.

"Find what?" I whispered.

"Oh, you know. Those...pictures of you girls." Her eyes had a scared-rabbit look. "They're around here somewhere, I just know it."

"I think they're in the hall cabinet. Why do you want to look at pictures?"

"It's a long story. It's...Sylvia. This morning I realized she would have started second grade today, and I tried to picture her climbing the steps onto the bus, leaving me...." She stopped and got that fuzzy look again. "When I tried to remember her face, all I could see was a round, doughy lump. No eyes. No turned-up nose. Not even the teeny, pink mouth."

Mama's fingers trembled. Taking her by the arm, I steered her toward the couch.

"It's all right, Mama." Like a robot, she sat down. I sat beside her as Scarlett wriggled her way up between us and rested her chin on Mama's lap.

"Well, anyway..." She took a deep breath and focused somewhere behind me. "I know this sounds silly, but my mind has played the awfulest tricks on me since those treatments. Nasty things. Meant to help me forget the bad memories so I can cope with the present." Her voice got stronger as she held my hand, squeezing it until I thought she would crush my bones. "You ask me, it's a shot in the dark. How do they know where to zap my brain? What if they get off a fraction of an inch and fry the good parts?" Her eyes flashed. "Where does that leave me?

"Here's the crazy part. After a while it's hard to tell if I'm remembering something that's real or forgetting something that's not. Like today. Had I imagined Sylvia? Had she even existed? I started looking for her pictures, to prove she had been real, and I couldn't even remember where we kept the pictures." She rocked back and forth. "I couldn't remember...."

"I'll get the box, Mama. Hang on." I went to the wall cupboard between our two bedrooms, a narrow set of doors, the inside shelves just deep enough for books. I found a blue shoe box on the bottom shelf and took it to Mama. She patted the couch next to her for me to sit down.

She lifted out a handful of pictures and sorted through them. Me holding Sylvia. Mama leaning against a car, pulling up the hem of her skirt, showing her leg to whoever was taking the picture (Daddy?). Mama and Daddy getting married. Me holding an Easter basket. Baby pictures of Sylvia with a bow stuck on top of her bald head.

Mama held them to her chest. "Thank goodness, I haven't lost my entire mind." She pulled out another stack and laughed at a snapshot of Daddy in a fishing hat.

And that's how Daddy found us—the house in a terrific mess, Mama looking a wreck, both of us giggling and pointing at the pictures.

"Looks like a tornado in here," Daddy said.

"Pert near." Mama shoved a picture at him. "Look at you, all gussied up. Thought you were the cat's pajamas, didn't you?"

"Handsome devil, that's what you always said." Scarlett pranced around on the floor. Daddy scooped her up and let her out the front door. "What's the occasion? Why'd you two decide to look at these old pictures?"

"It's a long story." Mama winked at me.

"Look at this one. Is this me or Sylvia?" I showed her a picture of a baby in a bonnet, screaming her head off.

Mama's eyebrows went together into a V as she pulled the photo in close. Her expression changed. The sparkle left her eyes as she pinched the edge of the picture.

"Poor thing. Crying all the time. Never could get her to stop. Colic, that's what everyone said. You'd think her own mother could ease it, though, wouldn't you? Not on your life. The more peppermint water bottles I gave her, the more she cried. Practically wore out the floorboards walking her." Mama's voice sounded far-off. "Never could do a thing with her. 'Just give it some time,' people said. I never got the chance. She was gone before I could make her happy."

"Sugar, let's not start the guilt again. You were a perfectly wonderful mother. Look at Sis here. She ain't turned out half bad."

"I miss her so much." Mama didn't take her eyes off the picture of the crying Sylvia. "If only..."

"Uh, Mama, Goldie told me not to question why God does things. Actually she said 'the Almighty,' but it's the same thing."

"I don't think I do that. I've prayed until I'm blue in the face, but the ache I feel, the longing to hold her, never leaves."

Daddy reached down and took Mama's hand. "I know, sugar." He pulled her up and said, "What say I help you clear this stuff away, and then Sammie can tell us about the first day of junior high."

"Right. Just clean up the mess and everything's fine again. I don't think you'll ever get it, Joe Tucker." Her eyes narrowed into slits, and I could almost feel Daddy flinch as if struck with an arrow.

I had my own ache inside. Selfishness, I know that's what it was, but sometimes I wished Mama would remember me. Just me—Sammie. I picked up my school things and went to my room, closing the door behind me. She hadn't asked one word about my first day in seventh grade.

Gathering up copies of the *Dandelion Times* to give Mrs. Gray, I could hear Mama and Daddy arguing. It was hard not to listen, so I crept over to the door and as quiet as I could, I turned the knob on my door and inched it open a crack.

"I'm trying to understand, but the doctor said he wanted to see you back in a couple of months."

"What does he know? Being committed the first time wasn't my idea if you remember correctly. But then I don't suppose you do. You just want to take me back so they'll lock me up again."

"That's a crock and you know it. Zeb Thornton said he takes his wife back periodically. Preventative, so the spells don't come back. All I want, sugar, is for you to be well. No more of this up-and-down business."

Leaning closer to the crack in the door, I slipped and the door went shut with a thud. But not before I heard Mama say, "I would rather die than go back to that place. You've no idea...."

Sweat beaded up on my forehead. *Daddy had Mama committed? My mama?* I couldn't catch my breath, like the air was there, but when I heaved my chest, it wouldn't go in.

Yanking on the doorknob, I walked into the front room and looked at both of them. Their eyes darted back and forth at each other.

"What did you mean, when Daddy had you committed? Last summer? Getting shock treatments was Daddy's idea?" It made sense now, how he'd talked to Zeb Thornton and decided that must be what Mama needed.

Daddy cleared his throat, and I could see his neck turning red above his shirt collar. "It was a joint decision. Doc's, your mama's, and mine, that's all."

Mama lowered herself to the couch, and that's when I noticed for the first time that she still had on her terry-cloth robe, hanging open, just like when she used to have her spells. She pulled her knees up to her chest and put her head down.

"Mama said it was your idea."

"Sammie, you're too young to understand. And I'm not trying to put her back in the hospital. Just get a checkup."

"What if they do that shock thing again? Did you think about that? What if that happened and Mama couldn't remember you like she couldn't remember Sylvia? Or that time about Patch? What if they zapped her so many times she couldn't remember me?" I ran over to Mama and knelt by the couch and let her robe rub against my cheeks. When tears ran down my face, I felt her velvet fingers wiping them away.

Mama smiled at me and tucked a strand of my hair behind my ear. "Don't worry, honey. Your daddy's just a fussbudget. Blowing smoke, that's what."

She patted the sofa for me to sit beside her, and we sat there curled up together while Mama asked me about school and if I'd picked a favorite teacher yet. I told her about Mrs. Gray and Gina inviting me for a slumber party.

Daddy sat in his rocker, and the way he kept his eyes on the television, it was hard to tell what he thought. One thing I knew. I didn't want Mama to go away again. Ever.

On Thursday, Daddy had to work late. Mama said she felt like taking a walk, so we strolled up and down the camp streets, waving to the neighbors and laughing at Scarlett scampering here and there.

In front of Tuwana's house, Mr. Johnson had his sleeves rolled up, rubbing a chamois over the hood of the Edsel.

"What a magnificent car." Mama ran a finger along the window chrome.

"Best thing I ever done, getting this doll for my princesses. I declare, Mrs. Tucker, you might be the only soul in Graham Camp who hasn't had a ride. Wanna go for a spin?"

"Oh, could we?" Mama's eyes widened, and just like that, we hopped in with Mr. Johnson reciting the Edsel's features. Tele-touch drive. Electric windows. I knew them all by heart now. Mama's hair blew in wild swirls around her head as we rode along with the windows open, just like the long-ago day when I was a little girl. Mama laughed and thanked Mr. Johnson for the ride when he dropped us off later at our house.

"Wasn't that glorious?" Mama's cheeks glowed pink from the cool evening. "So clever of Benny Ray to give his girls such a nice surprise. There's nothing wrong with being practical like your daddy, but spontaneity is fun too. Believe it or not, your daddy used to drag me off on an adventure once in a while, take me dancing for no reason...." She hummed and did a little spin on the sidewalk as Scarlett pranced at her feet.

"And you too. He'd come in from working on the rig, load us both up, and we'd go out for coconut pie at Findley's Diner. He loved showing us off."

"I remember that."

"I don't see how. You were just a tiny thing. All that changed after Sylvia, anyway. Everyone thinks I had all the problems, but your daddy changed too. Clammed up tight, that's what." She lowered herself onto the top step of the porch and gazed off into the distance.

A whisper inside told me to put my antennae up and stand guard. Just the mention of Sylvia did that to me now. From the corner of my eye, I watched Mama's face, looking for signs she might be working herself up. After a minute she lifted her shoulders and smiled at me. "I think I might have handled things better if your daddy had talked to me more. We all got our ways though. Nothing for you to worry about. Everything's going to be fine now."

In my heart I'd never believed anything more than I did at that moment.

## SEVENTEEN

THE NEXT MORNING I woke up late and made a mad dash getting ready for school and gathering my things for Gina's slumber party. The smell of waffles made my insides growl as I yanked the pink sponge rollers from my hair. One side of my pageboy had a crease I couldn't get smoothed out. No time to fiddle with it.

"Thanks for making waffles," I told Mama as I wolfed them down, dripping a blob of syrup on my white blouse.

"Here, let me help you." Mama wet the corner of a tea towel and scrubbed the spot. "It'll dry before you get to school."

"Today's the big day.... Mrs. Gray will tell us who gets to work on the school newspaper. Don't forget, I'm staying after for Gina's slumber party."

"I won't forget." She hugged me and handed me my books.

I gave her a peck on the cheek, and with my suitcase in one hand, an armload of books in the other, and my purse swinging from my shoulder, I hurried to catch the bus. Just before I got on, I turned around and saw Mama standing on the porch. She blew me a kiss.

"Running away from home?" Cly asked when I'd made my way down the bus aisle.

I collapsed into the seat, out of breath.

"Yes...I mean, no. I'm going to Gina Hardy's slumber party tonight. What about you? Going to the game?"

Cly shrugged. "Doobie's getting his learner's permit today. We're gonna see if his pop'll let Doobie chauffeur, us. Save me a seat, just in case."

"I didn't know Gina was having a sleepover," Tuwana said. "I wonder why she didn't invite me."

"I don't know. She didn't say who she asked."

"Hmmph." Tuwana looked out the bus window.

The suitcase I'd brought wouldn't fit in my locker, and lugging it between classes looked stupid. I trudged toward the office to ask the secretary if she had any ideas. When I saw her empty chair, I figured I had to carry it around. As I started out the door, Mr. Howard's voice boomed behind me.

"Something I can help you with?"

"Yes...well...I don't know." Seeing his red hair and buckteeth shining made me wonder if I'd broken one of the Howdy Doody commandments by barging into the empty office.

Mr. Howard cocked an eyebrow and crossed his arms. "If you have a question, I'm listening."

"I need a place to put my suitcase since it won't fit in my locker, and I'm staying after school today and spending the night with Gina Hardy and will need the things I've brought." I smiled and pointed to the bag. "The things in my suitcase."

"I see. You're one of the camp girls, aren't you?"

"Y-y-yes. Sammie Tucker. Seventh grade."

"Well, Miss Tucker. No problem. Miss Golightly—she's the secretary—will keep an eye on it for you. Better hurry on to class. Don't want you getting a tardy slip."

"Yes, sir. Thank you." I fast-walked, imagining Howdy Doody eyes boring into my back, and whooshed into my seat just as the bell rang.

By fourth hour, I still hadn't heard anything about the school newspaper and had decided two things. One—Mr. Howard wasn't as bad as I expected. Two—I must not have made the cut for the newspaper. Make that three things: If Cly came to the football game, I would make sure he had a seat beside me.

So with all the stuff tumbling around in my head and Mr. Apple, the history teacher, talking about the Boston Tea Party, I almost didn't hear my name called over the loudspeaker.

"Sammie Tucker, could you please report to the principal's office?"

*Mrs. Gray wants me for the newspaper! Please, please, please, let that be it.*

"You may be excused." Mr. Apple cocked his head in the direction of the door.

My heart pounded in my ears as I hurried down the hall, and I forced myself to take a deep breath. *Stay calm. Mrs. Gray won't be impressed by some ninny.* I slowed down and gulped one more big breath before entering the office.

Three people stood in a semicircle in front of the secretary's desk. Miss Golightly, her face as pale as cottage cheese. Mr. Howard, his cheeks flushed with perfect round circles, one on each side. And Goldie Kuykendall, wiping her hands on her aviary apron, her Buster Brown haircut a mess, and a look of agony distorting her face.

"You know Mrs. Kuykendall?" Mr. Howard's voice sounded croaky.

"Goldie, what's wrong? What are you doing here?"

Her arms, sturdy and strong, reached out and pulled me to her chest, smothering me in aviary smells.

"Sammie, Sammie..." Trembling, she tightened her hold on me. My chest filled with dread, and I couldn't catch my breath.

Breathing through my nose, I pulled away and looked into

Goldie's round face, her mossy eyes rimmed in red. "What's going on? Why are you here? Tell me."

"Your mama...she's gone." She swallowed hard.

"Gone? Gone where? She's left me and Daddy?"

"I don't know how to tell you. She's...gone. Gone to be with the Lord." Goldie wrung her hands on her apron. "Come, your daddy is waiting at home for you."

She steered me toward the door, and as she did Mr. Howard's voice crackled. "Your suitcase, Sammie. You might need your things."

I clutched the handle and followed Goldie into the fluorescent blue hallway, through the double glass doors, and into the midday sun. Inside I felt ice cold.

[ EIGHTEEN ]

GEORGE, GOLDIE'S HUSBAND, tossed a cigarette butt out their Buick window onto the school parking lot. I glanced over my shoulder to see if Mr. Howard was watching. *How weird to think of that.*

Goldie took my suitcase and put it in the front seat before crawling into the back with me. No one said a word. I closed my eyes, praying that when I opened them I would be in Mr. Apple's classroom learning about the evil tax the British had imposed on tea.

George started the car, grinding the engine. I turned my head away from Goldie and stared out the window where I saw a red and purple and yellow blur of grade-schoolers on the playground. I gnawed on my lower lip until the taste of blood came into my mouth.

"What happened?" *Was that my voice?* It sounded far away.

"Your daddy asked us to pick you up and tell you your mama was gone, to heaven, like I said." Goldie patted my knee, her breathing heavy. "He wants to tell you the rest."

"He won't tell me." I turned and looked into her eyes. "I know he won't. He'll gloss it over, make up some story about everything working out for the best. My mother is dead. That's what you said."

"I'm so sorry. . . ."

"It wasn't an accident, though, was it? You would have said,

'Your mother was killed' or, 'There's been a terrible accident,' but you didn't."

Goldie's face sagged with little bags around the corners of her mouth.

My insides twisted together as I tried to imagine what Mama had done. *How? Why? When?* My eyes burned, hot and dry. The blood from biting my lips had a metallic taste like the way a penny smells when you hold it in your sweaty hand. *What did Mama do?*

"Did she slit her wrists? Swallow some more pills? Please...you have to tell me."

Goldie didn't say a word. Just sat there, her jaw muscle twitching.

"She was my mother. I have a right to know." Inside I didn't want to know. If Goldie spoke the words out loud, it would be true. *Mama killed herself.* I waited for the answer, my muscles bunched into knots.

"Your daddy should be the one to tell you, but..." Goldie stopped, looked at George, and then told me in a voice like sandpaper. "Slim Wallace drove his truck along your street this morning, checking which incinerators needed to be cleaned out. He found Scarlett yipping and squirming out by your row of garages. He thought your mama forgot to let her back in, so he picked her up and took her to the back door. When no one answered, he opened the door and called. Scarlett nipped him on the arm and jumped down, running back to the garages and pawing at the closed door. That's where he found her." Goldie patted my hand, then picked it up and held it in her cold, clammy one. "Honey, your mama died from hanging herself."

Liquid rose in my throat, more bitter than a green persimmon, and I leaned my head against the hard vinyl seat of the Buick. The world swirled gray around me, and when I tried to speak, my mouth felt as dry as a cotton ball. No words would come. My fingers and toes went numb, then my arms and legs. When I tried to swallow, my throat filled with even more bitterness, and I screamed, "Stop. Stop the car!"

I waited until George pulled over before yanking on the door handle. I jumped out and heaved in the dry grass, letting slime and vomit pour out of me. Every time I retched, tears sprang from my eyes. Over and over, I puked. Twice, three times. Six. I lost count, just letting my insides roll out every time a cramp came until at last the puking stopped, leaving me empty. And hollow.

Goldie wiped the mess from my face with George's handkerchief and guided me back to the car. She held me quivering in her arms all the way home. Then she guided me into the house where Daddy sat like a stiff wooden soldier in his rocker. Other people were there too—faces I don't remember, standing like they'd been waiting for me to arrive. No one said a word, just looked from Daddy to me to Goldie.

Daddy pushed himself up and came to me. "Sis..." He wrapped his arms around me. "It's Mama."

"I know. Goldie told me."

He ran his rough hand over the back of my hair and everyone kept on not saying anything. When a knock came at the front door, George opened it and nodded for Daddy. A man wearing a black suit said Daddy needed to sign a paper. He stepped out onto the porch. I went to the window, saw Daddy shake hands with the man, and then the man in the suit walked to the end of the sidewalk. A long, black station wagon with darkened windows drove up, collected the man, and they drove off. No one said, but I knew Mama was in the back of that car.

I wanted to run after them and yell at Mama to come back. *Don't leave me. I'll be a better daughter. I'll stay home from school and take care of you.* The words pounded in my head so loud I figured everyone in the room could hear them. I watched, and when the black car turned onto the road up the center of camp, I bit my lip, then lifted my hand to my mouth and blew Mama a kiss.

*Mama!* The voice in my head screamed. My insides started shaking so hard I thought I would burst. Daddy came back in and put his arm around me, but I shoved him away. Daddy had done this. He could have stopped Mama. All that talk about going back to that hospital did it.

"It's okay, Sis. There tweren't nothing we could do." He put his hand on my arm, but I flung it off.

"It's all your fault! You wouldn't listen to her." I glared at him, his outline fuzzy through the tears staining my eyes. "She said she would die before she went back to that place. You could have stopped her."

I ran into my room, threw myself on the bed, and hammered on my pillow with my fists. I wanted to hammer Daddy and all those people who said Mama would be fine. Just fine. She would never be fine again, and neither would I. I beat on the pillow until my arms ached and I couldn't lift them anymore. Then I curled into a ball and shut my eyes to keep back the river of tears. *Dead. I wish I were dead like Mama.*

Inside I felt as cold as if I were.

I must've fallen asleep because when I woke up, a woolly blanket had been tucked around me. The morning haze filtered in my window, and far away, in some other world, Goldie's parakeets chirped. A faint smell of maple syrup drifted to my nose, and it surprised me that I still had on my school clothes from the day before. A small tan circle of the washed-off maple syrup remained on the front of my blouse. *Maybe Mama made waffles again this morning.*

A knot formed in my throat.

I turned to face the ceiling and noticed for the first time the faint pattern of lines left by a paintbrush. I followed the lines back and forth, up and down, not letting anything come into my mind. My stomach growled, and I needed to go to the bathroom, but my legs and arms felt like they had weights attached to them. Moving would take all my energy.

Daddy poked his head into my room, and I turned my head the other way.

"Sis…" He sat on the edge of my bed, but I shut my eyes tight to keep from looking at him. "Some of the neighbors brought food. It'd be best if you got up and ate a bite."

*How does he know what's best?* The urge to pee got stronger, so I swung my legs over the bed and, without looking at Daddy, shuffled into the bathroom. My mouth tasted sour, so I brushed my teeth and then let the water run hot so I could wash my face. In the mirror I saw the same old Sammie and wondered how I could look the same when inside I felt shriveled and old.

I found Daddy in the kitchen hunched over a cup of coffee. He looked as ancient as Slim. Our kitchen counters had enough food for a church bake sale. Cookies and pies covered with cellophane. Unknown dishes hidden under tinfoil. "Where'd all this come from?"

"Neighbors. Church ladies. I can recommend Irene Flanagan's cinnamon rolls, right there by the toaster, if you're hungry."

"I'm not….Maybe some juice." Hams, casserole dishes, and fried chicken jammed the icebox, but no juice. "Who's supposed to eat all this food?"

"You and me, I guess."

My stomach lurched up into my throat.

Daddy took a slurp of coffee. "Gotta go to the funeral home later and take the clothes for Mama to wear. I thought her blue dress with the lace collar. The dress matches her eyes."

"What difference does it make? Her eyes won't be open. Not now. Not ever."

"I just thought...well, that's the one I'll take, if it's okay with you."

I shrugged and got a glass of water.

"I'll have Goldie come over while I'm gone."

"I'll be fine. Just leave me alone."

"Sis..." He stood up and was fixing to hug me, I could tell. I turned around and ran into my room and slammed the door.

I waited until I heard Daddy leave before I got up to change clothes. When I opened my underwear drawer, I noticed something I'd never seen before. A little brown book with gold letters. *Holy Bible.* Inside it said *New Testament, Psalms, and Proverbs.* It had thin pages with gold edges. I flipped to the second page and found Mama's name written in blue ink. *Marguerite Samuels, presented on the day of her baptism, June 6, 1937.* Underneath the date, in a child's writing, it said *Me, Rita, age 10.*

I studied the page and wondered how the New Testament got into my drawer. Somewhere, floating around in my head, I knew Mama had left it for me to find. *Why?* That's what I couldn't figure out. A ribbon hung from the bottom, marking a page with some words underlined.

*Ask, and it shall be given you;*
*seek, and ye shall find;*
*knock, and it shall be opened unto you.*

I read them over and over. Did Mama mean to tell me something? Maybe she left a note for me somewhere and meant for me to find it. A note that told me how much she loved me. My chest had a tight feeling, and I tried to think where to look.

Then I remembered something else I'd seen in my underwear drawer. There on top of my nylon panties I found a smooth leather case about the size of a deck of cards, the color of honey. I opened it, and curled on black velvet inside the box, a strand of pearls, each pearl exactly the same size, shone with a luster. Not the flat, plastic look of the pop beads in my dresser, but smooth and satiny. With my finger I traced the curve of the strand. I lifted it out and looked under the velvet, hoping to find the note where Mama told me she loved me. The bottom of the case stared up at me. No note.

I lay back on my bed, clutching the testament and the jewelry case. When my fingers grew numb, I let the Bible rest on my tummy and opened the case. I lifted the pearls and closed my eyes, hugging the strand to my chest. Then with both hands I worked my way around, noticing that the pearls weren't perfectly round like I thought earlier. Each individual bead had a rise or a dent, small bumps that I could feel. When the clasp touched my fingers, the metal felt lacy, web-like. Beginning with the first pearl, I counted my way around. Eighty-four pearls joined to form a circle. I opened my eyes and stared at them, trying to think why Mama had put them in my drawer.

Scarlett jumped onto the covers beside me, her eyes like two lumps of dull coal. Tears rolled down my cheeks and Scarlett licked at them. Time seemed frozen, and even though it seemed I should be doing something, I couldn't think what.

The front door opened, and Alice Johnson yoo-hooed. "Anybody home?"

Quickly I coiled the pearls back in the case and stashed them with the New Testament under my pillow. Then I went to the front room. Mrs. Johnson had a peanut butter pie in one hand and a feather duster in the other. She went right to work stirring the dust around, chatting nonstop about how sorry she was. "Benny Ray just feels dreadful about your mama. Said she had the best time riding in the Edsel, and he went on forever and a day about how much she had improved over the summer. Which proves, you never can judge a book by its cover."

I plopped onto the couch while she kept on dusting and straightening. "I tried to get Tuwana to come with me, but she's in an awful state. Just one thing after another for her this week. Not getting to be a cheerleader. Finding out Gina Hardy didn't invite her to her slumber party. Not to mention your mother. Adolescence is such a difficult age, as I'm sure you've guessed by now. I lost my own mother when not much older than you. At least you've got a father you can depend on."

*Daddy?* It was all his fault, but I wouldn't tell that to Mrs. Johnson if she threatened to yank my hair or pull my teeth out. It was none of her business, and the more she dusted and chattered, the madder I felt. Who did she think she was, swooshing in here with her feather duster?

"Where do you keep the sweeper?"

"In my bedroom closet, but I don't want you to..."

She ignored me, and soon the whirring of the Electrolux filled the air. I stretched out on the couch, propping my feet on the arms to fully extend, thinking about nothing.

"All done." Alice wiped the back of her hand across her forehead. "Now, if you'll come in the kitchen, I'll show you what I've done."

She handed me a list. "These are the people who've brought food with what each one brought. If you'll notice, I've numbered them and Scotch taped the corresponding number on the cake plate, casserole dish, or whatever. This will simplify things when you write the notes, thanking people for their particular dish when you return the various containers. I would explain this to your father, but men are hopeless with this sort of thing so it falls on us women to take care of the niceties."

My head felt swimmy, but I took the paper from her. "I don't feel all that nice at the moment. My mother is dead, in case you hadn't noticed. I wish everyone would just leave me alone."

"Oh dear, I was afraid this would hit you pretty hard. Would you like a hug?" She held out her arms to me.

"No! Please don't touch me." My body started shaking again, just like when Goldie told me about Mama, but I took big gulps of air and glared at Mrs. Johnson. "I don't need you or Daddy or anyone else. I want to be left alone. A-L-O-N-E."

I ran from the room and flopped onto my bed, letting sobs escape from my throat and lungs. *All I ever needed was Mama. And she's never coming back.* I bawled until I thought my insides had turned to mush. Under my pillow, I felt for Mama's Bible and her pearls. They were all that was left of the only thing in the world I ever wanted—a regular mother like everyone else had. And I didn't think I could stand another minute of my life without her.

Somehow I made it through that day and into the next. Daddy tried to talk to me, but I wasn't having any of it. From my spot in bed, I heard people come and go, bringing food, food, and more food. At this rate we'd have enough to feed half the starving children in the Congo. Once I thought about getting up to number the dishes like Alice suggested, but I didn't. It was too hard.

Along in the afternoon, Daddy came into my room.

"Sis, we need to talk about some things."

"There's nothing to say." I turned and faced the window.

"At least hear me out. What your mama did was terrible. I know you blame me, and I can see where you might. Truth is, if I could,

I'd be the one laid out in that casket, not your mama. I loved her. You need to understand, no one could see what was inside her, what she was thinking. That's what depression does."

*Depression?* That's the first time I'd heard a name for her sickness. Always before it was *nerve problems* or *those spells.* It had a name. I repeated it in my head. I turned over and looked at Daddy. He looked terrible. Eyes drooping at the corners, whiskers sprouting all over his face, and sadness coming out of his eyes. A twinge of something fluttered inside me. Then, just as quick, I remembered his arguing with Mama, and I didn't know what to do. Mama was dead, and all I had left was Daddy. I lifted my hand to him, and he took it and knelt down by my bed. He put his head on my covers, holding my hand in both of his. His shoulders shook and gurgles came from his throat. He stayed like that a long time, crying beside my bed.

With my other hand, I touched his shoulder. Tears fell out of my eyes too, and after a while Daddy sat on my bed and hugged me to his chest. I could hear the *thump-thump-thump* of his heart through his shirt. It sounded good in my ears. Steady. Strong.

Inside I didn't feel quite so cold.

When a knock came at the front door, Daddy got up to answer it. A voice crackled from the front room.

"I swear, Joe Tucker, I thought I'd never get here. But here I am, plumb parched and as weary as a lost lamb. Where's that sugar-dumplin' niece of mine?"

"Sis, we've got company."

My stomach rumbled as I went to the front room in slow motion. "Aunt Vadine?" I hung back and eyed her for a second. "I...I didn't know you were coming."

"Of course I came. Now, come, give me a hug."

My legs moved me across the floor, each step slower than the one before, until I reached the outstretched arms of my mother's sister. I braced myself and felt her arms around me, pulling me to her plump bosom. Her breath reeked of Juicy Fruit.

"It's good you could make it." The words stuck like a wad of gum in my throat.

## NINETEEN

IRENE FLANAGAN PLAYED the piano as I sat squeezed between Daddy and Aunt Vadine in the second pew. Shivers danced up and down my spine while my eyes fixed on the paisleys in Mrs. Flanagan's shirtwaist dress. She swayed ever so slightly, each paisley swinging like a tiny noose.

In my head Mama swung back and forth in time to "Precious Memories" as I counted each tiny loop on Mrs. Flanagan's dress. I shut my eyes to stop the image, but they burned behind my eyelids, and I couldn't stop counting. When I reached fifty-four, Irene rose from the piano and took a seat off to the side of the platform. Brother Henry walked slowly to the podium. His words got lost in the muddle in my head and Aunt Vadine's sniffling beside me. The air felt thick and heavy; Brother Henry's words slurred together. I wanted to run away and hide from all the eyes I felt boring into my back.

Someone sang "In the Garden"—Deacon Greenwood, I think. I kept my head down and looked at the toes of my shoes when Irene went back at the piano. Brother Henry spoke again, but this time stood right in front of us. I raised my head and saw him holding his Bible and pointing to a page. I held my breath.

"In Matthew, it tells us to 'Ask, and it shall be given you; seek, and ye shall find; knock, and it shall be opened unto you.' We think of Jesus' words as being the key to heaven, and they are. But for you, Joe, Sammie, and Mrs. Cox, I encourage you to follow these instructions not for answers to what has happened or why, but to find peace and everlasting joy in the memory of your wife, your mother, your sister. May the God of all comfort fill your hearts today."

The air swirled around me, not heavy as before, but light and breezy. How had he known Mama's words, the verses she underlined in her New Testament? Before I had time to think about it, Mr. Johnson stood at our pew to usher us out, and I saw Hilltop Church filled with people from Graham Camp, my classmates from school, and near the back, Mr. Howard, his face flushed red as a ripe tomato. Someone whisked me to the car, and we followed the hearse to the Mandeville cemetery.

Tears welled up as we passed newly plowed fields and pastures of parched buffalo grass. As we glided by, a pump jack dipped its head and bowed.

When we got to the cemetery, Daddy guided me along to a row of folding chairs under a green tent held up with skinny poles. The rich, earthy smell of the newly dug grave filled my nose, and I breathed it in. Big gulping breaths so I would remember the tickle the smell made in the back of my throat. I got a whiff of Juicy Fruit. I turned to see Aunt Vadine, one hand dabbing her eyes with a hankie, the other linked in the crook of Daddy's arm. My neck prickled like a spider crawling inside the collar of my dress. The way Aunt Vadine hung onto Daddy twisted something inside me.

As soon as everyone sang "Amazing Grace" and Brother Henry prayed and dismissed us, I ran up to Mama's grave. I tore off the white gloves Aunt Vadine had insisted I wear and broke a rose from the pink bouquet spread across the casket. A thorn pierced my finger, and I sucked the blood off. Then I scooped a handful of Mama's grave dirt and filled one of the gloves.

When I turned around, Tuwana stood beside me, her eyes red and mascara streaking down her cheeks. "It was a nice service." She sniffled.

"Nice? It was my mother's funeral. I wouldn't call it nice." My voice trembled.

"Mother said Brother Henry did a good job under the circumstances. I'm sorry. I really am. Anything I can do?"

"No, Tuwana. I'd rather be left alone."

She frowned and opened her arms. "I'll still be your best friend. If you want me to, that is." She gave me a quick hug.

By now people started closing in on me, putting their hands on my arms and my back, offering hugs and crooked smiles that looked like their faces might break. Every time someone touched me, it felt like they took a part of Mama with them. I wanted her to myself. I wanted to see her casket and think about how she looked inside. *Stop touching me! Can't you see I don't want any of you here? All I want is Mama.* The words shouted in my head, and my skin felt dirty from all the arms reaching out, grabbing, clawing at me.

I broke away and ran to the car. In the backseat, tears leaked from my eyes, a few at first, and then a river of them splashing out. I laid on the seat and let them come. The sobs came in waves like the ocean, and I could hear deep groans snarling my throat. My fingers cramped from clutching the glove. I sat up, letting the last sniffles drain down my throat, and looked out the window. Overhead a clear blue sky circled the earth above the green funeral tent. Mama's copper coffin hovered over the open spot in the ground, and figures milled around like ants at a picnic. When I twirled the pink rose in my fingers and sniffed its sweetness, a glimmer of an idea popped into my head. A way I could keep Mama to myself.

I closed my eyes and leaned my head against the seat, waiting for Daddy and Aunt Vadine.

*　　*　　*

After the dinner the ladies at Hilltop Church laid out, Daddy, Aunt Vadine, and I went home. We sat staring at each other in our funeral clothes. Aunt Vadine had brought in a wooden sewing basket and pulled out a ball of thread, which she worked with a silver crochet hook. A toothpick bobbled between Daddy's lips. Any minute I expected to hear the splash of water and smell the scent of lilac wafting from the bathroom.

After a while Daddy mumbled something about fixing the squeak in the Chevy, the one that had been there since we went to Red River. He changed into Levi's and an old shirt, leaving me alone with Aunt Vadine.

"I thought it quite odd"—Aunt Vadine looked up from her handwork—"taking a handful of dirt from your mother's grave. What came over you?"

"It felt like the thing to do at the time. The smell and all…"

"We'll probably never get the dirt stains out."

"I'm leaving it in the glove."

"And ruin a perfectly good pair of dress gloves?"

I didn't answer.

Later she started in again. "Tell me, Samantha, about your mother, her last days."

I gritted my teeth. I hated being called Samantha. So prissy.

"Please, call me Sammie. And to answer your question, I don't care to talk about Mama right now." *I don't even know you.*

"Confession is good for the soul." She rested her hands in her lap. "I have needs to know about my own sister too, you know. Surely you had some inkling, some clues she left…."

"No. Nothing."

"You don't have to be so huffy. I hoped we could comfort one another. And your daddy. We're all he has left, you know."

My face felt hot, but Mama's sister or not, I couldn't tell her anything.

Aunt Vadine went back to her crochet, and when Scarlett, who'd been snuggling beside me, stretched and opened her mouth in a wide yawn, I stood up. "Scarlett needs to go outside."

"While you're up, would you be a sweetie and get me a glass of iced tea? No sugar."

After getting the tea, I took Scarlett outside. The elm leaves, browning around the edges like pieces of burnt toast, floated from the trees. The tingly air cooled my face, but not the burning ache inside.

Scarlett chased after a leaf. With my chin resting on my knees, I sat on the porch and watched her. A pukey-green feeling came over me when I remembered the three suitcases Aunt Vadine had Daddy lug in yesterday.

A glove full of dirt does sound crazy. But it was part of the idea that had come into my head. I wanted to keep a memory box of Mama—things I could touch and smell and look at that reminded me of her, that would keep her close to me.

After supper Aunt Vadine touched Daddy on the arm. "You know, Joe, I feel like taking a walk. Maybe you could show me around the neighborhood."

"Suits me. You want to go, Sis?"

I shook my head. With the house to myself, I went to my room and collected my penny-loafer box, the dirt-filled glove, and the casket rose, which I pressed between two layers of waxed paper. Next I dug to the bottom of my underwear drawer and got Mama's New Testament and slipped the sandwiched flower between the pages. To keep it from bulging, I wound a rubber band around it three times and did the same to the wrist of the glove to keep the dirt from spilling out. I closed my eyes and sniffed to get the earthy smell where Mama now rested into my head. My heart thumped loud and fast as I tried to think about her not as dead, but just off somewhere taking a walk. Maybe a cool stream trickled nearby where she could take off her shoes and stick her toes in the water.

From the bathroom I took a sliver of lilac soap from the edge of the tub, Mama's hairbrush, and a box of bobby pins. The last two things for the shoe box were Mama's pearls in their leather case and *Gone with the Wind*. I yanked a piece of notebook paper from a spiral in my desk and scribbled a note: *Mama's things, the day she was buried. September 8, 1958.* I hugged the box to my chest, then stashed it behind my old dolls on the closet floor and went to the kitchen.

Dirty dishes filled the sink. I put the rubber plug in the bottom of the sink, squirted in the Palmolive, and turned the water on hot. I scrubbed the dishes, rinsed them in a dishpan, and put them in the drainer to dry. Doing something ordinary that I'd done a hundred times before calmed the banging of my heart against my chest. Wash. Rinse. Drain. The hot water stung my hands and turned them red, but I kept on until every last dish was clean. I was running the dishrag around the countertop when Daddy and Aunt Vadine trooped in.

"Your father showed me around the neighborhood." Aunt Vadine took a clean glass I'd just put in the drainer. "Can I get you a glass of tea, Joe?"

"Mmmm." Daddy's answer could have been a yes or a no. He hung up his hat and went to the front room. Low voices hummed from the television.

"Nice setup here at Graham Camp; makes me wish I'd paid a visit sooner." She poured the tea and handed the empty pitcher to me. "Here, might as well get this too while you're at it. Funny how death draws people together, isn't it?"

"You think Mama's dying was funny?" I washed the tea pitcher and felt the pounding start up in my chest again.

"Not funny...that's not what I meant at all. Simply that death brings people together in mysterious ways sometimes, doesn't it?" She smacked her gum and carried the two glasses from the kitchen.

The only mystery to me was how Aunt Vadine could have ever been Mama's sister.

I dried my hands and went to the front room. Aunt Vadine had situated herself on the couch with her crochet, the fine yarn streaming from the box at her feet. Scarlett had nosed into the box, and when she heard me, she lifted her head, a tangled ball of crochet thread in her mouth.

Aunt Vadine grabbed a magazine from the end table and swatted at her.

"No, naughty dog. No!" She swung at Scarlett, who tried to run away, but the matted yarn ball caught in her teeth, hanging like a stringy Santa Claus beard from her chin. I reached down to pick her up. She jumped sideways and yanked the crochet from Aunt Vadine's lap, looping it somehow around my aunt's foot.

"Come back here!" Aunt Vadine screeched and fanned the magazine in the air. When she tried to stand up, her feet tangled up in the yarn. Petrified, Scarlett jumped onto Daddy's lap, dragging the unfinished, now unraveled creation with her.

"Here, girl, calm down," Daddy said, and chuckled under his breath. Looking at the mess Scarlett had made, I couldn't help it. I burst out laughing. Scarlett's scraggly yarn beard and Aunt Vadine's face, the color of pickled beets, sent me into a giggling fit. The more I tried to stop, the deeper the howls came. Tears ran down my face, and my sides ached. When I looked at Daddy, he smothered a grin on his face, which tickled me even more. Daddy's calm, steady fingers loosened the yarn from Scarlett's pearly white teeth, and when he finished, he held a slimy ruined mess.

Tears splashed on my face. Crying, aching tears, not those of laughter. *How did that happen?* My face grew hot. I ran into my bedroom and threw myself across the covers, sobbing until I thought my head would burst. My arms and legs ached, deep burning pain as if I'd just rounded the bases from hitting a home run. Weak and trembly, I wished I were dead for the hundredth time that day. Dead with Mama and baby Sylvia.

## [ TWENTY ]

THE NEXT MORNING Aunt Vadine shook me awake with her square hand. "Time for school."

"No, I can't. . . . Not yet." I turned over on the couch, my bed now since Aunt Vadine slept in mine under my chenille spread. How could I face anyone? Let them give me those creepy stares like I had a brand on my forehead announcing my mother died. No. I wouldn't go, and no one could make me. Not Aunt Vadine. Not Daddy. No one. I shut my eyes and drifted off.

Soft licking on my face woke me up a second time, and I rolled over, pulling Scarlett into my arms.

"You need to take that mutt outside. Why your daddy ever agreed to let you keep a dog in the house is beyond me." Aunt Vadine had on one of Mama's aprons over her shirtwaist dress. The smell of linseed oil hovered in the air. "Best get going. If you're staying home, you can help me." She smeared a rag along the baseboard. "Lord, I wonder how long it's been since this woodwork had a good oiling. One thing about your mother, she didn't put any stock in keeping house."

She rearranged the furniture, putting the couch under the watercooler and Daddy's platform rocker on the opposite wall, with the TV in front of the west window. I cringed. Daddy would not be able to see the six o'clock news with the glare of the evening sun. *Not good.*

"Now that we've freshened things up a bit, you can buff the furniture. Hard work is good for the soul. Helps work out the grief in a body." And that's the way the whole day went, her directing me to dust this, move that, until I wanted to scream.

After a while Aunt Vadine flopped onto the sofa and finagled a throw pillow under her feet. "Whew! Guess I did a bit too much today. Think I've strained my back. Maybe when you get through polishing the end table, you could heat up some of that ham. The one with the cloves, not the canned one. That slimy gel turns my stomach. Your daddy will be home soon, and he'll be hungry."

While I worked in the kitchen, heating up leftovers, Aunt Vadine called out, "Maybe an ice bag would help my back, Samantha, if it's not too inconvenient."

Then she wanted the television channel changed and asked me to fetch the Doan's backache pills from the medicine cabinet. On and on. I wanted to shove the pills down her throat. Maybe going back to school wouldn't be so bad after all.

Tuwana came by after supper, and we sat on the front porch. "You'll never guess who's playing for the fall formal. Sonny and the Spinners. Everyone says they are so cool. Mike's cousin is the drummer, which is why we were so lucky to get them. Can you believe it? Our first dance."

"Since when do they let the junior high kids go?"

"Since never, but they're trying it out this year. Mike's mom is on the committee, and he's already asked me. A real date. Maybe Cly will ask you."

"I don't think so. We're just friends—you know that. Besides, I don't have anything formal to wear." And going to a dance would not be right. Not so soon after someone's mother died.

"You don't have to wear a formal; they just call it that. Suits for the guys and nice dresses for us. Like that new ruby sweater and skirt your mom got you before school started. That would be perfect."

"I don't know. I'll probably wait until next year."

"The dance isn't until the first Saturday in November. You're going to have to get back in the groove sometime. Mother says the best medicine is moving on after a tragedy. You'll see."

She stood up and tossed a tennis ball for Scarlett to chase and then pulled something from her pocket. "I almost forgot. Mrs. Gray asked me to give you this."

She handed me an envelope with my name printed in neat block letters on the front. My heart skipped a beat.

"Go ahead, open it, before it gets too dark to read out here." Tuwana tapped her foot.

I slid my finger along the seal on the back flap and took the note out. It had a fresh, flowery scent.

Dearest Sammie,

How saddened I was to hear of your great loss. My innermost sympathy to you and your father.

I have reserved a place for you on the *Cougar Chronicle*, the name chosen for this year's junior high newspaper. Your writing and your summer paper impressed upon me your kindness and ability to capture the essence of good reporting. We would love for you to work with us if you can.

With regards,
Mrs. Gray

A catch came in my throat. *Mrs. Gray wants* me *for the paper.* A warm feeling came over me, and all of a sudden I couldn't wait for tomorrow so I could go back to school.

Cly waved me back to his seat when I got on the bus the next morning. He stood up and let me in beside him. Tuwana gave me a little finger wave from the seat in front where she sat with PJ. They had out their compacts and giggled while putting on mascara as the bus bumped along.

Cly stared straight ahead while I turned to look out the window. "Sam, I'm sorry.... I know I should have come over or something, but...well, I think you know what I mean." He smelled of Vitalis and something sweet.

"Yeah, I know. I saw you at the service. That was nice." I shrugged and smoothed out a wrinkle in my skirt. *Cherry Life Savers*. That was the smell.

"Got any more Life Savers?" I tilted my head toward Cly.

He peeled the foil and wax paper from the roll, handing me one.

I popped it into my mouth. "So, did you go to the football game?"

"Nah, Doobie's pop had to work. Besides, Slim needed company. He feels lousy about your mom."

"Oh."

"We all do."

A gap hung in the air. I sucked my Life Saver down till it was as thin as paper. "How's basketball?"

"I made the first cut on the team. Me and Doobie."

"Congratulations."

The rest of the ride to school he told me about basketball defenses and offenses, drawing X and O plays on the back of his algebra homework.

When we got off the bus, he handed me the roll of Life Savers. "Here, you might wanna suck on these once in a while...to get your mind off stuff. It helps me sometimes."

The day went by in a blur. I figured out if I let my eyes float in their sockets I couldn't see people giving me strange looks. Like when Gina hugged me and her lips got all quivery, I looked off at the blackboard and smiled. Things like that. Mostly kids barely nodded at me or acted like nothing had happened, and the teachers went on teaching in their ordinary way. When Mr. Apple announced a pop quiz in fourth hour, my stomach lurched, and I ran out of the class into the restroom and locked myself in the stall. I pulled out a cherry Life Saver and sucked it down to the last sliver. Cly was right, I did feel better, and later Mr. Apple told me not to worry about the pop test; he hadn't meant for me to take it anyway.

When seventh hour arrived, I marched into Room 12 and told Mrs. Gray I was ready to work on the *Cougar Chronicle*. Her topknot had slipped off center, and strands of toffee hair had worked their way out and flew about her face like wispy feathers.

"Hey, everybody, welcome Sammie Tucker, our newest reporter on the job!" She took my hand and pulled me into the circle of students. We discussed the first edition, dividing up who would cover what. Mrs. Gray tacked a mock layout on an easeled board and gave a lesson on choosing the best headlines to capture the audience. The paper would come out the last Friday in September. My first assignment would be an article for the "Meet the Teachers" section. From a box Mrs. Gray had with all the teachers' names, I drew out a name. Mr. Howard.

A ripple went through me. Not the scary kind, but the head-to-toe thrill you get from riding the monkey cages at the carnival. *Sammie Tucker. School Reporter.* I couldn't wait.

The tingle carried me all the way home. That, and a couple more cherry Life Savers. Like when Belinda Zyskowski smiled at me through the gap in her front teeth when I got on the bus after school.

"I'm sorry about your mother. My fish Bubbles died, and we flushed him. Mommy says I can get a new fish soon, so maybe you could get a new mother too." I knew she didn't mean it like that. Still, it cut through me.

When I got off the bus, I found Scarlett at the end of a rope, one end tied to the leash, the other to the fire hydrant beside the driveway. "Don't tell me; let me guess. You're in trouble with Aunt Vadine." I set my books on the porch and unsnapped the leash from her collar, and together we trooped into the house.

"I'm home," I hollered.

"Take that mutt right back outside. She's been nothing but a nuisance all day." Aunt Vadine emerged from the bathroom smelling like ammonia. More cleaning?

"I don't think she liked being tied up."

"Then keep her out of my way."

I took Scarlett to my room to change clothes. When I opened my dresser drawer to get a pair of pedal pushers, I found it filled with cotton panties and long, chiffon nightgowns. Aunt Vadine's undies? In my drawer? A quick check, and I found the next drawer also held her things. She'd left the bottom two for me. I raced to the closet. Her three suitcases stood at attention on the floor.

A clammy, sick feeling came over me. *Mama's memory box!* I rummaged in the far corner, throwing out a stuffed bear and my old Betsy McCall doll, and felt my heart skip a beat when I found the shoe box on the floor. Looking inside, I found all of Mama's things. Untouched.

What to do? I couldn't keep it in the dresser or the closet. *Think.* Somewhere safe. Nothing seemed safe from Aunt Vadine. I jammed everything into my purse except *Gone with the Wind.* That went in my desk under a stack of old school papers.

"Samantha, I could use your help," Aunt Vadine barked from the other side of the door. Sweat broke out on my forehead as I threw on my clothes and reached for my Keds. Then I stopped.

What made her think I wanted to help her? That Daddy and I even wanted her here? She wasn't my mother, even though she seemed to think she could boss me around and yell at me. Not to mention the way she insulted Mama. I didn't have to face her if I didn't want to.

Sitting at my desk, I pulled out a sheet of notebook paper and wrote down the questions for Mr. Howard's interview. Name. Where he went to college. Why did he want to be a principal? Things like that. When I'd exhausted my choices, I doodled in the margins.

Aunt Vadine stuck her head in after a while and glared at me. I smiled and pointed to the books on my desk. "Homework." I pulled out my math book and did my assignment on fractions. Then I read about Patrick Henry and the minutemen in my history book. By the time Daddy got home, all my makeup work from school was done. And I hadn't had to listen to Aunt Vadine or do any fetching for her.

## TWENTY-ONE

THE DAY OF MY INTERVIEW with Mr. Howard, I wolfed down the beanie weenies, spinach, and fruit cocktail in the lunchroom so I wouldn't be late.

Tuwana raised her eyebrows when I stood to leave. "What's the rush?"

"Big interview for the paper."

"And who, pray tell, would that be?"

"You'll see." I tried to act mysterious to cover up the nervous twinges in my stomach.

Heading to the tray dropoff, I felt Tuwana's eyes following me. I turned and gave her a finger wave before leaving the cafeteria and marching toward Mr. Howard's office.

"Come in, come in." Mr. Howard waved me in, his mouth stuffed full, a piece of lettuce ruffled around his lips.

"Thanks. I'm here for the interview for the *Cougar Chronicle*. You've been chosen for our featured teacher of the month, although technically you are the principal, not a teacher." The words flew out of my mouth, and my knees shook. *Calm down.*

"True, quite true. Although I did do a semester of student teaching before I went on to get my principal's credentials."

"What did you teach?"

"Geography. Quite a subject for a poor farm boy who'd never been more'n fifty miles from Happy, Texas."

"Good. You just answered one of my questions. Your background." I fumbled with the paper in my hands, trying to read the questions I was supposed to ask. "Where did you go to college?"

"West Texas State Teachers College. Down in Canyon. Please, Sammie, have a seat. This might take a while since I've got a few questions for you too."

Mrs. Gray hadn't mentioned him being allowed to ask questions, but then, as principal of the school, he did have *credentials*, like he said. I sat down on the edge of the chair, scribbling about his family, why he wanted to become a principal.

"Actually, I didn't. I wanted to be a tree surgeon. My parents promised me a new car if I went into education. Sweetest roadster you've ever seen." His face flushed red.

"What's the most important thing you'd like to say to students here in Mandeville?"

He thought a while, chewing the last of his sandwich. He scrunched his face. "Keep your nose clean. Abide by the rules. Don't take any wooden nickels." He stuffed wax paper into a bag and slurped milk from a lunchroom carton. Then he leaned back in his chair, folded his arms across his chest, and looked at me with a stern expression.

"From all accounts, I've learned you're a good student, Sammie. Dreadful thing, your mother. How're you doing?"

Goose bumps popped out all over me. I rubbed my arms trying to get them to go away so he wouldn't notice. I lifted my chin and smiled. "Great, everything's fine."

"It may seem fine now, but..." I braced myself for the *If there's anything I can do* speech I'd heard from all my teachers and the people at Graham Camp. Mr. Howard leaned forward on his elbows. "It's been my experience that children in homes with only one parent make poorer grades and have more detentions than regular kids. Some even become problematic in their encounters with the law. Juvenile delinquents, so to speak."

"Is this something you would like me to include in my article?"

"No, this is about you. A friendly precaution, shall we say?"

"Me? A juvenile delinquent? Is that what you think?" I sucked in my breath.

"No, no, of course not. At least we hope not. Fact is, you've got a double whammy. Mental illness in the family *and* being raised by a lone parent—a father at that. You'd be wise to heed my advice, what I told you earlier. Keep your nose clean. I'll be checking on you regularly."

"Uh, well...you do that. Thank you for the interview, Mr. Howard." My head felt like it was spinning. I gathered up my notes. *Mr. Howard thinks I'm a looney tune.* No way. I took a deep breath through my nose. "And just in case you were wondering, I am not a mental case."

I stumbled from the office toward my math class. Too bad he hadn't become a tree surgeon—he would have been good with a chain saw.

The idea that I might turn into a juvenile delinquent stayed with me all day. I tried out different scenes in my head. Flouncing around in a skimpy outfit, smoking a cigarette, and hanging out on the steps at Willy's store. Stealing cars and whizzing through the countryside with my hair blowing out the window. Personally, I didn't think I'd ever seen a juvenile delinquent, so it must be Mr. Howard's way of scaring me. Like telling us to be on the lookout for Communists. How many Communists had I seen? None that I could recall.

So I didn't have a mother. Well, I did, but she left, and now all I had was a big hole inside where she should have been. A hole that hurt so bad I couldn't stand it. And that wasn't something I could discuss with Mr. Howard.

That afternoon I found Scarlett tied to the fire hydrant again.

"Which one of Aunt Vadine's projects did you interrupt today?" I unhooked her and rubbed her chin. So far my aunt had alpha-betized the soup cans and spices in our kitchen cabinets, stripped the floors and put on a new layer of Johnson wax, and washed and ironed all the curtains. When I pushed open the screen door, lemony, waxy smells filled the house. I wished for once when I came home a whiff of lilac bubble bath would hit me in the face. Instead the smell of Juicy Fruit lingered in the air.

All of Mama's clothes—dresses, underwear, silk nighties, shoes—lay in mounds on the couch and Daddy's chair. Sparkly hair clips, tangles of beaded necklaces, and rhinestoned brooches had been piled on the end table.

"What's going on? Why are Mama's things out here?"

"Helping your daddy out. You know men aren't good at figuring out what to do with the effects of the deceased."

"But..." My eyes took it all in. The dress Mama wore to Alice's furniture party, the robe she'd worn for days and weeks on end, her white pumps with the loose heel that clicked on the pine floors...

"You're too tall to wear your mama's things, and I'm bigger boned than she was. No sense keeping any of this. I heard on the radio the VFW is having a rummage sale in town. We'll take a load off your daddy's mind doing this for him. Besides, it behooves us to help the veterans of foreign wars after the sacrifices they made for our country." With her hands on her hips, hair the color of a bird's nest, and thin slashes for lips, she didn't look one ounce like her own sister, my mother. Wasn't it enough she messed with my stuff? Now she was messing with Mama's.

I piped up, "The rummage sale isn't until next spring. Once a year, that's how they do them. So there's no rush."

"No sense putting off 'til tomorrow what you can do today. You'll want to look over these things, keep a bauble or two in remembrance...."

All of Mama's things, and I could pick a bauble or two? Why did Aunt Vadine have the right to dispose of Mama's possessions?

"...doing our Christian duty to give what we can." She snapped her gum.

The shiny strung beads and screw-on earrings with dangling rhinestones, the tortoiseshell sunglasses with lenses as big as saucers, teeny flag pins, blues and golds and soft aqua, cool and smooth surfaces... *a bauble or two*? I scooped up a handful and knew I could never choose just one or two.

"No! You can't do this. These are Mama's things. Who cares if they fit or not? They're hers, and... besides, you don't know if this is what Daddy wants or not."

"Your daddy doesn't know what he wants right now. He'll thank me for it down the road, and so will you, when you realize how my being here has filled the maternal void you've had in your life for so long." She reached into the front of her blouse and pulled out a hanky I recognized as being one of Mama's. Aunt Vadine dabbed at her eyes, then straightened up. "We mustn't let our emotions get in the way. We've a job to do, and the Lord frowns on those with idle hands. Here, you can help me put these things in boxes."

I rubbed the material of Mama's dresses between my fingers, dawdling and thinking. Then I grabbed Mama's robe, a blue gingham blouse, a sundress. I snatched up one thing and then another, as many as my arms would hold and ran to Mama's room and threw them on her closet floor. I grabbed a pillowcase from the bathroom cabinet and scooped up her jewelry, every last piece, and stuffed it all in.

"Sammie, you have to get a hold on yourself. You're acting as crazy as your mother."

"My mama wasn't crazy. She had depression; that's what Daddy said. Is that a sin?" My breaths snorted out through my nose as I glared at Aunt Vadine, who flipped the hanky in the air. The lemony smells and gum popping closed in on me, and I felt pressure building in my chest. I ran from the room into Mama's closet and threw myself on the pile of her clothes. I hugged them to my chest, breathing in Mama smells and hating Aunt Vadine for babbling on about doing her Christian duty. Most Christians I knew didn't act like her at all. Not one bit.

After a while I sat up with my back to the closet wall and stroked Mama's clothes. The thick warmth of her robe, the starchy feel of her yellow pedal pushers, the silkiness of one of her nightgowns. I took the robe and slipped my arms into the sleeves. Something seemed off about Mama's robe being here. Every time I thought about the day she died, I figured she had been wearing her robe since she practically lived in it. Why hadn't she worn it that day?

A picture kept coming into my head of Mama swinging from a rope. I tried to keep from thinking about it, but I couldn't help myself. What had she worn that day? Did she put on her makeup? Earrings? Maybe she took a lilac bath and was going somewhere. Daddy said she needed to go to the doctor for a checkup. Maybe she was going to town to see Doc Pinkerton. To get those pills again. Was that what she was doing?

I leaned my head against the wall. *Slim.* I could ask him about that day. *Daddy.* Had he seen her? Would either one of them tell me? My stomach went sour. Maybe I was crazy. Like Mama. Which was better, being a juvenile delinquent or being crazy? Or dead?

The truth was I didn't want to be any of those things, but how do you turn around when you're speeding off down the wrong path? If only I had a mother, I would have someone to talk to, someone who would let me cry and not tell me I was crazy or ask me to bring the Doan's pills.

It was bad enough thinking all those weird thoughts. Then

Tuwana had to stick her nose in. One Saturday we sat in the Edsel listening to KIXZ and not talking about much of anything when she asked how long Aunt Vadine would be staying.

I shrugged. "She hasn't said."

"Mother says if she's got a grain of sense, she'll stick around. Grieving widower, free meal ticket, that sorta thing, ya know?"

"What do you mean?"

"The obvious. Vadine's going to be your new mother, get it? Mother says after the proper length of time, she'll make her move. It makes perfect sense. You need a mother. Your dad needs a wife. There you go."

"No way. All she's doing is helping out, cleaning and organizing. Doing her Christian duty, she says. I'm sure she's got a job and better things to do in Midland. Besides, she and Mama didn't get along all that well. Why on earth would she want to live with us?"

"Who knows? Maybe she likes your dad better than you think. Mark my words. She'll be your new mother."

Tuwana and her ideas! I gritted my teeth. Not that the thought hadn't come to me, but Aunt Vadine for a mother? It made me want to puke.

## TWENTY-TWO

THE REST OF SATURDAY and all through church the next day, I couldn't get Tuwana's prediction out of my head. I watched the way Aunt Vadine buzzed around Daddy and brought him cups of coffee, asking him if he'd like to have his neck rubbed, things like that. Then at church she sat close to him, sharing a hymnal. She fluttered her eyelashes and smiled at Daddy after Deacon Greenwood prayed one of his famous around-the-world prayers. By the time we finished lunch, my insides felt like they would burst if I didn't talk to Daddy and see what he intended to do about Aunt Vadine.

I found him puttering on the back porch, a Camel hanging from the corner of his mouth.

"I thought you gave up smoking." I sat on the back steps.

"I did for a fact. Took it up again." He flicked the butt into the grass and scratched the top of Scarlett's head. "How're you making out at school?"

I told him about the school paper and doing the interview with Mr. Howard.

"You know, I always thought he looked like that Buffalo Bob puppet Howdy Doody."

"Yep. That's his nickname. We don't call him that to his face, of course, but his ears do stick out."

Daddy laughed and measured a piece of lumber he had laid out on the cement slab.

"What are you building?"

"Thought I'd make a doghouse for Scarlett."

"You mean she can't sleep in the house anymore?"

"She's getting bigger, needs her own place. Think we'll run a picket fence around this cement here, keep her safe in the day."

"Is this Aunt Vadine's idea?" I didn't have to ask. I knew from the way she carried on about dog hair and whacked Scarlett with a flyswatter every time she got near her crochet.

"Partially." He stood up, walking in the direction of the garage. The garage where Mama died. How could he go in there? Somehow he just went in and out, carrying a hammer, a saw, a rusty can of nails. Then two or three more trips, bringing sturdy planks and slabs of flat siding. He measured and marked the wood with a stub of pencil he kept perched on top of his ear.

"Speaking of Aunt Vadine..." I tried to find the right words. "I've been wondering..."

"Were we?"

"Were we what?"

"Speaking of Vadine."

"Well, I'm trying to."

"Sis, can you hand me the saw?"

I handed it to him and blurted out, "How long is she staying?"

Daddy stopped and looked up at me. "Awhile. Seems we're not the only ones having a hard time."

"She wasn't all that close to Mama." The words spat out stronger than I intended.

"Not that. Her job. The manager of the truck stop ran off with all the money, and now the owner can't pay her anything but tips, so she's going to help us out awhile."

"And when were you going to tell me this?"

"Today, as a matter of fact. Later on I'm gonna get my old army cot from the garage rafters."

"Army cot? She's going to sleep on an army cot?"

"No. We figured you would. We got a feather bed topper for it in town. Set it up so you're sharing a room. Won't have to hang your legs off the end of the couch anymore."

"I'm not sure this is a good idea."

"Look, I know you've had a rough time. Vadine's right worried about you. Told me yesterday how upset you get at times, that you need female companionship. Heaven knows I've pert near worried myself into an early grave about that very thing. Mama's treatments last summer and then her...well, her being gone now. It's a good thing Vadine came along."

He made her sound like Saint Vadine, the angel of mercy.

"Don't you think about Mama though? About the day she died? Like, did she leave some kind of note?"

"None that anyone found. I'd give my eyeteeth to figure it out myself, but..." He blew a puff of smoke and ran his hand through his hair. "Sis, if she ain't coming back, it don't do no good revisiting it." He took a long drag off the Camel.

"Maybe not for you, but I need to know. Like what she was wearing and did she think about what would happen to us?" That was the big question. Did she even care?

"It's not something I aim to dwell on. And neither should you. She made her decision, and we have to move on."

He picked up the saw and started cutting. I looked at the garage. Would I ever be able to go in there? All I saw from my spot on the steps was a gaping black hole. I hugged my legs to my chest and felt a cold wind skitter across the yard.


That night someone screamed in my sleep. My eyelids felt glued together, and the more I struggled to open them, the tighter they clamped shut. I felt myself being sucked down into my sheets like

I was drowning in quicksand, only it was feathers. Mountains and mountains of them. More screaming. Strangled groans filling my ears. I tried to raise my arms, but they felt like lead. I would get one hand free and try to push up, but the feathers pulled me down deeper. Finally I was able to squint into the light shining in my room. Hulking figures hovered over me and pushed against me, deeper and deeper. I closed my eyes and fought against them, thrashing my arms, as the groans became grunting, huffing noises.

"Sammie! Wake up, Sis." Daddy's voice brought me into a sluggish half-awake, half-asleep kind of trance. My heart pounded, trying to escape my body. My head stayed filled with blackness, a hole that had no end and tried to suck me into its swirling nothingness. Daddy was outside the blackness, pulling me up, his hands rough and strong, one on each shoulder, freeing me from the drowning feeling. My breaths came faster, and I forced my eyes open. The groaning and screaming stopped, and Daddy pulled me to his chest.

"Shhh. It's all right. It was a nightmare, that's all." His hand felt like sandpaper on the back of my head.

I looked over his shoulder and saw Aunt Vadine, her arms crossed against her flimsy nightgown, a hairnet hugging her head. She yawned and sat on the bed that used to be mine.

The person screaming must have been me, but everything seemed off-kilter. Inside my body shook, shivery and cold.

Daddy stayed beside me, one knee bent, the other on the floor. I fished around under my covers and found Mama's robe and held it next to me, letting it warm me. When I closed my eyes, the black hole had gone. No more screaming. Just something foggy and soothing. Warm like a nice bath. I relaxed and let my head sink into the pillow. The last thing I remember was Daddy's lips brushing my forehead.

★   ★   ★

Every day at school, people talked about the fall dance, who was asking who, and what new outfits they were wearing. I made up my mind I wasn't going. It didn't seem fair to Mama even though Tuwana kept after me all the time.

"If I were you I'd let Cly know you're interested. I've heard Linda Kay Howard wants him to ask her."

"Well, you're not me, okay? I'm just not going this year. And if Cly wants to ask Linda Kay, he should."

It wasn't that I didn't like Cly. I did miss playing backgammon with him over at Slim's, but Slim was the problem. What would I say to him? I wanted to ask him about Mama, that day he found her, but I couldn't. Sometimes I thought I wanted to know; then I didn't. Daddy said we had to move on, but I felt frozen in time. Like I might wake up tomorrow and Mama would be there and everything would be fine again. Going to a dance or playing back-gammon didn't seem right.

I didn't really want to stay home all the time with Aunt Vadine either, but she had been nicer since I'd had that nightmare. Of course, Daddy had been home most evenings too, and she always put on her drippy sweet disposition around him. Sometimes it gave me the heebie-jeebies, but if Daddy meant for her to stick around permanently, he would've gotten me a real bed and not just a featherbed on top of an army cot. Maybe when Aunt Vadine left, Daddy and I could get back to normal. Not that I knew what normal was. Still, I kept my fingers crossed.

One good thing was seeing Mrs. Gray every day. She always had this breezy way of helping us come up with good ideas when we did our layouts for the *Cougar Chronicle*. And she loved my article about Mr. Howard.

"Excellent! Who would've guessed our own principal once had

a dream to shape and nurture trees and gave it up to shape young lives instead?" Mrs. Gray's reading glasses hung on a chain around her neck. Shiny, black sticks bobbled in her topknot. *Japanese princess* popped into my head. She smelled good too. Like Ivory soap.

The day after the paper came out, Linda Kay Howard scooted her lunch tray next to mine in the cafeteria.

"Your article sent my mother into hysterics." She crunched a carrot stick. "She's been trying to get my dad to prune the roses for two years, and come to find out he had horticultural tendencies all along." She laughed like a donkey braying.

I went through each day numb, answering questions in class, turning in my homework, laughing with the kids in the lunchroom. Still, nothing felt right. In the back of my mind, the word *depression* whispered to me over and over. And I couldn't get it out of my head.

## TWENTY-THREE

ONE AFTERNOON I HAD Scarlett outside when Daddy came home from work whistling.

"Sis, I thought we ought to pay Slim a visit this evening." He threw a stick for Scarlett to fetch.

My stomach knotted up. "I don't know. Why do you want to visit Slim?"

"Just bein' neighborly. Maybe he could teach me that game you're so fired up about."

Could this be Daddy's way of moving on? After supper he took his everyday cowboy hat from the hook and told Aunt Vadine our plans.

"What? No dessert? There's still some of your favorite coconut cake."

I noticed she'd put on a nice dress and had started wearing rouge and lipstick.

"Not tonight. Gotta watch my figure."

Aunt Vadine's eyes squinted for a flash. Then the corners of her lips tilted up. "Don't be too late."

I put my plate in the sink and grabbed my purse.

The wind had picked up, a bit of a chill in the air, so Daddy said we'd better take the Chevy instead of walking. When we got to Slim's, he was lugging a basket from the garden. "Green tomatoes." He set the basket down. "Accordin' to *The Old Farmer's Almanac*, we could have a frost tonight. Another week or two and we could get a hard freeze. Don't want these 'maters going to waste."

"Definite nip in the air. Sis and I wondered if we might keep you company this evening."

"You betcha. Come in, and I'll fix you a skillet of these babies. Best things you ever had." Slim battered thick slices of the tomatoes, rolled them in cornmeal, and fried them in bacon grease.

"Delicious." Daddy took a second helping. *Watching his figure, huh?*

I helped Slim clean up. I'd forgotten how homey his house felt.

"The reason we came over..." Daddy leaned on the door frame, working a toothpick around in his mouth. "Couple o' reasons. I've been wanting to thank you for putting up with Sis here, letting her come around all summer and all."

"She's good company. Been good for young MacLemore too, who, if I'm not mistaken, promised me he'd come by tonight for a rematch. That scoundrel beat me six for eight a couple nights ago." Slim handed me the last plate to rinse and put in the drainer to dry.

"That's the other thing. Figured I'd see for myself what all the fuss is about this game. I thought maybe Sis and I could play this winter while her aunt knits her fingers to the bone."

"Crochet, Daddy. That's what she does."

"Beats me. Some frilly fancy work's all I know."

Just then Cly hollered at the screen, "Hey, Big Daddy, didn't know you had company."

"Just a regular hive of activity. Seems we got another taker on backgammon. Unless, of course, you'd like to play dominoes. Old fogies against you *cool cats.*" Slim winked at Cly.

Slim got out the dominoes and shuffled the "bones" as he called them on the enameled kitchen table.

*Click.* Cly slapped a domino down and scored ten.

A teakettle whistled on the stove. Slim put Sanka in two cups for him and Daddy. "You kids want some Ovaltine?" He filled our cups and brought them steaming to us.

Cly and I won the first game.

"Some sorry partner your pop makes." Slim gave a husky chuckle and shuffled the bones.

Daddy clicked a double five on the table. "Give me ten, Sis."

Cly groaned and played without scoring.

The whole time I sipped my Ovaltine and listened to Daddy's tapping one of his dominoes end over end, I kept trying to think of some way to ask Slim about Mama and the day she died. Every time I'd think of a question, Slim would score five or it would be my turn to shuffle the dominoes.

Then, out of the blue, Slim brought up the subject. "Tough go on your own, without Rita." He looked at me. "And your mother."

Daddy cleared his throat but didn't say anything.

"I ain't over my Dottie yet. Young Cly here'll tell you, I keep myself company talking to her."

"Bonkers, that's what he is." Cly slapped down a domino and scored ten.

"You gotta remember the good times. Yessir, Dottie and me sitting on the porch swing, counting the lightning bugs and dreaming about our girls growing up."

"Your girls? I thought you only had one daughter." I remembered he'd bought an extra paper last summer. *For my daughter*, he'd said.

"Two, actually." His fingers, knobby at the joints, gripped a domino. "Some dreams turn out different than you plan. Can't be helped, I reckon."

Daddy leaned back in the kitchen chair and rubbed his chin.

"The good times, huh? The trip to Red River'll be worth remembering, huh, Sis?"

I smiled and nodded. Except for Mama's mixed-up memories, it had been a good vacation.

"And dancing. My, how Rita loved to dance. Met her that way."

Slim must've put something in Daddy's Sanka the way he started talking. "After the army, I came strutting home to Midland, and the first night back, some buddies took me out on the town. Whoo-ee. Met Rita that night, with her flaming red hair, twirling to Bob Wills and the Texas Playboys..." His eyes had a faraway look—not sad, but like remembering the sweetest thing that ever happened.

"That's how Tuwana's mother met her dad," I said. "I think it was in Pampa, some dance at the armory."

"Is that a fact?" Slim clicked his last domino on the table. "Twenty-five. And I'm out. What's the score?"

Groaning, I shoved the paper full of Xs across. "You win."

"Tied up." Slim pushed back from the table. "Think I'll go out and check the weather. See if that pesky almanac is right."

Daddy followed him, and I wanted to kick myself for not saying something about the day Mama died. Maybe Slim wouldn't tell me, but he *was* the one who found her. And as near as I could tell, I was the last person on earth to talk to her. Maybe she was still breathing when he found her and said something, some last-minute thing she wanted me to know. I stared at my hands and fiddled with the dominoes.

Cly waved his hand in front of my face. "Hey, anybody home in there?"

"Yeah, just thinking." I took the last sip of my Ovaltine, which had turned cold with a grit in the bottom of the cup.

"Me too. I've been thinking about that big dance coming up. Doobie can't go with me. He got himself a date with PJ."

"So I heard."

"Uh...I was wondering..." Cly lined up the dominoes in piles of three. "I guess to be cool at Mandeville you have to have a date."

"Tuwana says Linda Kay Howard wants you to ask her. She's really pretty nice."

"Have you ever heard her laugh? She sounds like a hyena. Besides, I know who I'm going to ask to the dance."

The Ovaltine mixed with fried green tomatoes sloshed around in my stomach. "Who's the lucky girl?"

"You...if you'll go with me."

My forehead broke out in a sweat, and the first thing that popped out of my mouth was, "A donkey. That's what Linda Kay laughs like."

"You numskull. What kind of answer is that?"

The lightbulb over Slim's table made tiny pear-shaped lights in Cly's dark eyes, and I started laughing.

"Yes. My answer is yes. And don't call me a numskull."

## TWENTY-FOUR

ON THE WAY HOME I told Daddy about Cly asking me to the dance. In the dark of the car, I couldn't see his face, but when we pulled into the driveway, he put the car in park and said, "The MacLemore kid seems all right. Slim's pretty high on him. Don't rightly figure you're old enough for a date—"

"It's not a real date—just a school dance. Tuwana can't stop talking about it. Her parents are chaperones." I half-wished he'd say I couldn't go. Why I'd blurted out to Cly without thinking, *I* couldn't even figure out. For one thing, I didn't know anything about dancing, except the square dancing we did in fifth grade music class. *Do-si-do* and all that.

In the faded moonlight, I could see a funny grin on Daddy's face. "You'll always be my little girl, but you'd be in good hands with the Johnsons. Maybe it's time you had a little fun."

*He said I could go?* I thought I might faint. Or throw up. Why else would I feel light-headed and tingly?

"Sis, you think you could open the garage?"

I sat glued to my spot. Open the garage? Pull the door open where all that blackness waited? I gripped the armrest on the door. When Daddy cleared his throat, I yanked on the handle and ran into the house.

That night I had the dream again. The black hole that tried to pull me in. Like the garage. Black and empty. I didn't hear the screaming this time, but when I woke up, I had cold sweats and Daddy had his arms wrapped around me. He pulled Mama's robe from the tangle in my covers and held it up to his face. He closed his eyes, and I thought he was trying to get a whiff of Mama. Tears ran down my cheeks as I buried my face in Daddy's undershirt. It smelled of BO and Old Spice.

Tuwana jumped up and down when I told her I had a date to the dance. "See, I told you if you acted interested, Cly would ask you."

"All I did was play dominoes over at Slim's with him and Daddy."

"Which is repulsive in itself. How you can stand to be around that creepy old guy is beyond me."

"Slim's not creepy. He had a wife once and two daughters."

"And why don't you ever see his daughters coming around? Think about it. He murdered his wife. That's what Mother says."

"I like him, and I think your mom got her information mixed up."

"Forget Slim. Let's plan for the dance. Ask Cly if y'all can ride with us. Since Mother and Daddy are sponsors, they said I could just meet Mike at the VFW. Oh, and Mother's taking me shopping to buy a new dress...."

Sometimes I just wanted to scream when Tuwana talked about her mother. Not that I didn't like Mrs. Johnson, but it was always *Mother this* and *Mother says*, like Tuwana had her own private dibs on everything about mothers. So I didn't have a mother to talk about. So what? It just wasn't fair. Sometimes I tried to remember the look on Mama's face when we picked out the ruby sweater and skirt from the catalog. She hadn't known I'd be wearing it to my very first dance. Would she be happy? Would she look down at me from heaven and say, "That's my daughter"?

On my cot I held her robe next to me and rubbed it against my cheek, trying to remember how she smelled and the exact shade of red in her hair, and everything blurred in my mind. And every night I asked God to let me please, please, please get up the nerve to go in the garage and see and feel the last place on earth where Mama had been. But when morning came, I couldn't even look at the garage.

One night when Daddy had evening shift, Aunt Vadine had one of her moods where nothing I did suited her. After supper I told her I needed to take Scarlett for a walk. She hollered as I went out the door, "It's nearly dark. Why your daddy lets you run wild..."

I shut the door behind me before I had to hear any more about what a juvenile delinquent I had turned into. Wild? How could taking Scarlett for a walk be wild?

A couple of blocks from home, Scarlett took off after a cottontail that jumped under the Bradys' hedge. She yanked the leash out of my hand, and I ran after her. She streaked across three yards before I caught her. I picked her up and scolded her, then went back toward the street and saw Cly coming from the direction of Doobie's house. I don't think he saw me the way he bounced his basketball on the street, cut to the left, dribbled, and made another quick turn. Then he held the ball up like he was getting ready to shoot.

"Hey, pass over here." I set my purse down and looped Scarlett's leash around my arm.

Cly looked up sorta sheepish and tossed me the ball. I dribbled up to him and asked him how basketball was going. First string on the B-team.

"Congratulations. Bet your uncle is proud."

He shrugged and went over to scoop up my purse. "Hey, cat, what do you carry in here? Bricks?"

"Maybe. Maybe not. Be nice and I might show you." I started toward home, and he fell in step beside me. A patch of grass, now crusty brown, grew between our incinerator and the garages for our block. You couldn't see the garage door from here so it didn't creep me out too bad to just see the side of the tin building. I motioned for him to follow me, and we sat down with our backs against the warm incinerator.

"I always wanted to know what you birds carried around in those bags. You gonna tell me, or do I have to wrestle you for it?"

"I'm thinking about it. You'll probably think I've flipped my wig if I show you."

He reached into his pocket and took something out.

"Shut your eyes and open your mouth." When I did, he put a cherry Life Saver on my tongue.

"All right. I'll show you."

I pulled out my wallet, a compact, a skinny notebook for school assignments, two tubes of lipstick, one called "Party Pink" and the other a shiny lip gloss, and a pencil with no eraser. Should I show him the rest? Mama's stuff? So far, I hadn't shown that to anyone. Tuwana would laugh. Gina would probably be okay with it, but it hadn't come up. But Cly? Should I or not?

"Come on, what else you got in there?"

"Promise you won't think I'm crazy?"

Cly nodded, and I took out the New Testament, the glove full of grave dirt, and last, the leather box with Mama's pearls.

"These were Mama's things." I explained what they were. "I feel connected to her somehow by having them with me."

Silence. I stared at the toes of my loafers. *He probably thinks I'm nuts.* My fingers went numb from clutching the pearl box so tight.

After a while Cly peeled off another Life Saver and offered it to me. "You're lucky, you know?"

"How's that?"

"At least you've got something to remember your mom. Me, I don't even have a picture. Just a bunch of rotten memories."

"I'm sorry. Does it make you sad?"

"Sometimes. Mostly I just don't think about it."

We sat in the dark, not saying much, just looking up at the sky. I tucked the things back in my purse and leaned back into the warmth of the incinerator. "That's all I think about."

"I figured. Sometimes you're off in another world."

"Have you ever been afraid to do something?"

Cly spun the basketball between his fingers and didn't answer. "Well?"

He cleared his throat. "I don't think about it much anymore, but there used to be rats in the place where my dad and me lived. Scared the bejeebies out of me to shut my eyes at night. I could hear them scratching when it got dark, and I would lie with my eyes open, keeping a lookout. When I fell asleep, they came in my dreams. My dad laughed, called me a sissy."

"You were afraid of rats, but you killed a rattlesnake."

"Slim pushed me to it. Then when I started hitting it, I thought about those rats, and that's why I beat the bloody pulp out of that thing. You know what? I don't have those rat dreams anymore." He stretched out his legs and whistled for Scarlett. "Why'd you wanna know if I'm afraid?"

"There's this thing I'm afraid to do."

"If you don't do it, you'll always be afraid. You gotta put it on the front burner and just go after it. You wanna tell me what it is?"

"Maybe someday."

"I'm all ears."

I took a deep breath and looked up at the sky. Stars looked down, millions of them, winking at me. Why, of all the guys in

California, had the one without a mother shown up at Graham Camp? What did it mean? The stars twinkled while I wondered whether or not to tell Cly tonight. Or ever. A falling star shot across the Milky Way.

Feeling braver, I told him. "It's the garage. Where Slim found Mama that day. I want to go in there, but I can't. I'm afraid to ask Slim how Mama looked, if she said anything...." My voice broke, and I couldn't finish.

Cly reached over and put his arm around me. I rested my head against his shoulder.

"You'll do it someday, cat."

My stomach growled and made us laugh. Tinny, echoing laughs.

"I'd better go before my aunt gets worried." She'd probably had forty conniptions by then already, but facing her wasn't half as scary as the thought of stepping into the garage.

Cly stood and pulled me up. "Here. You might need these." He tucked a half roll of Life Savers into my palm and went off dribbling the basketball.

The kitchen clock read only eight o'clock, but Aunt Vadine snored from Daddy's rocker. I got a drink of water and tiptoed into the bedroom. At my desk I pulled out a sheet of notebook paper and wrote Mama a letter. I let her know I thought Cly was a good friend and that I was thinking about wearing the pearls to the dance. I tucked it in an envelope and wrote *XXX* and *OOO* on the back before I took it to her room and propped it on her pillow next to Daddy's.

[   TWENTY-FIVE   ]

NOTHING SCARED SCARLETT O'HARA. She took care of dying soldiers, and when she was flat out of food and money, she made a dress out of her curtains. One Saturday, I decided to read *Gone with the Wind* again and see if I could figure out what made her so brave. When I went to get the book from my desk, I couldn't find it, so I asked Aunt Vadine if she'd seen it.

"A child your age shouldn't be reading such filth. Books like that give girls ideas, and boys can smell it on 'em coming and going."

"It's just a book about the Civil War, people caring for each other even though Atlanta burned to the ground and thousands of men lost their lives."

"Phooey!" Her lips drew together like the top of a drawstring purse. "Trash. That's all it is. Totally inappropriate for you to be reading. And don't think I didn't see you behind the incinerator, cavorting with that boy, Sly somebody or another."

"Cly. His name is Cly. And we weren't cavorting. I don't even know what that is. We were talking. And I would like it very much if you would give back my book."

"Get it yourself. It's in that incinerator you're so fond of." She picked up her crochet, jabbing the shiny hook in and out of the pot-holder-sized creation in her hands.

I ran out the back door over to Goldie's, my face burning from her words.

"Cavorting! Why would she say that?"

Goldie listened patiently while I told her everything.

"Maybe she feels responsible for you, wants to be a substitute mother, and doesn't know how to go about it." Goldie handed me a glass measure with her special vitamin mix and nodded toward the mating parakeet bins. "She'll either come around or tire of Graham Camp and move on. Sometimes you have to let things slide off and stick it out."

For once I didn't find Goldie's advice all that comforting. Why did I have to make all the adjustments? None of this would've happened if Mama hadn't killed herself. No tiptoeing around one disaster after another. No Aunt Vadine snooping through my stuff, taking over my room. No Scarlett being banished to the doghouse. No Mr. Howard with his Howdy Doody eyes on me.

Slamming the screen between the parakeet pens and the work area, I glared at Goldie. "You know what I think? None of this would be happening if Mama hadn't *you-know-what* to herself. It's all her fault. Did she give one thought about me and Daddy? No, she had to go off and be with her precious Sylvia." I smacked the measuring cup on the worktable and felt the blood pumping in my ears. Once I started, I couldn't stop.

"You know what else? She didn't just up and decide that morning to slip a rope around her neck. She knew the night before." My breaths panted out like Scarlett after she'd been chasing a rabbit. "Why else would she tell me everything was going to be just fine? How could she know that unless she knew she was going to do it? And another thing. When I left for school, she stood on the porch and blew me a kiss. She never did that before."

Goldie wiped her hands on her dirty apron and led me out of the aviary and into her front room. By now my whole body shook, and when Goldie tried to sit me down, I shoved her away.

"And what about Daddy? All these years, while Mama moped

around in her bathrobe, he left me to worry whether she took her pills or supper got put on the table. Smiling like we were just the most ordinary people on the block, telling me things would get better. Then you know what else he did? He tried to get Mama to go back to that hospital. Just a checkup, he said, but he knew something wasn't right. Mama said she would rather die than go back to the hospital. Not once did she think what would happen to me. Now Mr. Howard at school thinks I'm two steps away from being a freak show. That's what Mama did—turned me into someone I don't even know anymore. I hate her! Do you hear me? I hate her!"

The words gagged me, closing my throat off. I raced into Goldie's bathroom and vomited, my head over her toilet, clutching the sides of the cold porcelain. Rivers of bile, sour and yellow, puked out over and over again. I got the hiccups, which felt like being punched in the belly every time one came. I held my breath and counted to fifty. My head got all swimmy, and I gulped for air. Tears and vomit wet my face, and I felt as hollow as a dead tree. And just as rotten.

Goldie washed my face and walked me into her front room. Lowering me on the couch beside her, she held me in her arms, rocking back and forth. When she talked, it wasn't about Mama, and her voice sounded far away, like coming up from a deep well.

"When my Jimmy died, nothing and no one could console me. I blamed God and George and my own stupidity for letting him go off to that swimming hole. Like a cancer, it devoured me, robbing me of every joy I had in life. George looked like death himself, and one day he said to me, 'Goldie, we've let fear get the better of us. Fear of what might happen if we choose to go on and live a normal life.' Soon after we moved here and chose to go on."

She stopped for a minute, then cleared her throat and said,

"You've been through a lot in your young life, more than your share." Her rough fingers stroked my cheeks. "The Lord says we'll have troubles. Guaranteed. Listen to me, child. Your mama made her choice, and you have to make yours. You can keep your anger and hate everyone around you. You can blame God or your mama or your daddy. Or you can choose to face life, wherever it takes you." Goldie held me tight and kissed the top of my head.

"It's too hard and not fair...." Daddy's words echoed in my head: *Life is not fair.*

"You're not alone—there's your daddy and me, and don't go discounting the helpers the Almighty brings your way. Irregard-less...you, and you alone, have to choose."

My choice? What helpers? Aunt Vadine? Mr. Howard? Even Alice Johnson and her showing me the proper etiquette of grati-tude? If this was the work of the Almighty, it was a big fat joke.

Goldie had never lied to me before. Never. She couldn't if she tried.

What if I had it all mixed up? It wouldn't have been the first time. Still. Mama had known what she was going to do, and she didn't care.

She.

Did.

Not.

Care.

But...what if Goldie was right?

Deep inside I felt a burning spot, a hot coal that wouldn't stop. *How could Mama do this to me?*

## TWENTY-SIX

GOLDIE'S WORDS RANG IN my ears. *You decide.*
What I decided was to write Mama another letter and tell
her what a rotten mother she was. Tears splotched the notebook
paper as I scribbled.

Why didn't you think about what would happen to me? How
could you do that? Leave me so Aunt Vadine had to come
and take over, telling me how I upset the organization of her
cupboards by putting the cinnamon next to the pepper? Her
cupboards? Did you get that? Everyone thinks Aunt Vadine is
going to be my new mother. I want a mother, but she's not the
one. You are. Now I'm stuck with her.

I'm going to my first dance, and she lectured me about the
evils of dancing just because Brother Henry preached about
that. She puffed up like a toad when I told her you met Daddy
at a dance. Why can't you be here to see me dressed up and
wearing your pearls?

After writing three more pages, I didn't feel so mad anymore. Just
sad. And lonely. I folded up the pages and stuck them in an envelope.
No *XXX* and *OOO* on the outside. I thought about Cly and going
to the dance. Maybe Cly was one of the helpers Goldie talked about.
He even said someday I would be able to go in the garage.

*Today. It has to be today. Before I chicken out.*

I grabbed my jacket and stuffed the letter to Mama in the pocket. When I did, my fingers curled around the Life Savers Cly had given me. I peeled off the paper and put one on my tongue. The sharp cherry taste made me feel braver. I buttoned my jacket and went outside.

The sky was bright, a blinding blue that hurt my eyes when I looked up. And the wind bit my cheeks, making them feel hot and cold at the same time. With my hands stuffed in my pockets, I lowered my head and walked from the back porch toward the driveway and the garages. Scarlett bounced beside me, wagging her tail, like I might take her for a walk.

When my feet crunched on the gravel drive, I raised my head and looked at the row of garages. Six on our side for the houses on our half of the block. Six identical doors, all shut. Two of them had padlocks. Finally I let my eyes focus on ours. Second from the right. Shut tight. No lock.

In the background Goldie's parakeets sang—crisp, chirpy noises. Had Mama heard the parakeets that morning? I listened for a minute and took a deep breath. Even with the sun out, I felt chilled and shrugged deeper into my jacket as I walked to our garage. I lifted the metal latch and let the door creak open. I waited for a second, hoping more light would fill up the space. I stepped inside and noticed how quiet and still the air was. Scarlett scratched in the dirt floor and sniffed around the walls. I watched her and then made myself walk to the center of the garage. A nervous energy surrounded me. That and the shadows.

When I looked up, I saw that metal beams crisscrossed below the slanted ceiling. How had Mama done it? Did she throw a rope up and loop it around or climb on something? How did she know how to make a noose? I studied the beams and didn't see anything at all. Like nothing had ever hung from them. A stepladder leaned against the back wall. I walked over to it and dragged it back to the middle, where I opened it. Daddy had used the ladder to paint my room blue when I was in the fifth grade, and blobs of blue paint dotted the steps. Steadying myself, I climbed up until I got to the third step. I reached up and touched the metal crossbar. Mama must've done it from this step, right here. A shiver went through me as a picture of her dangling from a rope flashed through my head.

I tried to step down, but the hem of my jacket caught on the hinge of the ladder. When I pulled it free, I saw a spot of green. A tiny piece of material, no bigger than a postage stamp, was stuck in the hinge. I gulped for air. Mama must've worn her green dress that day. The same one she wore the day I got my hair cut in a pageboy.

I hurried down the steps and half-folded the ladder so I could pull the scrap out. I rubbed it between my fingers, a tiny triangle with two sides frayed where it ripped. My throat got a knotty feel as I remembered the way the skirt swished when Mama walked. Did it hang limp or float in the stillness of the garage that day? I sat on the folded ladder and let the cold numb me—my face, my toes, my fingers, so that after a while I could no longer feel the smoothness of the green fabric in my hand.

Scarlett came up and sniffed the patch, then jumped up and licked my face. I picked her up and tucked her inside my jacket, needing her close to me. After a while she squirmed out and ran into the corner of the garage where Daddy kept paint buckets and oilcans on a metal shelf. I shooed her away, and when I did, I noticed a hatbox on the bottom shelf.

*"Seek and ye shall find"* popped into my head. I hauled the round box out, trying to remember where I'd seen it. Mama's closet? Maybe Aunt Vadine put it in here. Or Mama. A lavender ribbon, grosgrain I think you call it, held the lid on. Quickly I undid the knot and peered inside. A crocheted baby bonnet lay on the top. The one Sylvia had worn in the picture. No doubt this had been

one of Aunt Vadine's creations the way she spent half her life with a ball of yarn in one hand and a hook in the other. It felt delicate and lacy. Under the bonnet were two stacks of letters with rubber bands around them. In the dimness of the garage I couldn't tell what they were or who they were from. I decided to take them into the house. I put the lavender ribbon and the green scrap inside the box, leaned the ladder against the wall, and whistled for Scarlett. Before I left, I turned around and looked into the empty garage. It didn't scare me anymore. No more black hole. Just my heart feeling like a squeezed orange knowing that's where Mama died. Died and left me.

I creaked the door shut behind me and looked up. Cly leaned against the end of the garages.

"You did it." He winked at me.

"It wasn't so bad. Not good, but..."

"No rats?"

"Nope. I found this box though. I think it's some more of Mama's things. Were you watching me?"

"Just got here. You want to come over to Slim's for a little backgammon?"

"Sure. First, though, maybe I ought to put this box back. Aunt Vadine would just snoop in it." I flipped open the garage latch and carried the box back to the shelf. In and out, like I did it every day of the week.

When we walked by the incinerator, I stopped, fished the rotten mother letter out of my pocket, and threw it into the lake of fire.

While we played backgammon all afternoon, the wind howled outside Slim's windows. Slim got up to check the weather. "The sky's darkening up. Looks like there's rain a-coming." He craned his neck to look through the front room window. "Best if you young'ens get goin'. Sammie, I'll drive you home."

Cly sprinted across the street to his house while I ran toward Slim's truck. The sky opened up, spitting rain that blew sideways, stinging my face like bits of glass. Slim helped me in, then let the engine warm up a minute before hunching over the steering wheel to drive me home, muttering about the blasted weather in the Texas Panhandle. Him and Daddy...always talking about cold fronts and high-pressure systems like they held the secrets of the universe.

"Thanks, Slim. Be careful driving back."

"You bet. Hurry on into the house now."

I wanted to go to the garage to get the box I'd found earlier, but the wind about knocked me down when I started up the sidewalk. When I made it to the porch, I turned around, waved at Slim, and opened the door. Scarlett appeared out of nowhere and whooshed past me into the house.

"I'm home!" Stomping the wet off my feet, I slipped out of my soggy jacket. Scarlett ran into the kitchen and shook her wet fur, spraying water all over the cabinets.

"Good heavens, throw that thing out. Nothing worse than the smell of a wet dog." Aunt Vadine came from the bedroom tugging a sweater on over her dress. Scarlett raced at her, barking and pouncing on her front paws, doing the hokeypokey in and out and around her legs. This time I saw the fire come out of Aunt Vadine's eyes, and I moved fast.

I grabbed Scarlett by the collar and whisked a towel from the cabinet to dry her off. "Poor baby. You're so cold and wet." Pulling her to me, I whispered into her ear, "Don't worry, you won't have to go back out. I'll fix you a spot in here."

"Nothing doing. The dog stays out." Aunt Vadine wouldn't budge when I suggested making a spot for her under the kitchen table.

"I'll watch her. I'll even sleep out here with her. It's inhuman to make a dog sleep in the cold and wind. What if it snows?"

"It's not going to snow...how you get these ideas astounds me, but since you won't let me hear the end of it, you and the dog can sleep under the table."

Grabbing the feather topper and my pillow from the army cot, I fixed a spot. When Scarlett curled right up and went to sleep, I got up and went into the front room. Aunt Vadine sat in Daddy's rocker poking a crochet needle in and out of her latest project.

"Would you like some hot chocolate?" I got out a pan and the milk.

"That would be nice."

We sipped the chocolate while rain hammered the roof. The windowpanes rattled like bones in the wind, and I wondered if Daddy would make it home from his evening shift. Looking out the front window, I couldn't even see the elm trees at the edge of our sidewalk, just a blur like the television warming up. If the rain *did* turn to snow, we could have a blizzard. *My baby sister, Sylvia, died during a blizzard.* Immediately I pushed the thought out of my head. I picked up one of Aunt Vadine's *Crochet World* magazines and flipped through it. Baby bonnets, baby bibs, baby everything-you-could-think-of.

"Hmm, I was wondering...." I closed the magazine. "Is this what it was like the night Sylvia died?"

In and out. Poke. Poke. Poke. No answer.

"Mama said she couldn't get Sylvia to a doctor because of the blizzard. It doesn't matter, I guess, but all this wind and blinding rain scares the bejeebies out of me."

"What kind of talk is that? Bejeebies?"

"Better than saying pee-waddings, I guess."

"Samantha, you've got a filthy mouth. As for your question, I wasn't there when Sylvia died. We did have a snow flurry or two, but your mother kept herself in such a state, she probably didn't know a blizzard from a hole in the ground."

"What state? Like she was scared or nervous or something?"

"Something. Never was right after birthing Sylvia. Cried for weeks on end. Brought the baby over to your grandma Grace and me to watch, said she just couldn't take any more."

"Mama cried or Sylvia cried?" This had turned out more confusing than I thought.

"Who knows? Sylvia had the colic and you were such a meddlesome child, always running off to the neighbors, getting into things, just being a general nuisance. More than once I told Rita she should take a switch to you—after all you were five years old, big enough to at least behave yourself. Handling two of you made her berserk."

*Me?* She was saying I was a brat. Was she saying it was my fault Mama had problems?

"Didn't Daddy help?"

"Your daddy provided a living, a car, a place to live. The oil field paid well, but only when there were jobs. Men need to know they're appreciated. I'm not one to speak ill of the dead, but your mama never showed an ounce of appreciation for your daddy. If she had, she wouldn't have done what she did and be in hell today."

Her words hit me like a slap in the face. *Mama in hell?* How could she, Mama's own sister, say such a thing? I knew, though I don't know how, Mama had done what she did to go to Sylvia, to escape the hell in her mind. *Seek and ye shall find.*

Aunt Vadine poked her crochet hook in and out, studying the web of loops and chains, her face hard like it was made of stone. Her saying those things about Mama made my blood boil. Not to mention the way she treated me. *So I'm not an angel all the time.* One thing I knew, Aunt Vadine must not have helped Mama back then, so why did she think she could help us now?

I put on my flannel nightgown and crawled into my feather bed with Scarlett under the table. In the dark I reached for my purse and felt inside for the leather jewelry case. Holding the pearls in both hands, I counted. One, two, three...all the way around to eighty-four. I went around again, counting in twos this time. *Sylvia cried all the time, and Mama couldn't take it. Is that how she felt when Penelope screamed that day in Alice's front room? Like a failure? Was I really a horrible child?* I counted the pearls again. *Sylvia died before Mama could prove she was a good mother. Is that what depression does?*

Scarlett whimpered in her sleep, and I pulled her close.

*Please, dear God, say hello to Mama, and in your spare time, maybe you could look down and see things aren't going too well here. I'd like to feel normal again. Just plain old Sammie. I've tried choosing happy thoughts. Instead here I am, sleeping under the kitchen table. That's odd, don't you think? Do you think you could give me and Daddy some answers? I don't think Aunt Vadine's the answer we need. Maybe we could try something else.*

*Oh, and bless all the children in the Congo. Amen.*

I returned the pearls to their case, and after a while Aunt Vadine shuffled off to bed. Outside the wind howled. A window screen had come loose, banging like a bass drum. *Bum-bum-bum.* I dreamed of dancing to Sonny and the Spinners, twirling in Cly's arms with Mama's pearls—all eighty-four of them—shining and perfect.

## TWENTY-SEVEN

NOVEMBER 1. The day of the dance finally arrived. It took thirty minutes to do my hair, and I'd borrowed some mascara from Tuwana, who said it would define my eyes—my best feature according to Miss Fashion Expert of the state of Texas. Through the stiff mascara, I blinked at my image in the mirror. *No zits. That's good.* I slipped into my ruby sweater with the matching straight skirt. Holding my breath, I lifted the pearls from the case and fastened them. My heart pounded as I took another look at my reflection.

*Mama, I wish you could see me now.*

Aunt Vadine knocked sharply on the door. "Your friend is here." She said *friend* like it was a disease.

Daddy and Cly chatted about basketball while I grabbed my purse and my coat.

Cly's eyes widened a bit when he first looked at me, and his smile told me he approved of how I looked. He had on a dark suit and a slim tie with circles printed on it. My heart fluttered.

"Aunt Eva said you'd like this." He handed me a box.

"Wow…" I lifted out a miniature white mum with a glittery net and ribbons. "Thank you. Was I supposed to get you something?"

"Beats me." He shrugged and stood with his arms at his sides, shifting from one foot to the other.

"Did you see what Cly brought?" When I turned to show Aunt Vadine the mum, she had the oddest expression on her face, her eyes locked at a place near my neck.

"Those . . ." She started to raise her hand to point at something. She straightened her whole body and inhaled through her nose. "Your necklace. How lovely."

"Those are Mama's pearls, aren't they?" Daddy said.

I smiled and nodded.

Aunt Vadine mumbled something, then fixed her lips in a tight, wrinkled prune pose.

Daddy helped with my coat and Cly held open the door. We hurried out to Mr. Johnson's Edsel with its scooped-out sides glowing in the moonlight. For a second I felt like Cinderella.

Black and gold streamers decorated the VFW with balloon bouquets tied along the sides between pictures of uniformed veterans from the two world wars and Korea. Four guys with pompadour hair tuned their guitars on the stage directly under the American flag. Their tight pants rode low on their hips, their white satin shirts unbuttoned halfway down their chests. Sonny and the Spinners. As soon as we got there, Cly headed for the guys bunched on one side, and I saw Gina in a circle of girls on the other. She pinned on my mum and said, "Nice outfit."

When the music started, a few couples danced—the ones you'd expect. Tuwana and Mike hopped by while Pug and Mitzi, the homecoming king and queen, twirled and spun. Most of us just anchored the sides of the VFW, looking nonchalant, tapping our feet to the music. My first dance, and I had no idea what to expect.

"They're all a buncha goons." Gina cocked her head toward the boys. "Not that it matters all that much. I'm four inches taller than Spunky, even in my flats. We'd look like Mutt and Jeff out there if he ever asked me to dance."

The band played two slow songs next, and the same three or

four couples snuggled and shuffled around in time to the music. On our side Linda Kay Howard kept things lively with her hee-haw laugh.

After the band ended "That'll Be the Day" in a ragged, off-key *bum-bum-bump*, Mrs. Alexander, Mike's mother, took the microphone and gushed about how great the band was and urged us to give them a hand.

"The next song will be ladies' choice. Come on, y'all, don't be shy. We want everyone to have fun."

A flurry of activity, like a VFW game of Fruit Basket Upset, started as the band began playing "Party Doll." I looked around to see what Gina was going to do and bumped into Linda Kay, dragging Cly out onto the floor. My heart sank, and I stood during the whole song wishing I could be swallowed up by the streamers and balloons. I had the urge to go to the bathroom, and I considered running downstairs. Instead I chewed on a hangnail and watched Linda Kay tilt her head up and smile at Cly, who danced stiff-legged, like a windup toy. I heard a cackle above the slow music. *Linda Kay?*

*Okay, Sammie, you've got two choices. You can stand on the WW II side of the VFW all night, or you can go up and rescue Cly from Howdy Doody's daughter. What'll it be?* I'd gnawed my index fingernail down to the quick, rolling the choices around in my head. At the last strands of the song, I squared my shoulders and looked around for Cly. Ladies' choice or not, I'd come to my first dance, and Mama's pearls were not going home without me dancing. Craning my neck, I looked around the room.

"Why aren't you dancing?" Tuwana appeared at my side, a glow on her face like a neon sign flashing *I'm in love.*

"I am, if I can ever find Cly...."

"Over there..." Tuwana pointed across the room. Linda Kay had both of Cly's hands in hers, claiming him for another dance.

My face flared, and I thought if I let out a breath, fire would come out. I ran for the refreshment arrow aimed at the basement. *A drink of water, that's what I need.*

The cold water from the fountain tasted good. I looked around the basement. Cookies and punch at one end. A Ping-Pong table at the other, where Doobie and PJ slammed the ball back and forth.

"Having fun?" Mr. Johnson came from the refreshment table eating a chocolate chip cookie. My sick smile must've given him the answer.

"Me neither. Tuwana said she'd throw herself across the street in front of the school bus if I embarrassed her by dancing. I'm banished to the basement." He laughed and nodded toward the Ping-Pong table. "Tell you what. Let's get Doob and PJ to play us a set of doubles."

That's where Cly found me when the band took a break and everyone stampeded to the basement for lemon sherbet fluff and homemade cookies.

"Here you are. I've been looking all over for you."

Mr. Johnson handed his paddle to Cly and went off to chaperone the punch bowl. PJ and Doobie played a couple sets with us before PJ dragged Doobie off to dance with her. "Or else," she threatened, and bugged out her eyes behind her glasses.

Cly and I played singles with the drumbeat of the band coming through the ceiling. We didn't even bother to keep score, just slammed the ball back and forth.

Finally Cly stopped, loosened his tie, and said, "Punch?"

The chaperones had already cleaned up the refreshment table, so we filled paper cups with water from the fountain.

"Wanna play some more Ping-Pong?" Cly asked.

Doing my best imitation of Tuwana—hands on my hips and slitty eyes—I said, "You know, I didn't put on Mama's pearls so I could beat you at Ping-Pong. Before the night is over, I'd like to at least have one dance with Eva MacLemore's nephew."

"I thought you'd never ask."

Climbing the stairs, Cly kept his hand on the small of my back as if guiding me on a snipe hunt. Chills zinged up my spine. The lights had been lowered on the dance floor when we arrived, and the band member named Sonny whispered in a husky voice in the microphone, "For all y'all lovers out there, one last dance—'Love Me Tender.'"

Beads of perspiration broke out on my forehead. *An Elvis song.* Cly's arm tightened around my waist while he took my right hand in his left, and we danced, heads close together. Cly's suit, no longer stiff, melted into my ruby outfit as we dipped ever so slightly to the right, sliding to the left.

"You smell nice," he whispered in my ear, and he squeezed my hand a little tighter.

"It's just lilac water." The music carried us like dandelion puffs across the floor. At the end of the song, Cly pulled my hand in close to our bodies. His moist breath flickered on my neck. Then, right there under the pictures of a dozen veterans, he lifted my chin and kissed me. If I lived to be a hundred and six, I'd never forget that kiss—like velvet and marshmallows, and tasting of cherry Life Savers.

All the way home in the backseat of the Edsel, Cly held my hand. My face got hot every time I thought about him kissing me. If that was what juvenile delinquents did, I liked it. When Benny Ray dropped me off, Cly gave my hand an extra squeeze, and my heart skipped a beat. I took a deep breath and went in the house.

Daddy asked the usual questions about if I had a good time while Aunt Vadine stared at the crochet in her hands. I chattered away about the punch and cookies and how well the band played.

I floated into my room. Slipping out of my skirt and sweater, I ran my tongue over my lips. The taste of cherry Life Savers lingered. I undid the clasp on Mama's pearls, ran them across my cheek, and set them carefully on the chest of drawers before sinking into my feather bed.

In my dreams Sonny and the Spinners played all night as Cly and I swirled and danced past the VFW soldiers, who smiled and winked from their frames on the wall. The pearls around my neck blinked off and on, becoming cherry Life Savers in one flash and Mama's pearls the next. When the first rays of sun streamed through my window the next morning, I swung my bare feet to the pine floor and stood to take the real pearls in my hand and hold them. I blinked once. Twice. A light-headedness came, making me so woozy I thought I might faint.

Mama's pearls were gone.

## TWENTY-EIGHT

I TURNED MY ROOM INSIDE OUT and upside down looking for the pearls, playing the tape in my head of when I'd returned home from the dance—kissing Daddy good night, undressing, undoing the clasp, and running the pearls across my cheek. They didn't just up and walk off my dresser by themselves.

During church the next morning, I shot a desperate SOS toward heaven when Ernie Greenwood prayed. *Ask and ye shall receive; seek and ye shall find* hadn't produced any results. *Of course not, dummy. God's not interested in your selfishness.* My stomach twisted until I was sure my insides were tied in knots.

It didn't take a Madame Curie to figure out what had happened. Aunt Vadine took them. I hated myself for thinking it, but deep down I knew she had. The look on her face when Cly had picked me up. The chipper way she said, "Your necklace. How lovely." Her tight lips. But why? What had I done?

After church she fixed oyster soup for lunch, just the two of us, since Daddy was back on daylights. I thought perhaps she'd decided to play a cruel trick on me by having me find the real pearls swimming among the canned oysters. No such luck.

"I'm going to clean my room." I put my empty bowl into the sink.

"I should think so, the way you sling everything around in there. Didn't even hang up your clothes last night after the dance."

I bit my tongue and smiled, then rinsed out my glass.

An hour later I'd been through all of Aunt Vadine's drawers, all of mine, pulled out the dresser, and looked under the beds. I found dust bunnies, but no pearls. My last resort was to retrace my steps from the car and then go over to Tuwana's and search the Edsel.

"I think I left something in Tuwana's car."

"Oh? What was that?"

"Uh...just something. I'll be back later."

To Tuwana I confessed my suspicions about how the pearls had disappeared, but to be on the safe side, I wanted to check the Edsel.

"No problem. Besides, we can talk better without all the little ears here in the house." She gave Tara and Tommie Sue a *this-means-you* look, and we went out to the car.

She chattered while I searched. Under the front seat, I found two clippies and a red rag.

"You should've seen Linda Kay when Cly kissed you."

The blood rushed up my neck to my face. My first kiss, and the whole world witnessed it.

"What's it to her? He was my date."

"Said she'd make sure her father knew about the PDA."

"What's that?"

"Public display of affection. Commandment number five on Howdy Doody's list."

"I'm sure we weren't the only ones. I thought I saw Mike nibbling your ear. That's PDA if I ever saw it."

"You were the only one *she* saw, bein's how she's so love struck with Cly."

"Who doesn't return the feeling, I assure you." In the backseat, I ran my hands between the cushions, still hoping for a miracle. A pencil, two pennies, and a used tissue turned up. No pearls.

"Mr. Howard thinks I'm a delinquent in the making anyway, so

I'm sure Linda Kay will give him a reason to keep his eyes on me."
I bugged out my eyes as I said it, which made Tuwana laugh.

"You'll never believe what else."

"Not more Linda Kay whining, I hope."

"No. Something cool. Mike's mom told Mother that the bank in
town needs a receptionist. Well, it just so happens, Mother's been
hinting around to Daddy she needs a career. No sense wasting her
steno school certificate, you know." Tuwana's eyes shimmered.

"Your mother? Going to work? Why?"

"For the money, what else? This isn't the Dark Ages anymore.
Mother says women today have real jobs, not just running the cash
register down at the Piggly Wiggly. She interviews at the bank
tomorrow."

"Too bad Aunt Vadine can't have the job. Give her something
to do besides wear out the couch cushions all day."

"Mother says she's just waiting to make her move."

"Who?"

"Your beloved aunt, that's who."

"How's that?"

"Etiquette requires a certain period of mourning, which is what
your aunt is doing, letting your daddy get over your mother. It's
a known fact men can't manage without a wife, so think about it.
She's just waiting in the wings for him to need a woman, then,
bingo, *here I am*. She'll turn on the charm, and before you can say
Robinson Crusoe, they'll be tying the knot, giving you a new
mother."

"That's the stupidest thing I've ever heard. Not only that, it's
sick. Daddy doesn't like her much better than I do. Not in a million years."

"Don't say I didn't warn you."

\*     \*     \*

On Monday, Mr. Borden, the science teacher, assigned a research paper for the third six weeks—a survey of a scientific career. I chose veterinary medicine since I was crazy about Scarlett. And Goldie's parakeets. I was determined to make an A so Mr. Howard wouldn't think I'd become a moron. Every time I saw him patrolling the halls, creepie-crawlies worked up the hair on my neck. *Has Linda Kay tattled yet?*

*Brucellosis, trichinella roundworms,* and *canine rabies* rolled off my tongue at the supper table just as easily as if I were discussing the latest fashions or what the lunchroom ladies served at school.

"Interesting," Daddy said, and then excused himself to sit on the porch and smoke.

The minute he left, Aunt Vadine told me how disgusting it was to hear about worms at the supper table after her efforts to provide a pleasant family meal, and it was no wonder Daddy had to go outside and smoke. My behavior must be a great disappointment to him, blah, blah, blah.

In my opinion, her cooking could have been the cause of his quick exits. That or the Evening in Paris perfume she drenched herself in.

Daddy started keeping to himself more. No more thumps on the arm and "How's it going, Sis?" Sometimes he'd be outside for two or three hours, way after dark, sitting on the porch or off walking somewhere. Aunt Vadine camped out on the couch, watched her Westerns on television. *Gunsmoke. Maverick.* That new show *The Rifleman.* She watched them all. I thought she must be homesick for West Texas. I hoped so, anyway.

Tuwana went on forever and a day with her crystal-ball predictions about Aunt Vadine becoming Daddy's new wife and about her mother's new job. "I don't care if I am paid fifty cents an hour, babysitting every day is humiliating. And I get zip for fixing supper." Or, "Mother says with her new job we can afford braces for my teeth. This time next year, I'll be the girl with the Pepsodent smile!" Her fake grin revealed only the teeniest ripple of unevenness along the bottom.

Cly started staying after school for basketball practice and riding home with Doobie, who now had his license. When Doobie got his brother's hand-me-down, rusted-out Mercury, he acted like it was a Rolls-Royce. Cly waved at me in the halls at school, but that was about it.

The only one who cared if I existed was Scarlett, who licked my face and loved me because I took her for long walks.

Not a day went by that I didn't think about Mama's hatbox. Who were the letters from? What did they say? A part of me was even more afraid of the letters than I had been of the garage. What if I found out Mama had a past she was ashamed of? Or that she was ashamed of me? Was it right to read someone's confidential mail even though they were dead? Then fury would bubble up like a hissing teapot—a fury with Mama's name on it. Nothing could erase the terrible fact that she killed herself. Leaving me. And Daddy. That wasn't right either.

The week before Thanksgiving, I made up my mind. So what if they were personal? Maybe they held a clue about why Aunt Vadine acted like she did. With Scarlett at my side, I went to the garage. The door was cracked open. Daddy's voice came from inside, but I couldn't tell who he was talking to. I listened for a minute, but the talking had stopped. Should I go in? As I stood there trying to decide what to do, I heard a muffled sound, like the time when Daddy sat beside my bed and cried.

*Daddy goes into the garage and cries about Mama?* It shocked me. All this time I thought I was the only one who cried. Or cared.

## TWENTY-NINE

THE KUYKENDALLS INVITED US for Thanksgiving dinner, and Goldie promised to make her famous blueberry cobbler. I went over early to help Goldie, who had me take care of the general aviary duties while she bustled around the kitchen, basting, chopping, whipping, and what all.

The birds chattered and ruffled their feathers at me while I scrubbed and refilled their water and food bowls, measuring out the different seeds and vitamin mixtures (tonics, Goldie called them). I knew the parakeets all by name and chattered bird talk back at them as I yanked dirty liners from their trays and put in new ones. When I got to the last row and shooed out the parakeets, a rush of wings and sassy twittering met me. I kept up the tempo of cleaning and watering even though the smell of turkey and sage dressing coming from Goldie's kitchen made my stomach rumble in anticipation.

When I unlatched Lady Aster's box, I stood back since she always came out like a streak of lightning, heading straight for the bird bath, splashing water every which way announcing this was her kingdom. She didn't swoop. Didn't come out at all. Nothing. I peered inside and saw her huddled in the far corner, a heap of blue and yellow feathers. Dull black eyes, like a pair of peppercorns, stared back.

A familiar knot formed in my throat. I couldn't even tell if she was breathing.

Just like Mama.

I ran through the workroom into the kitchen. "Help! There's something wrong with Lady Aster."

Goldie dropped the pan in her hands, and a crash of metal echoed from the walls. She hurried past me. I followed and pointed to the open cage, hoping to see Lady Aster swoosh out and peck at us, like the joke was on us, but she didn't. No cheeping. No flying out. Goldie reached deep inside and lifted the bird in her thick fingers, cradling her in the palm of her hand as she cooed, "What is it, baby? You can tell Goldie." The confetti-sized yellow beak opened, but no peep. Then the downy head went limp in Goldie's hand, Lady Aster's bead-like eyes opened in a frozen stare.

Goldie carried Lady Aster, her fragile treasure, into the front room and dropped to the couch like a sack of potatoes.

"Goldie, what is it?" George came from the bedroom, buttoning his shirt. "Your arm—you've burned it. Quick, Sammie, get the butter from the icebox."

I ran to the kitchen, found a stick of butter, and brought it back. Goldie waved me away, still cradling Lady Aster against her blueberry-stained apron.

George lowered himself beside Goldie, wiping a tear from her cheek with his fingers. An ugly blister as wide as a Curad bandage had risen on her right wrist. I handed George the butter and remembered the mess in the kitchen.

Gas flames, blue and orange tongues, licked up from an empty burner, and a Dutch oven lay on its side on the countertop. Potatoes tumbled from the pot, into the sink, on the floor. I switched off the burner and started picking up the scattered potatoes. That's when I heard Daddy and Aunt Vadine arrive.

Aunt Vadine marched right into the kitchen, carrying a dish in her hands.

"Samantha." Extra syllable on the *Sa-ma-an-tha*. "I thought you'd come to help Goldie, and instead you've made the most horrendous mess. Where do you want the pea salad?"

Gravy bubbled on the stove, and I'd ground a potato into mush on the floor. Whiffs of Aunt Vadine's Evening in Paris cologne and roast turkey swirled around in the tiny kitchen. I gritted my teeth and took the bowl from her hand just as a green and yellow parakeet flew past my face, flapping and screeching.

*Oh no!* I'd left the door to the aviary open.

I slipped on the smashed potato and leapt across the dining space to secure the door before a whole swarm came through. Aunt Vadine flailed her arms around her head when the poor thing tried to land in her hair.

"I've been attacked! Get that nasty thing away from me." She stumbled into the front room as Daddy and George came to see what had caused all the excitement.

I looked around the kitchen, and for some reason the whole thing struck me as hilarious. Potatoes every which way. A parakeet—Charlie, I thought it was—on the loose, and Aunt Vadine, who came in without a clue about Lady Aster. It wasn't Aunt Vadine's fault, but every time I thought of her fighting off her attacker, I let out another giggle.

*Pull yourself together, Sammie.*

I cleaned the mess up and made one last check to see that everything was okay before I went to the front room and sat with Goldie, who was still holding the clump of feathers.

Her eyes, bleary and red, stared at a spot on the floor just past the tips of her lace-up black shoes, the same ones she wore every day of her life. Putting my head on Goldie's shoulder, I told her how sorry I was and ran a finger over the lifeless blue and yellow feathers.

Aunt Vadine sat in an armchair wearing one of her starchy Sunday dresses and her face made up with cranberry rouge. She looked out of place, empty without a wad of crochet in her lap. Once she said, "Shouldn't someone see about the turkey?" But no one did.

After Daddy and George returned the runaway parakeet to the aviary, they went outside to get some air. Every once in a while, a puff of smoke drifted by the open curtains.

A while later they came in, George carrying a small cardboard box. He lifted Lady Aster from Goldie's cupped hands and laid her on a soft nest of cotton wadding.

"We're gonna miss this one, Goldie. Your favorite." When he started toward the door he whispered, "And mine."

I snuggled closer to Goldie, my head resting on her bosom, its softness swallowing me. When she slipped her arm around me, the smell of her deodorant and kitcheny odors made me want to cry. Instead I closed my eyes and pretended it was Mama who held me.

Aunt Vadine let out a long sigh and refolded her hands in her lap. "Maybe we should go on home, Joe."

Daddy hooked his thumbs in his pockets and said, "Goldie makes the best blueberry cobbler this side o' the moon. I'm sticking around to get a taste."

At the mention of the cobbler, Goldie jumped into action and whisked herself back into the kitchen, me on her heels. In no time we had Thanksgiving dinner. And Daddy was right—the blueberry cobbler was worth the wait.

The next day I wrote the avian section of my term paper, poring over the books Goldie had lent me. Together she and I decided Lady Aster must have had a respiratory infection, which meant the aviary had to be scrubbed from top to bottom.

"Work is good for the soul," Goldie said, as she and I talked and laughed our way through scouring everything from top to bottom with soapy water laced with Clorox. We talked about Lady Aster and chanted back and forth to the other parakeets, *cracker, cookie, pretty*, trying to improve their vocabularies. By the end of the day, a fat yellow and lime green female with a long tail had risen to the top of the pecking order. Kiwi, Goldie called her. The feisty bird strutted about, saying, "Cuckoo, Kiwi." Goldie's face beamed, tiny parakeet-feet wrinkles fanning out from her eyes.

After church on Sunday, Daddy split the minute we cleared the dinner table. I went to my room to change clothes, and just as I was pulling on my jeans, the phone rang. Two long jangles. Through the crack in my bedroom door, I heard Aunt Vadine's crisp "Tucker residence."

Then a short pause.

"Bobby, I've told you not to bother calling."

I stood up and moved closer to the door, cracking it open a sliver. Who was Bobby?

I could hear her heavy breathing. "Fine, thanks for asking."

A long silence, while I guessed she listened.

"The answer is still no. My home is here now, and I don't need your affection, mind you."

She snorted after the next remark, then covered the phone with her hand, muffling her response. All I heard was, "... tell that sorry loser what he can do with his offer. What a pathetic worm." She slammed the receiver down.

Curious, I squared my shoulders and marched into the front room.

"I thought I heard the phone. Was it for me?"

Aunt Vadine looked up, a surprised look on her face. She half-smiled, her eyebrows arching up.

"Some salesman. I swear you'd think people wouldn't call on the Lord's day of rest." She rolled her eyes and popped her Juicy Fruit.

"Hmmm. I thought I heard you say Bobby something."

"Samantha, your imagination is surpassed only by your impertinence. Eavesdropping on phone conversations is another example of the lack of training your mother supplied you with. Just this morning in church, I prayed for the wisdom to provide you with godly instruction and admonition."

"I know what I heard." I looked into her yellow-speckled eyes. "Is Bobby a friend of yours? Someone who misses you back in Midland? It sounded like you turned down a job offer."

She drew up her shoulders and inhaled through her nose, like a bull getting ready to charge. Instead of pawing at the ground and coming at me, she spun around and went into the bathroom. *Slam. Click.* She locked the door.

What was that all about? Aunt Vadine had a boyfriend? It sounded gross even to me. Even so, a little flicker of hope went through me. Maybe she would go back to Bobby and leave us alone.

## THIRTY

AUNT VADINE DIDN'T MENTION her mysterious telephone conversation to Daddy. I thought about bringing it
up, but if I did, it might make her more determined than ever to
stay at Graham Camp. I felt like my life was in limbo. I hardly
ever cried or got furious about Mama anymore. Mostly I had these
visions of her in hell, thanks to Aunt Vadine. Every time I thought
about it, the hair on my arms stood up.

Brother Henry would know about things like that, so one Sunday after church I asked to talk to him. Privately. He took me into
his tiny office and closed the door.

"What's on your mind today, Sammie?"

I decided to get right to the point. "Do you think Mama went
to hell because she killed herself?"

"Oh dear. That is a common notion nowadays." Brother Henry
pointed to a folding chair for me to sit down. "One of the Ten Commandments is *thou shalt not kill*, and suicide is a form of killing."

My heart raced, afraid of what he might say next.

"But the other side of the coin is we live under grace, and by
rights, any one of us could break one of the Ten Commandments
and get hit by a train, and no one would condemn that person to
hell."

"Mama definitely believed in grace. I have her New Testament...." I took it out of my purse and shoved it across to him.

"She got it when she accepted Jesus and was baptized in the name of the Father, Son, and Holy Ghost. Right here it shows the date." I pointed to the first page.

"I never doubted your mother's faith. Although some would disagree, I believe God Almighty would not cast one of his own into hell purely based on a single act. If so, then God's grace would only extend to those who are perfect, and heaven knows, none of us are that. I believe the Bible is clear that nothing can separate God from his followers." He thumbed through Mama's New Testament. "Here it is. Romans 8:38 and 39." He read it to me.

I liked the part about how neither life nor death could separate us from God's love.

Brother Henry handed me the New Testament, his eyes kind and sad. "How do you feel about that?"

I shrugged. "Okay, I guess." I gnawed on a hangnail.

"You don't sound okay."

"She shouldn't have left Daddy and me. If she loved me, she wouldn't have."

"You feel like she didn't love you?"

"How would you feel?" My face got hot.

"Like you, I suppose. Remember, Sammie, your mother had an illness, and I'm willing to wager she would have preferred to stay here and be your mother. Some things only God knows. That's his job. Our job is to trust him."

"Trust him to make Aunt Vadine my mother? Ha! No thanks."

"That's not what I meant at all. Trust him to heal your heart. The pain may never go away, but someday you will be able to laugh and feel joy again. Trust him."

Before I left, Brother Henry said a short prayer and told me his door was always open.

Later that week, during our seventh-hour newspaper class, Mrs. Gray asked if I'd thought of a topic for a Christmas essay for the *Cougar Chronicle*. "I've decided to call it 'Christmas in Heaven.' It will be from the viewpoint of my mother and what it's like to be with Jesus and the angels."

"Very creative." She stood close enough that I could smell her Ivory fresh soap. My fingers itched to reach over and touch the fuzzy lavender sweater she wore, to tuck the sprig of hair that tumbled from her topknot back into place. Instead I held my breath as she addressed the others. "Okay, group, think this is a good idea?"

Everyone nodded, although Nelda thought we should still include the legend of Father Christmas for the grade-schoolers who got copies of the paper. We agreed to do both, and Mrs. Gray moved to the front of the room to check off each article she'd printed on the blackboard. I couldn't help staring at her left hand as she wrote. No wedding ring. Where was Mr. Gray?

The Montgomery Ward Christmas catalog had a dreamy sweater almost like Mrs. Gray's. Soft, with a monogrammed initial in cursive on the left shoulder. Page three. I loved its mint green color and showed it to Aunt Vadine one afternoon.

"Mama always had me make a list for Christmas. Three things. Here's something I would like." I showed her the sweater.

She sniffed and called it faddish. I went ahead and left it on my list as number two. For number one, I put a typewriter. Ever since I saw the notice on the school bulletin board selling their old machines for ten dollars, I'd wanted one. Number three: a gold compact like Tuwana bought in Amarillo. I propped the list beside the coffeepot so Daddy would see it. Maybe he wouldn't think the sweater too faddish.

A few days before Christmas vacation, Mr. Borden, the science teacher, let us play charades. While Roseanne Swanson acted out a movie, I daydreamed, looking out the window, and saw Aunt Vadine march up the sidewalk through the front door of the school. My heart skipped a beat. *She's come to see about the used type-writer.* Roseanne finished her turn, and I watched out the window while the boys groaned about playing a sissy game. By the end of the class, Aunt Vadine hadn't come out, but in my heart I knew I'd be getting the number one thing on my list.

The next day I went to Slim's. I'd plotted with him to help me get a backgammon game for Daddy, and the order from the "Monkey Ward" catalog would be sent to his house. Waiting for the mail, we pulled out Slim's game and played for a while.

"What're you doing for Christmas?" I asked.

"It's my turn to have my daughter over this year, even though she does the cooking."

"Once you told me you had two girls. Do you still?"

"Yes." Slim moved a double three and blocked one of the corners. "And no."

"I'm confused. Do you or not?"

"I do, but one of my girls has never forgiven me for something long ago, doesn't acknowledge I even exist." Slim's voice sounded like sand had blown in and lodged in his vocal cords.

"Something you did?"

"Yes. Unintentionally, but it resulted in the greatest loss of my life."

"You don't have to tell me if you don't want to."

"It's like a sore festering. The longer you let it go, the more infected it gets."

"I don't understand."

"I haven't spoken of it in a while, and the festering is inside of me. If you want, I'll tell you what happened."

I nodded, but wasn't at all sure I wanted to know. It sounded like that holy of holies place Brother Henry preached about where not many people have gone and come out alive.

"Dottie and I had two girls, twelve and fourteen, when it happened." Slim leaned back in his rocker and rubbed his chin. "We'd gone to Amarillo to do some shopping, left the girls with their grandmother. We got a late start home, and on the drive back, I musta dozed off. Woke up in Saint Anthony's hospital with half a dozen busted bones and the news Dottie had died in the accident."

His cheeks looked sunken, like hollowed-out moon craters.

"It took three months in the hospital to patch me up. By then Dottie's mother had taken the girls. She blamed me, wouldn't let me see them, even went to a judge and got custody. I got a job driving trucks in the oil field. Ambled over half the state of Texas, sent my girls every spare penny and called whenever I was in town, but none of them would see me."

"That's terrible." I felt sorry for him. "But one daughter, she forgave you?"

"Just in the last few years. Her husband, a sergeant in the army, got blown up in Korea when he stepped on a mine. Somehow, losing him, she decided not to let her own bitterness fester any longer. Perkiest thing you ever saw now. God's been good to give me back one of my girls."

"But the other one, surely by now..."

"One hopes and prays. I must admit, it's drawn me to the Almighty, beseeching him every day."

"It's Christmas. Call her. You probably have grandchildren, kids you could be teaching how to play backgammon...."

"Anybody say backgammon?" Cly hollered at the front door.

"Hey, stranger." Slim pushed himself away from the game. He clapped Cly on the shoulder and steered him to the place opposite me. "This girl's too hot for my blood. See if you can teach her a lesson or two."

"First game, double or nothing." I lifted my chin.

Slim slipped on his beat-up hat and a jacket with the elbows worn through. "I'll go check on the mail."

"You ready for Christmas?" Cly asked me.

"Ready as I'll ever be. How about you?"

He shrugged. "Norm's got a wild hair we should drive down to Dallas and see Big Tex."

"Who's that?"

"Some fifty-foot cowboy statue at the fairgrounds. Supposedly he talks and wears a seventy-five gallon hat. Sounds crazy to me, but Uncle Norm's bent on going to see it."

"Sounds fun."

"Yeah, Aunt Eva's got some kin down there. Gonna be a real family Christmas." He sounded pleased.

I threw a dud roll. Cly got two doubles in a row. We played back and forth, me getting stomped.

"You've lost your touch, cat."

"I was just thinking about Slim. Did you know he has two daughters?"

"He's mentioned it a time or two. He told me I oughta write my old man a letter. He says no matter what he did, he's still my dad."

"Are you going to?"

"I'm still rolling it around in my head. You don't know what it was like living with a hothead drunk. He'd just as soon kick me as look at me."

Because I couldn't think of anything to say, I stood and went to see if Slim had started back with the mail. An empty slate sky filled the view in the window. A tumbleweed skittered across Slim's garden. At least Cly's dad didn't kill himself.

"The only decent thing he ever did was bring me to Norm and Eva's house. Now I get a chance to play basketball, hang around with dolls like you, even ride in Doob's old rattletrap. Norm treats me half decent nowadays. Tells me all the time how he wanted to play college basketball till the war came along and thinks I'm a chip off the old block."

I knew what he said about Norm was right. When I went to see Cly play basketball, you could hear his uncle holler, "That's my boy!" every time Cly scored. Who would've thought? "Dolls like me? At least you didn't call me an ankle biter."

"Naw, ankle biters don't kiss like you did."

I picked up a throw pillow from Slim's couch and creamed him.

## THIRTY-ONE

SCHOOL DIDN'T LET OUT until December 23, the same day Tuwana left for Lubbock to visit her grandparents on the Johnson side. They lived in a brick house and owned their own insurance company, in which, if Benny Ray had a lick of sense, according to Mrs. Johnson, he would become a partner. Then Mrs. Johnson could join the Junior League and they would live happily ever after.

Cly also took off the next day with Norm and Eva to go visit the Dallas relatives and Big Tex.

Everyone had plans for something exciting. Even Goldie. George's brother from Pampa was coming, so she gave me my present early. A new copy of *Gone with the Wind*, which I had to leave at her house to keep Aunt Vadine from incinerating it. How I longed to curl up in those pages and read Mama's favorite book again, thinking somehow I could touch her in a tangible way and bring her home for Christmas. Instead I thanked Goldie for the book and went home.

Tempted to get Mama's letters from the hatbox, I decided against it. A queasy gut feeling told me reading her private letters might ruin Christmas. Not that I was looking all that forward to it.

Christmas without Mama felt like the manger with no baby Jesus. Or Santa's reindeer without Rudolph and his nose-so-bright. Mama loved Christmas. She made gingerbread cookies and hinted for weeks that I'd never guess what I was getting that year. We had paper chains on the tree, mugs of cocoa, tinfoil stars hung from the ceiling with fishing line.

This year I had Aunt Vadine.

No paper chains or gingerbread men, although I did decorate the little pine tree Daddy bought from the Boy Scout lot at the VFW. Lots of tinsel and the box of ornaments Daddy pulled down from the attic. He had to work on Christmas Day, so I stretched out on the couch and read a library book while Aunt Vadine stationed herself in Daddy's rocker with a new crochet project, counting off stitches. "Four single, two double...oh fiddle, I forgot to double back."

Aunt Vadine put a ham in the oven for "our nice little family Christmas." She smiled and raised her eyebrows toward the tinseled tree. None of the packages looked big enough for a typewriter, so I figured it was like the time I got my Radio Flyer bicycle, when Daddy went out on the porch and came in saying, "Oh, look what Santy Claus left outside." Of course, the possibility of my *not* getting a typewriter did occur to me, so I went back to reading rather than think about that.

Daddy came home *ho-ho-ho-ing*, and after he cleaned up, we had our Christmas dinner. Ham, scorched potatoes, pea salad. Aunt Vadine never claimed to be Betty Crocker, but she did make the best pea salad, dotted with pimiento and just the right mix of Miracle Whip and lemon juice. Then for dessert we each had a wide slice of pumpkin pie from Piggly Wiggly with a squirt of canned whipped cream on the top.

"Ready for the big event, Sis?" Daddy rolled his eyes toward the front room.

"You're going to be so surprised," I told Daddy, and surprised myself by feeling a tingle of excitement.

"I'm going to freshen up." Aunt Vadine gave Daddy a wink,

which I took to mean she'd be going to get my "big" present, the one kept secretly hidden since it would be too obvious otherwise.

Daddy and I settled in the front room, admiring the tree.

Aunt Vadine came out wearing a silky purple dress with a swirling skirt and three-quarter sleeves, one I'd never seen before. She took teeny little steps in a circle like a ballerina. Apparently she'd popped a fresh piece of Juicy Fruit gum in her mouth too, as the sickly sweet smell overtook the pine scent of the lighted Christmas tree. She gave another twirl, and then I saw them. Around her neck she wore Mama's pearls.

The room spun around me, and an *aack* escaped from my mouth.

"You okay, Sis?" Daddy asked.

"Hope you like the dress, dear," Aunt Vadine cooed to Daddy and then turned to me. "He gave me the money to buy my own present."

"It's not the dress.... It's...uh, you're wearing Mama's pearls." Pea-flavored bile rose in my throat.

"Perfect with the dress, don't you think?"

"Rita's pearls?" Daddy had a blank look on his face.

"Sammie's much too young for them. Besides, they weren't Rita's to give. Our mama should have passed them on to me, bein's I'm older. I knew Sammie wouldn't mind."

I waited for Daddy to say something. To protest. He didn't. What could I say? She's a thief? A liar? After all it was Christmas, a time of good will.

I wanted to puke.

We proceeded right into the opening of packages. My first one was a compact, not the gold one I'd asked for, but a nice plastic one with CoverGirl Ivory Blush powder.

Aunt Vadine gushed over the hankies I bought her. "Don't these purple forget-me-nots match my new dress just perfectly?"

"They're pansies." I forced a smile.

Daddy shook the package I gave him and made a big deal of guessing. "A box of rocks? New fishing tackle?" He did seem tickled with the backgammon set, which folded into a box like a miniature suitcase and held the dice, their holders, and the brown and tan playing pieces.

"You think you can teach an old dog like me this game?" He winked and handed me another box with my name on it.

I shook it and thought it felt about the right weight for the sweater I wanted and guessed that before opening it. Aunt Vadine smiled and said she picked it out *special* for me. My fingers trembled as I opened it and undid the layers of tissue paper. My heart sank as I lifted out a navy and white sailor dress with a collar as big as a flag.

"Oh, I'm...uh, speechless." A vision skipped through my head of Shirley Temple in ringlets singing about the good ship Lollipop.

"I knew you'd love it. Just the thing for a girl your age." Aunt Vadine gave a smug wiggle from her spot on the couch. "And now, for the grand finale..." She stood up.

*Ah, this is it. The moment we've been waiting for. Now she'll get my typewriter.*

She didn't though. She pulled the last box from under the tree, a square one with gold foil paper, the expensive kind Mama and I always admired but passed up. She took it to Daddy and knelt at his feet. "My gift to you, for all you mean to me."

Daddy's neck turned crimson. Then his whole face got a splotchy purple look to it as he lifted out a sapphire blue scarf—at least a yard long and made of a slippery fabric. It looked like water running through his fingers when he held it up.

"What the devil?"

"Silk." Aunt Vadine scooted closer to Daddy. "Nothing like a natural fiber to ward off the cold. I wanted you to have something useful but extravagant, so you'd know how much I care." She half rose on her knees, took the scarf from Daddy, and began bundling it around his neck. With her face smack-dab up to his, she leaned in and kissed him, her fingers lingering on his sideburns.

The pearls had been bad enough. Now I watched Aunt Vadine drool over Daddy, smacking her gum and carrying on like Tuwana predicted. *Biding her time. When the right moment arises.* I tossed the boxes aside and glared at her.

"How can you do this? Coming here, trying to steal my daddy like you did my mama's pearls. Don't you care what I want, what Daddy wants?" The words flew out of my mouth before I could stop them, and I felt even more hateful ones forming in my throat, choking me. A clammy vapor clung to my skin, suffocating me.

*Away. I have to get away.*

I rushed out the door, not even grabbing my purse or my coat.

As I flew down the steps of the front porch, I heard Aunt Vadine say, "My goodness, I wonder what brought that on."

The cold stung my eyes, but inside I fumed. I ran and ran, paying no attention where to, just escaping, and getting as far away as I could.

My lungs burned, and after a while I slowed down, still walking fast, up the middle of camp. Christmas bulbs, strung like glowing popcorn chains along rooflines, lit my way. No moon or stars. Lighted trees, twinkling from Graham Camp front rooms, mocked me. *Ho-ho-ho*, they said. *Peace on earth.*

The cold seeped into the furnace roaring inside me, and I pulled my arms inside my thin sweater to warm them against my rib cage. I marched along, my feet now freezing. And wet. Looking down, I saw I was slogging through fresh snow. Above me flakes the size of silver dollars drifted from heaven. I stuck out my tongue to catch them, but my face, my entire body, in fact, had grown numb.

*Tomorrow someone will find me. Sammie, the ice statue.*

*Are you crazy? Is Aunt Vadine worth all this? Trust him. That's what Brother Henry would say. Please, dear God in heaven, can't you see I'm trying here? Running away may not be the brightest thing I've ever done, but maybe you can help me undo this mess.*

A light flickered ahead.

Moses was led through the wilderness by a pillar of fire by night. *Is that you, God? Showing me the way?*

The light twinkled, a tiny speck just ahead. I ran toward it. I thought I saw Moses himself.

"Who's there?" the voice called out, sounding familiar, but far away.

*Faster. Go faster.* My legs wouldn't go. I kept trying to reach the light.

*Go to the light. Right foot. Left foot.*

The light barely glowed. Dimmer and dimmer. I worked my arms back into my sleeves and reached for the Moses figure, but nothing touched my fingers. I reached again, stretching my arms, and toppled into blackness.

## THIRTY-TWO

*H*ELP! HELP!

Was that me yelling? I tried to concentrate in the blackness.

Something or someone lifted me up, strong like Moses, who'd carried the stone tablets down Mount Sinai, and a voice, maybe Moses himself, told me I could make it. *Floating. I'm floating up.* Then warmth pressed in on me, heavy like a blanket. Lights swirled overhead.

My teeth chattered like pebbles rolling around in my mouth, and my eyes focused. It wasn't Moses at all, but Slim Wallace.

"Sammie, what on earth?" His face looked like he'd seen a ghost.

Mrs. Gray, her hair circling like a golden halo above her head, hovered beside the colorless Slim, and I closed my eyes to stop the hallucination.

When I opened them again, the braided circles of the rug in Slim's front room, his high-backed rocker, and the backgammon board set up in the middle of a game came into focus. Slim and Mrs. Gray remained close by, and I tried to clear my mind. Nothing made sense.

"Sammie, are you all right? What were you doing?" Slim's voice was stronger now.

I looked from him to Mrs. Gray.

"What is she doing here?" My brains still felt scrambled.

"This is Olivia, my daughter. She's been telling me you're one of her students."

"Your daughter? How? Why didn't you tell me?"

"It didn't occur to me—that's a fact."

Mrs. Gray, just a vision a moment ago, sat beside me, putting her arm around me, pulling me close. She kissed the top of my head.

"I...I guess I ran away from home." An explanation seemed necessary all of a sudden. Not every Christmas does a juvenile delinquent turn up on your doorstep. And by now I'd figured out Mr. Howard's prediction about me had come true. What next? Stealing candy from Willy Bailey? Letting the air out of tires? All because Aunt Vadine kissed Daddy?

Slim got up to answer a knock at the door. Daddy came in, stomping the snow off his boots, already going into a spiel about me disappearing and asking if they'd seen me. Our eyes met, and I couldn't tell if relief at seeing me or the possibility of strangulation flashed in Daddy's dark eyes.

"Thank God you're all right," he said. "What in tarnation came over you?"

"Calm down, Joe. Olivia and I were just playing a friendly game of backgammon when we got an unexpected visitor. Take off your coat and stay awhile."

Mrs. Gray (I couldn't get it in my head her name was Olivia) slipped into the kitchen and came back with a cup of coffee for Daddy and steaming Ovaltine for me. The feeling came back in my fingers and toes as Daddy and Slim talked about the weather.

"Just a flurry tonight, that's all. *The Old Farmer's Almanac* says we're in for an inch or more the end of the month," Slim said. "Can't go wrong with the almanac. Hits it on the head every time. Sure can use the moisture though, that's for sure."

Mrs. Gray went into one of the bedrooms and then motioned for me to come in. She gave me a woolly sweater and a pair of corduroy slacks that bagged around the seat but fit okay otherwise.

"Here, some dry socks will help your feet."

"Thanks. Sorry I'm so much trouble."

"Pooh, no trouble at all. And when you feel up to it, I'm a good listener."

"Thanks. Maybe later."

Slim protested when Daddy said we ought to be getting back.

"The night is young. Why, Olivia and I here had pert near bored ourselves to death talking about the weather. Sammie, you ever played pinochle?"

"Nope, but if it's anything like backgammon, I'm willing to learn."

"Totally different game. Most folks down at the church frown on card playing, but I've been playing since I was knee high to a tadpole. You'll like it. You can be on my side."

"I haven't played pinochle since the army." Daddy set his hat on the end table. "Olivia here won't be getting much of a partner." It was settled. No more talk about rushing home, back to the disaster I'd caused. It *was* my fault, I knew that. I also knew I would have to untangle the mess. Just not tonight. *Thank you, Jesus.*

Pinochle turned out to be trickier than backgammon. For one thing, the card deck only had face cards, plus aces, tens, and nines, two of each in the four suits. You had to know a jillion combinations and what each one counted in order to bid and lay down your meld. Nothing simple like crazy eights or go fish.

Daddy caught back on as quick as a jackrabbit and laughed as he and Mrs. Gray slaughtered us the first game. While Slim dealt the cards, Daddy looked over at Mrs. Gray. "You know, I've been wondering.... What would happen if I took those knitting needles out of your hair?"

She held up her hands and widened her eyes. "I'd unravel, that's what. Such a mess!" Which made Daddy laugh, a deep belly laugh I hadn't heard in forever.

On a scrap of paper I wrote down how much all the pinochle combinations counted and kept it as a cheat sheet. The next game I got the hang of it, and Slim and I won by fifty points.

"Eggnog anyone?" Mrs. Gray scampered off to the kitchen. She brought short, squatty glasses for everyone, and we laughed until our sides ached from seeing who could make the biggest mustache of the creamy, sweet drink—nonalcoholic, Mrs. Gray assured us.

Daddy and Mrs. Gray beat us at the last game of pinochle, partly because I could barely keep my eyes open.

"Better get Sis home before she falls asleep and I have to carry her."

"Oh, Daddy, it's been years since you've done that."

The ground was barely white when we stepped outside—no more snow. Slim was right, only a flurry, but still, a biting wind went through me. Thankfully Daddy had driven the car, and while we sat there waiting for it to warm up, he brought up the earlier part of the evening, the part I wished had never happened.

"Sis, I expect you to apologize to your aunt for your actions. This may not have been the Christmas you were expecting, but rudeness is never acceptable."

"But Mama's pearls—she took them from me."

"Borrowed them. She's trying to help you, help me, the best way she knows how. You've got to give her some credit now and again."

My jaw tensed.

Daddy continued, "You'll apologize first thing tomorrow."

"Yes, sir. I'll apologize." What else could I say? My bones ached from being frozen and thawed out. Ovaltine and eggnog gurgled in my stomach. All I could think of was flopping onto my feather bed.

One thing kept dancing in my head. This *had* been a memorable Christmas, both the worst and the best I could remember. The worst being the disaster with Aunt Vadine; the best—hearing Daddy laugh again. Something inside me hummed right along with the car's heater as Daddy drove us home.

## THIRTY-THREE

WHEN I WOKE UP the next morning, the house was quiet. My stomach ached as I remembered my promised apology to Aunt Vadine. Pulling the covers up to my neck, I tried to swallow. Too dry. Scratchy. My eyes burned, and a heavy dull ache pressed against my skull. I fell back into a deep sleep until Aunt Vadine's voice brought me out of my feverish dreams.

"You going to sleep all day, Samantha?" Hard and raspy, like the soreness in my throat.

"Sorry. Could I have a drink please?" My bed felt like a toaster, burning my skin.

"Your legs aren't broken. Hurry up. We need to get the tree down before your daddy comes in from work."

My head flopped from side to side to tell her no, but she stood with her hands on her hips, waiting for me to get up.

In the bathroom, I cupped my hands and splashed cold water on my face, slurping a mouthful from my hands. *Dizzy. And hot. I've got to sit down.* I took a deep breath and held my wet hands over my eyelids to ease their burning. I stumbled into the front room, where ornaments and tinsel from the tree covered the couch and Daddy's chair.

"I'm going back to bed. My throat is sore, and I think I have a fever."

"It's no wonder with your inexcusable behavior last night. Your failure to think of anyone but yourself does have repercussions, you know."

The way she spat out her words hit me like I'd heard them all before. Was it the fever talking? A revelation from heaven? My head felt swimmy.

Aunt Vadine had talked to Mama the same way a while back, maybe a very long time ago. My head pounded as I tried to remember. Did Aunt Vadine hate Mama for some reason? Had she decided to take it out on me? Why? And if so, why did she care what happened to Daddy and me? I mean, really, if she wanted to help, she had a strange way of showing it.

My throat felt like I'd swallowed a flaming sword, but I plunged right in to my apology. "About last night, I'm sorry for what I said and did."

"I should hope you'd have a scrap of remorse after scaring your father and me that way. What were you doing blundering off into the night without even a coat?"

No answer would have satisfied her, so I changed the subject.

"My head hurts. Can I go lay back down?"

"Might as well. You're used to doing whatever suits you. Even after we tried to give you a pleasant family Christmas."

As I sank into my feather bed, something else flitted about in my head. If Aunt Vadine hadn't come to school to get the typewriter I'd asked for, what was she doing there?

When Daddy got home, he brought me a cool rag and smeared my neck with Vicks before wrapping a clean handkerchief around it. "Get some rest, Sis."

All night and most of Saturday, I felt so hot I couldn't catch my breath. I dreamed of being a marshmallow on the end of a stick, poked into a campfire. My body shook under the covers. When the fever broke, my sweat drenched the sheets. I got up to put on dry pajamas and change my sheets and noticed my throat didn't feel raw anymore. No headache. Just stuffiness, like a head cold.

The next day I felt well enough to go to church. Aunt Vadine handed me the sailor dress, which I laid gently on the bed. "No thanks."

"It's a perfectly stunning dress. Any girl should be so fortunate—"

"Okay, I'll tell you what I'll do. I'll wear the dress if you give Mama's pearls back to me."

Her face splotched. "Over my dead body." She snatched the dress up and huffed off.

That afternoon Tuwana came over gushing about her trip to Lubbock. "Granny bought me the coolest sweaters. Look at this, real cashmere...." She twirled around in our front room in a tulip pink twinset that matched her rosy cheeks. Her arm rattled like a wind chime every time she made the slightest movement. "Don't you love this charm bracelet?" She dangled her wrist in front of my face. We went into my bedroom and closed the door, where she recited what each charm represented.

"Your bracelet's great." I tried to sound happy for her. "How were your grandparents?"

"The usual—presents, presents, presents. The best holiday ever. Except for the big to-do about Daddy."

"What's that?"

"Pops announced his retirement from the insurance company and wanted Daddy to come work with Uncle Reggie, to keep it in the family. Of course Daddy said no thanks, he and Mother were doing all right with her new job. Mother went on and on about the golden opportunity, no more grease under his fingernails and wondering where our next meal was coming from. Tara and Tommie Sue sided with her, babbling on about going to Granny's house for slumber parties."

"What about you? Did you stick up for your dad?"

"I remained neutral. Actually, I don't want to have to start my whole life over, going to a new school, wondering if I'll fit in. Besides, I've decided to try for cheerleader again next year. I'm growing my hair out so I can wear a ponytail with those cute see-through scarves I saw everyone in Lubbock wearing."

"I'm surprised at your mom. I thought she liked her job."

"She did—until she found out she made ten cents an hour less than the janitor. Now she's thinking about quitting. All the way home she and Daddy argued about how they would pay for my braces. Mother said if he'd quit acting like the black sheep of the family, we'd have money to burn."

"Both sides have their points, I can see that, but I hope you don't move."

"Me too. How was your Christmas?"

I told her all about the pearls and the sailor dress.

"Well, what are you going to do about it?"

"You mean, am I going to wear the dress? Not for all the tumbleweeds in Texas—no way."

"No, about the pearls."

"I haven't figured it out yet. What do you think?"

"Your mom gave them to you. I say take them back."

"Tuwana, that's stealing. Besides, I don't know where they are."

"It's not stealing if you're taking what was yours to start with. You're reclaiming stolen property. Pure and simple."

"If only it were simple...."

Tuwana had already started pulling out drawers, digging in Aunt Vadine's undies, scrambling them up, and slamming the drawers shut. She lifted the mattress and peeked under it.

"Stop. Even if you found them, I couldn't take them. It would just make matters worse."

"Worse than what? My gosh, you have some rights, you know. It'll only get worse when she starts making her move to become your new mother."

"Don't talk like that. Daddy's not interested."

"Mother says all men are interested. Interested in someone to cook, clean, and share the sack with." The last part she whispered, cocking her head toward the front room.

The blue scarf Aunt Vadine had wrapped around Daddy's neck flashed through my head. The way she touched him, her merry "Whatever you'd like, Joe." Best friends or not, I couldn't bring myself to tell Tuwana about that. If I said it out loud, the possibility of it coming true would become real. For some reason, I also kept the part about going to Slim's to myself, although that *had* been the best part of Christmas.

"Nothing good is going to come of this. Trust me." Tuwana's blue eyes bored into me.

"Meanwhile, back at the ranch..."

"Whatever. Just remember, I told you so, and if you need any help, you can count on me." She jangled her wrist and dug into her oversized coat pocket. "I almost forgot. I got you something."

Inside the reindeer-printed paper was a small diary with a clasp and a tiny silver key.

"It's perfect! The best present I've ever received." I clutched the powdery blue diary to my chest with one arm and gave Tuwana a hug with the other. "Thank you."

January 1, 1959

Dear Diary,

We had ham hocks and black-eyed peas today. Good luck, you know. I could use it after this last year. I've made my New Year's resolution. I am going to quit running away from my problems. I have to stand up for myself. I just have to.

SJT

\*　　\*　　\*

I couldn't wait to get back to school and see Mrs. Gray. On the first day of classes, Cly told me all about Big Tex and Eva's cousin who had a used-car lot. Norm promised they'd go back to Dallas and get Cly a car when he passed his driving test. "I'm holding out for a ragtop."

The day dragged by slower than molasses. Finally last hour came, and I hurried to Mrs. Gray's class with the clothes she'd loaned me in a paper sack. Her head jerked up when she saw me, the bun on top of her head bouncing lightly. She seemed surprised to see me. Ever since Christmas night, I'd had conversations with myself about what I would say to her and how funny it was to find out she was Slim's daughter. She hurried over to me.

"Sammie, I'm sorry. I thought you had gotten the message. Mr. Howard wishes to speak to you." Her fingertips rested on my shoulder for a second.

"No, no message, but I'll go if I'm supposed to. Here are your clothes. Thanks for letting me use them."

She took the bag from me, her eyes sad. A twinge went through me, the teensiest bit of panic. Was it Goldie? Daddy? Maybe something had happened to Scarlett.

Mr. Howard's door stood open behind the empty secretary's chair. He waved me in. Cheerful, rosy-cheeked, he pointed to a chair for me to sit down. He picked up a folder, put on thick, black-rimmed glasses, and studied a sheet of paper.

"Mmmm…all A's for the semester. Quite a pleasant surprise in view of all that's happened." He smiled and seemed to expect a response.

"I like school and know I have to make good grades for college."

He cleared his throat. "Keeping up with my students is of particular interest to me, one of the qualities of a good principal, I like to think."

Did he think we were doing a follow-up on him for the newspaper? If so, it was news to me.

He went on. "I must admit, I had a few worries about you, but I can tell having your aunt in the home has been a stabilizing factor, of which you are no doubt aware. Maxine, I believe her name is."

"Vadine. Her name is Vadine Cox." How did he know her?

"Yes, quite a mesmerizing woman. So perceptive too. She's pleased with your academic progress, but expressed some other concerns to me when we visited before Christmas."

My fingers gripped the metal arms of my chair. That's what she was doing at the school—talking to Mr. Howard. What concerns? Obviously not the typewriters.

"She says you're headstrong, with a tendency toward impulsive actions and disregard for others. She's noticed a pattern, and having grown up with a mentally unstable sister—that would be your mother—she's worried about you. What brought her to me was the article you wrote for our school newspaper. Not the one about me—you did a fine job on that. The Christmas article you did. I'm afraid it concerned your lovely aunt greatly."

"What?" She never said one word to me about it. I racked my brain trying to remember if she even read the school paper when I showed it to Daddy.

"Your aunt says your fanciful ideas in the article are in direct opposition to your family's religious beliefs, and your confusion about the most basic things you've been taught has caused her much grief."

"Yes, sir. She believes my mom died and went straight to hell."

"Sammie, we don't allow swearing at school, and in matters of religious issues, we steer completely clear. That is why you've been released from working on the paper. Best all around, I think.

Working with families is one of the strengths I bring to my position here. You've been assigned to study hall for this semester. Any questions?"

"Mentioning heaven could hardly be called religious. More of just imagining what Christmas in heaven would be like. You know, would there be snow, Christmas trees, or would every day be like Christmas?"

"I see your aunt's point. Your fantasies now might be just the tip of the iceberg toward deeper delusions. I'm afraid my decision stands. Anything further you'd like to say?"

*Aunt Vadine did this. How could she?*

I studied my fingernails, trying to decide what to say.

*Does he expect me to blurt out an apology? Or fly off my rocker like he thinks Mama did? No! I won't let him get to me. Face. Your. Problems.*

I took a deep breath and scooted to the edge of my chair.

"Mr. Howard, did the typing department sell all the used typewriters?"

"What an odd question for the matter at hand." He shuffled the papers on his desk.

Seeing his confusion gave me a tingle of excitement. A riddle for Howdy Doody? "Well, did they?"

"No, as a matter of fact, we couldn't get rid of them so we donated them to the VFW rummage sale."

"Thanks, that's all I needed to know." Let him think I'd flipped my lid. He already did anyway.

When I left Mr. Howard scratching his head, I knew the time had come to try out my New Year's resolution—I would not run away from my problems. I had some serious questions for Aunt Vadine.

## THIRTY-FOUR

I'M HOME," I HOLLERED, tossing my bag onto the end table.

Aunt Vadine came from the bedroom, looking like she'd just woken up from a nap.

In the kitchen I banged a few cupboards, poured a glass of milk from the icebox, and dipped a Lorna Doone in the milk.

"How was school?"

"Oh, you know, the usual. First day of the new semester. Math review." I looked her straight in the eye. "Study hall last hour."

Aunt Vadine smoothed her hand over her sparrow-colored hair and plopped onto the couch, picking up her crochet.

"Mr. Howard called me into the office." I sat in Daddy's rocker.

"Mmmm..." The crochet hook zipped in and out, a steady line of thread unwinding from the yarn ball. I drummed up my courage.

"He wanted to discuss your visit to the school before Christmas." My insides bubbled with emotion. "I saw you that day, you know. At the time I thought you were coming to get one of the typewriters I had on my list—you remember, the used ones from the typing department."

"We don't have room for a typewriter, and the *peck-peck-peck* I'm sure you'd be doing day and night would drive us all crazy."

"You could have said something, or we could work out a schedule."

"You're too young for a typewriter. Besides, they were gone."

"Not according to Mr. Howard."

She stopped in midair and turned toward me, but said nothing.

"I found out what you were doing at school." My jaw ached from tensing it so tight.

"Writing such nonsense will only get you into trouble."

"Mrs. Gray didn't think it was nonsense. Neither did Brother Henry."

"Lawsy, Samantha, what did you do? Wag your fantasy all over creation?"

"That's not the point. You interfered in my life. You had no right to go behind my back, kiss up to the school principal, and get me kicked off the school paper. You have violated my rights." My voice squeaked higher with every word.

"Children don't have rights."

"That's a lie. Was it your idea or Daddy's?"

"He doesn't have time to chase off after every ridiculous incident you pull."

"Ridiculous? To you maybe. To me it was a big deal to work on the newspaper. As a matter of fact, I hope to talk to Daddy in the morning and see what he thinks."

"Your father is busy making a living and grieving the loss of his wife, and I fully expect he will support me in this. I've tried my best to be here for him, to fill in the gaps and give him comfort...."

"And be my new mother?" The words gagged me, but I couldn't stop them.

Aunt Vadine's spine straightened, and she sucked in a deep breath. "Well, certainly, if and when your father is ready, I believe we could make it work. I've known him even longer than your mother did."

*She knew Daddy before Mama did?*

"What do you mean?"

"It's really none of your affair. What your daddy and I had is between us." The crumpled crochet rested in her lap, her fingers tangled in the yarn. A faraway look came into her eyes.

"You *dated* Daddy?" I thought I might vomit.

"That's not so hard to believe, is it?"

"Daddy said meeting Mama at that dance was the best thing that ever happened to him."

"Of course he would say that. He wasn't the first to have his head turned by a good-looking woman. She could be quite charming when there was something in it for her."

"Were you mad at Mama for stealing your boyfriend?"

"Of course not." She drew her shoulders up in a huff. "It's all water under the bridge. Sometimes God gives us a second chance."

"Is that what you were thinking when you came for Mama's funeral? That Daddy might give you a second chance?"

"Don't be absurd. I came to help. It was the Christian thing to do." She stood up, straightening a doily on the armrest of the couch.

"Tuwana was right then."

Her eyes narrowed and turned from muddy brown to flashes of gold, like a cat ready to pounce on a garden snake.

"Tuwana said you came to be my new mother, that you're just waiting for the right time."

"Men have needs, things you're much too young to know about." Her words were aimed at a spot over my head like she was addressing an invisible person behind me.

"Like your boyfriend Bobby?"

She sucked in her breath. "Eavesdropping on my conversation was a nasty thing for you to do. I will not allow you to interfere in my life."

"But you can interfere in mine? Throw my books into the incinerator? March off to school and get me thrown off the paper? Steal Mama's pearls? Kiss my daddy?" The words flew out of my mouth, and I didn't try to stop them.

Aunt Vadine stepped toward me. Her arm flew at me, her open palm slamming against my cheek. My brains bounced from one side of my head to the other. My face stung, and hot tears filled my eyes. I blinked, refusing to let them fall. She would not make me cry.

"This conversation is over, you ungrateful little ninny."

"No, it's not. You *will not* be my new mother. I will talk to Daddy. You'll see."

The feel of her hand on my flesh burned, but I didn't care. I threw on my coat, hat, and gloves and slammed the front door behind me. I whistled for Scarlett. My breath huffed out in white clouds, and the air tingled my cheeks, easing the ache in my jaw from Aunt Vadine's slap. She could knock me silly for all I cared, but I would tell Daddy about Bobby and the newspaper and her lighting in to me. At least Mama had an excuse for all the times I'd come home and found the house dark, dirty dishes in the sink, and her curled in the quilt in her bedroom. She had depression. Aunt Vadine was just plain mean.

Tuwana was right. Not just about Aunt Vadine thinking she could become the new Mrs. Joe Tucker, but also about the pearls. They were mine, and I would take them back. Call it stealing if you want, but...they...were...mine. Mama wanted me to have them. And her New Testament. *Seek and ye shall find.*

My stomach tightened. While Scarlett scampered from one yard to the next, the cold bit me, creeping through my coat, my hat. The January dusk turned quickly from furry tan to a deep gray.

The elm trees stood with their bare arms reaching up in jagged angles to the sky. I looked up, hoping someone in heaven would reach down for me.

An achy spot inside wanted someone to hold me, to ask about my day at school and laugh with me. Daddy did those things, but a mother is what I wanted. Daddy deserved better than Aunt Vadine. We both did.

From my feather bed, I waited, listening for Daddy to come home from work. Morning seemed an eternity away, so I'd decided to stay awake until his shift ended.

Soft giggling pulled me out of the half sleep I must've fallen into. Moonbeams slanted through the gauzy curtains above my bed, ending on the twin bed where Aunt Vadine slept. Empty. No snoring from her side of the room. Then another giggle.

*From the front room?* I strained my ears, trying to tell where the sound came from.

Daddy's room? Possibly. Was that Aunt Vadine giggling?

A creaking sound. Then a gruff, low sound. Cold sweat covered my body. I lay there listening, trying to piece it all together for what seemed like hours. I wanted to get up and talk to Daddy, but my body felt paralyzed.

What did they think? That I was just a kid who couldn't put two and two together and figure out what moaning and creaking meant? I'm no expert, but I would have to be a certified idiot to not figure out what Aunt Vadine was doing with my daddy.

*No! No! No! Don't let her trap you, Daddy!*

Low voices came like radio static to my ears. No more giggles or squeaking sounds. Maybe I'd heard something on the television. The toilet flushed, and Daddy's voice came through loud and clear. "'Night, Vadine." He shut the door to his room.

When I woke up the next morning, Aunt Vadine's bed had its normal crumpled look, and I smelled bacon and coffee. I'd overslept by ten minutes and threw on my clothes, brushed my teeth, and combed my hair, still determined to talk to Daddy for at least a few minutes.

"Juice?" Aunt Vadine swooshed around the kitchen in her flimsy robe.

"No thanks. Toast and milk will be enough."

"Back to school, huh, Sis?" Daddy chewed a mouthful of scrambled eggs.

"Yeah, there've been some changes I wanted to talk to you about."

Aunt Vadine glided to the table and poised over Daddy's cup, refilling his coffee from the pot in her hands. "Your daddy and I visited last night." Her words flowed like Aunt Jemima syrup.

*And what else?* It was on the tip of my tongue. I gulped a big swallow of milk. How I could even think about breakfast at a time like this shocked me. And they acted as if nothing had happened.

"Aunt Vadine didn't realize how badly you wanted a typewriter, said we ought to see about getting one for your birthday. It's coming up, February thirteenth." He winked at me.

"Yes, I do want one, but..."

"Samantha, better get your shoes on. Here's your coat. I heard the bus beeping down the street." Aunt Vadine scurried like a tornado was coming, collecting my things and shooing me out the door.

A heavy frost had snapped every blade of dried grass to attention, glistening in the sun like a sea of glass sequins. My feet crunched as I walked toward the bus. In the light of day, I tried to remember what I had heard last night. Had Aunt Vadine gone to Daddy's room, knowing as a man he'd be *interested*, as Tuwana put it? Would she do that? Aunt Vadine said men had needs. My head told me she didn't mean the universal human needs for food, water, and shelter like we'd learned in science class. But she and Daddy acted everyday normal this morning, except for the mention of the typewriter.

It must've been a dream or my fanciful imagination, like Mr. Howard said.

I climbed the steps of the bus, more uncertain with every step, and by the time I slid into the seat beside Tuwana, I knew it had just been a nightmare. But it seemed so real.

After that I started having the same dream almost every night. Not the swirling black hole, but scary just the same. Daddy and I would be having a picnic or walking along a stream, the sun making sparkles around us. The picture would flash, and Aunt Vadine would appear. Daddy wore his army uniform, and Aunt Vadine had long brown hair, painted red lips, and golden eyes. She held Daddy's hand, and when I yelled, "Wait for me!" she glanced over her shoulder at me, the holes in her eye sockets empty. Then she walked the other way, pulling Daddy with her. I tried to run after them, but I had turned into a cardboard girl, flat like a paper doll. The more I tried to move, the thinner I got, until just an outline remained. That's when I would wake up, trying to turn back into Sammie so I could run after them. Sweat covered my body, and the air never let me suck it in. I pinched my arm to make sure I had skin and flesh. Then I would lie in bed, hugging Mama's robe to my chest and listen until I heard Aunt Vadine's snore, thankful once again she hadn't run off with Daddy.

The next morning my arms would have red spots from the pinches I gave myself. Bruises, some purple, some fading to yellow and green, spotted my arms. Thank goodness it was winter and I could wear long sleeves without raising suspicion.

\*     \*     \*

The middle of January, Daddy took us to a basketball game. Our Chevy had a clunk Daddy wanted to look at, so we took Aunt Vadine's car. We invited Slim to go, but he said he felt a bit under the weather, so Aunt Vadine came instead. And Tuwana of course. All the way to town, Aunt Vadine clucked about what a nice place Mandeville was and how she couldn't wait to see Cly play. Tuwana rolled her eyes at me as we sat in the backseat.

"Mother decided to keep her job at the bank. Says there's a teller's job opening up soon, and she's determined to go through the ranks. The way she talks, she'll be vice president by the time I'm through high school."

"Say, Aunt Vadine. Maybe you could see about the secretary job if Tuwana's mother is getting a promotion." A job might get her mind off being my new mother.

"I've always felt the woman's place is in the home." Aunt Vadine giggled and patted Daddy on the arm.

Tuwana nodded her head like *See, I told you so.*

Between the girls' and boys' games, I went to the concession stand. Waiting in line, I spotted Mrs. Gray, laughing, the bun on top of her head bobbing as she chatted with someone. She saw me and came over.

"Sammie, I've been wanting to see you. How are you?" She wore the sweater and corduroy pants she'd loaned me, and they looked much better on her, showing off her nice figure.

"I'm fine." My fingers itched to touch her sweater, give her a hug, but it didn't seem right, so I fiddled with the catch on my wallet.

"We've missed you dearly on the newspaper. I feel dreadful about what happened."

"Me too. I keep hoping I can talk to Daddy about it, see if he'll come and see you."

"You mean it wasn't your father's idea to ... uh ..."

"Not hardly."

"But Mr. Howard said your aunt came at his insistence. Then I met your dad at Christmas and he seemed so nice—I thought there'd been some misunderstanding."

"May I take your order, please?" the boy behind the concession counter asked.

"No, not right now. I'll be back." I stepped out of the line and turned back to Mrs. Gray. A catch in my throat kept me from talking for a moment. I looked down at my penny loafers. "My aunt and I have had some problems."

"So I gathered. When I told you that night at Slim's I was a good listener, I suspected something, but I won't interfere. Slim's told me a lot about you. He's crazy about you."

Looking up, I smiled at her. "I think he's swell too. Why do you call him Slim and not dad?"

"It's a long story, but we'll get together sometime and chat. I lost my mother when I was your age, and life can throw you some mighty big curves. I know."

"Thanks. Can I have Daddy come and talk to you?"

"Nothing I would like better." She turned to go back into the gym, and I got back in line.

"Make up your mind yet?" the guy behind the counter asked.

I ordered a Dr Pepper and M&M's. That's when the first glimmer of an idea formed, and by the time I sat back down, I knew I'd thought of a way to get Daddy's mind off Aunt Vadine as my future mother. Something had to be done before she pulled him any farther into her web.

## THIRTY-FIVE

FOR DAYS I PLEADED with Tuwana to help me with my plan. Personally, I thought the idea of getting Daddy interested in Mrs. Gray was nothing short of brilliant.

I thought reasoning with Tuwana might help. "Mrs. Gray is one of the most popular teachers in school."

"Yes, but probably because no one knows about her past, at least her father's past. If they knew..."

"All I'm asking is for you to go over there with me, friendly like, as you're so fond of saying, and we can ask if Mrs. Gray has a boyfriend."

"That sounds weird. Old people don't call it that, I'm sure. Maybe we should ask if she has a love interest."

"So you'll go with me?"

"Only because you won't shut up about it. And Mother can't find out or she'll kill me."

"How about Saturday? She takes your sisters to piano lessons then, doesn't she?"

"All right, all right. Saturday. Have you looked for the pearls any more?"

"Every place I can think of. I've become a regular Nancy Drew."

On Saturday it snowed again. The wind howled, and we stayed in the house the whole weekend. Daddy and I played so many games of backgammon, I saw the spots on the dice every time I closed my eyes. Double six. Snake eyes. A four and a three.

I tried to think of ways to talk about Mrs. Gray, but Aunt Vadine kept herself planted on the couch, you know what in her hands, just whipping the hook in and out. This week she made baby bibs with ruffled edges in yellow and green. When I asked her what she was going to do with all those baby things, she lifted her chin. I swear, for a minute I thought her eyes were hollow, like the dream. Then the corners of her mouth tilted up, and gold specks reflected off the bulb of the table lamp. She never said what she would do with the baby bibs. And I never got a chance to tell Daddy how nice it would be if he talked to Mrs. Gray.

The rest of January and the first week of February had the same nasty weather—sometimes just cold and wind, sometimes snow flurries. Cly still had basketball after school, and it was too cold to ride bikes or go to Tuwana's after school. Besides, she had to watch her sisters and start supper.

My insides tingled every time I thought about Mama's hatbox. I desperately wanted to get it from the garage, but Aunt Vadine watched my every move. If I tried to sneak it into the house, she would blast me with questions or spout her opinion about Mama roasting in hell.

Then there was the deal about the pearls. I still hadn't found them. I had to stay on my aunt's good side if there was any hope of seeing them again.

One night, when Daddy had evenings and the house had that choking-close feeling, I gathered up Mama's things—her hairbrush, the lilac soap, the glove full of dirt, her New Testament, her robe—and took them into Daddy's closet. Sitting in a dark corner with Mama's clothes I'd rescued from the VFW rummage sale, I sniffed the soap. The scent brought tears to my eyes, but I inhaled deeper, determined not to cry. *Mama, I miss you.* I picked long, coarse strands of Mama's hair from the brush and wondered what she would think about Aunt Vadine and Daddy.

Then I remembered the feeling I had from a long time ago. At first it seemed more like a dream, but when I leaned my head against the closet wall, the pictures came into sharp focus. Mama held my hand while we stood in front of a casket. Grandma Grace, that's who it was. Aunt Vadine and Daddy stood off to the side, Aunt Vadine clutching onto Daddy. That surprised me. Had she always had these feelings for Daddy? Mama whispered something, but I didn't catch the words, only that she seemed upset. That would be right. After all, it was her mother in the casket. The next thing I knew, we walked around the cemetery, looking at grave markers. Mama pointed to this one and that, but I didn't remember the names. I don't even think I could read, or if I could, I was only in the second or third grade. I ran off to chase a butterfly and turned around when I heard Aunt Vadine's sharp voice.

"Would you look at that? Someone has chipped a corner plumb off this stone." She knelt by a grave maker, not one of those that jutted up like the headboard on a bed, but a shoe-box-sized rectangle flat on the ground. Under the writing and the numbers, I saw an imprint of two tiny feet. When Aunt Vadine looked up, her eyes had the same hollow look as in my dream.

Baby Sylvia? For some reason that didn't seem right. Who was buried under the chipped stone? I curled up on Mama's clothes, using her robe for a pillow. In my hand I clutched the lilac soap, its sweet, clean smell enveloping me in my meandering thoughts.

The next Saturday, one week before my birthday, Daddy and Aunt Vadine went to town. I called Tuwana to come over to look for the pearls and then go visit Slim.

"Think. Where would you hide the pearls?" Tuwana stood in

the middle of the floor with her finger on her cheek as if a bolt of lightning might come through the ceiling and provide the answer.

"I've looked through everything in the bedroom and the bathroom."

Tuwana pulled the cushions from the couch, looked behind the books on the shelf beside the television, all the logical places. Then, standing with her hands on her hips, she pointed to Aunt Vadine's wooden sewing box.

"It's worth a try." I had my doubts since Aunt Vadine dug in that box every blessed day of the week, pulling string out to create mountains of doilies. Pineapple pattern. Rose pattern. Single crochet. Double crochet. After the bibs, she'd started crocheting baby bonnets and booties. Why, I had no idea.

I unlatched the tiny golden clasp at the top, allowing the two halves to open outward. Taking a deep breath, I lifted out the latest project attached to a ball of No. 2 thread, the shiny hook jabbed into the side. Scissors, a tape measure, instruction books, and six skeins of thread still in their cellophane wrappers all came out, leaving the bottom of the wooden box staring up at me, empty. Tuwana picked up the softball-sized skeins, wound around in such a way that they were hollow in the center.

"Listen." She shook one of them. It rattled. She turned it around and over and found a hole, no bigger around than a pencil, slit in one end. Inside we found the strand of Mama's pearls. We shook the yarn ball until the metal clasp came to the opening, then pulled the necklace through.

"Right in front of our noses." Tuwana laughed a tinkling *hee-hee-hee*. We joined hands and danced in a circle.

"Good work. Best place to hide something—in plain sight! Quick, let's get this all back together like we found it."

Satisfied that we'd arranged it all as we found it, I redid the clasp and held the pearls.

"I feel so evil doing this. Like button, button, who's got the button. The sneakiest one wins. Now we have to figure out where to hide them so she won't find them."

Tuwana thought for about two seconds and said, "How about if we bury them? Like a treasure?"

"I thought of that. But where?"

It ended up, we found the cocoa tin from my brownie-making frenzy the previous summer and dumped the last bit down the drain. Placing the pearls in a stretched-out bobby sock, we then stuffed the whole thing in the cocoa box, pushed the lid on tight, and took it to the camp playground.

Tuwana and I had discovered a special hiding place years ago. Cedars had sprung up, making a perfect circle except for a gap on one side, which, if you slanted your body and shielded your face with your arm, you could slip into without getting scratched. Once inside, you couldn't see out, and no one could see you. We'd take our dolls in there and play for hours. In third grade, Tuwana had brought one of her mother's sewing needles. We pricked our fingers, smeared them together, and became blood sisters.

Now we found our secret spot, overgrown but with a gap we could still squeeze into. Sunshine had melted the Christmas snow, leaving the needled ground underfoot spongy with the smell of moist earth. With the tools we'd brought—a red-handled serving spoon and a meat fork—we dug a hole and put in the cocoa tin. Finally, we covered the spot with dead leaves and cedar fans and slipped out. We headed for Tuwana's.

Going past the row of garages for Tuwana's block, we saw her dad hauling out boxes, old rags, broken toys, and the like.

"Whatcha doin', Daddy?" Tuwana kept her voice light.

"Your mother's been after me to clean out the garage. First nice day we've had in a month of Sundays, so here I am." He laughed in that big throaty way he had and disappeared into the blackness of the garage. The Edsel was nowhere in sight, so we knew Tuwana's mother had taken the girls to their piano lessons. We cleaned up at Tuwana's kitchen sink.

"Phase two," I said as we picked the cedar needles off our coats. "Slim's house to do some investigating."

For the eleventh time, I had to convince Tuwana we were doing the right thing. She drove me crazy the way she could see crystal clear how to handle someone else's situations but froze in terror when it came to her own.

"Mother will kill me if she finds out I went into Slim Wallace's house."

"Stop saying that. She won't find out. Now come on."

Slim opened the door on the first knock and let us in.

"And to what do I owe this unexpected pleasure?" he asked. "Want to teach Tuwana how to play backgammon?"

"No, we were just out in the neighborhood and thought we'd drop in," I said.

"I just made a fresh pot o' coffee. Better not offer you any though. You know what they say: It'll turn your feet black if you're not old enough to drink it."

Tuwana, who had been standing on one foot then the other, like she might wet her pants or something, giggled. "That's what Mother says to Tommie Sue when she begs to have a sip of Daddy's coffee."

"Is that a fact? How about some Ovaltine?"

Tuwana stood in the front room, scanning it like a ghost might pop out any minute. I followed Slim into the kitchen and opened the cabinet for the cups. From the corner of my eye, I saw Tuwana move over to the table where the backgammon board and Slim's Bible sat in their usual places. She picked up the Bible, silently fanning through the pages. Praying for deliverance, no doubt.

Slim reached in his pocket for a handkerchief when a rattly cough interrupted him from fixing the Ovaltine.

"You still got the crud, Slim?"

"Can't seem to shake it. Doc Pinkerton's got me on penicillin shots. Says I'm on the verge of pneumonia. Olivia's been after me constant to take care o' myself."

Tuwana's head was bent over something in Slim's Bible, her eyebrows puckered.

"How is Olivia?" I asked, anxious to get around to the real reason for our visit.

"Fine as frog hair."

*Whack!* Tuwana slammed the Bible shut, threw it on the table, and hollered she had to go. She ran out the front door, slamming the screen behind her.

"Wonder what scared her off?" Slim asked.

"Tuwana gets nervous. I'd better go check on her."

She had already run half a block before I got out the door. As I called for her to stop, a boom filled the air. *Oh my gosh, the plant's exploding!* I looked toward the towering smokestacks to see what had happened. Nothing looked any different. I thought of the underground maze of natural gas threading its way all over creation. Another boom sounded, so near I jumped. Smoke billowed above the garages.

An incinerator. Near the Johnsons'. Running as fast as I could to catch up with Tuwana, we both arrived at her house at the same time.

"Fire! My clothes are on fire!" Mr. Johnson's bloodcurdling screams filled the air.

Tuwana screeched as loud as or louder than Mr. Johnson. "Daddy! What should I do? Help! Somebody, help! Daddy, please don't die!" She ran toward him and then jumped back from the heat of Mr. Johnson being on fire.

I looked around, trying to think what to do. *Stop! Drop! Roll!* The fire drill words rang in my head, but Tuwana's dad had already dropped and rolled on the ground, moaning and drawing his arms and legs up to his body. People scurried up from all directions. Mr. Nash threw an army blanket over Mr. Johnson, stopping the smoke but not his howls.

Tuwana knelt by her dad, sobbing, saying she was sorry. For what, I didn't know. I tried to put my arm around her as some men bundled Mr. Johnson into a car and roared off. She pushed me away. A stink filled the air. Not like normal trash burning, but something much worse. Like singed chicken feathers, but I knew it was charred flesh. Bile came up in my mouth, and I spit on the grass.

The next thing I knew Tuwana's mother pulled up in the Edsel. "What happened? Why is everyone here?"

Tuwana stood frozen, staring at her mother. When someone repeated what had happened, Mrs. Johnson fainted, and Tuwana ran to her, sobbing and shaking. "Daddy's going to die. I just know it. He caught fire...."

Ernie and Lola Greenwood pulled Tuwana away from Mrs. Johnson, whose eyes fluttered open. Mrs. Greenwood helped her up, then piled Mrs. Johnson and the girls into the Edsel and got behind the wheel. Mr. Greenwood followed in his Pontiac.

The incinerator didn't send off any more explosions, but we all stayed back just in case. Daddy came up behind me just then, and I blurted out the awful news. He put his arm around me and led me off. I cried all the way home, babbling about Mr. Johnson cleaning out the garage and how something he threw in the incinerator must have exploded and caught him on fire. "You always told Mama and me to stand back and be careful with aerosol cans. Do you think that's what did it?"

Daddy kept his arm around me. "We can't rightly know. We'll just pray he makes it. Don't do no good putting any blame."

I wanted to blame something though. For Mr. Johnson. For Mama. But what? Goldie's words about not questioning the Almighty popped into my head, but still I couldn't help thinking, *Why? Why Mama? Why Mr. Johnson?*

Aunt Vadine fixed lunch, and we ate in silence. Around five o'clock the prayer chain called to say Mr. Johnson had severe burns on his face and upper body and had been taken by ambulance to Amarillo. His chances of recovery looked good, but he would be in the hospital for several weeks. Maybe months.

Poor Tuwana. Her mother would be crushed. Now she would hate Graham Camp more than ever.

I couldn't get my mind off Tuwana even when I went to visit Goldie. Later, taking Scarlett for a walk, I tried to think. Tuwana ran from Slim's house like she'd been shot. What had she seen in Slim's Bible? Did she read something about Slim's wife? What if she hadn't died in the wreck like Slim said? No. Slim wouldn't lie. Maybe Slim was drinking when the wreck happened and that's why he couldn't get over it. It didn't sound like Slim, but people change after a big shock, so maybe he quit drinking. What was in Slim's Bible? A clipping of some kind? What? The only one who knew was Tuwana, and she was at the hospital with her dad.

It probably wasn't anything in the Bible at all. Maybe Tuwana had stashed an Aqua Net can in the garage and suddenly remembered her dad throwing stuff in the incinerator. How awful for

Tuwana if that's what caused the explosion. Was that why she screamed she was sorry? For causing her daddy to catch fire?

As soon as she got back from Amarillo I would ask her about it. Or maybe I'd go over to Slim's and look in the Bible myself. The rotten thing was—we still hadn't found out anything about Mrs. Gray.

## THIRTY-SIX

February 13, 1959

Dear Diary,

My thirteenth birthday, can you believe it? I'm a teenager!

Not only that. The minute Daddy got off his graveyard shift, he surprised me with my gift. Not a surprise, really, since Aunt Vadine had planted the idea in Daddy's head on what to give me. Still, an Olympia portable typewriter just for me. Not a used one from the school either, but a brand-new one with its own carrying case. I have to wait until Daddy wakes up to try it out. So now I'm stuck studying the instruction manual and learning where to place my hands on the keys. Just think: in no time words, paragraphs, and whole pages will flow from my fingers. Now I really wish Aunt Vadine hadn't gotten me kicked off the school newspaper.

Speaking of which, you know who keeps coming in my room like she's dying to say something. I think she's discovered the pearls are missing. Should I say something? I think not. Ha. Ha.

SJT

When Daddy woke up, I went straight to work. I rolled a new sheet of paper into the typewriter and plunked a thank-you note to

Daddy and another one to Aunt Vadine. *Tap-tap-plunk*. The sound made my heart race.

I folded the notes and put them beside Daddy and Aunt Vadine's plates when I set the supper table.

Aunt Vadine came into the kitchen looking for the aspirin. "All that racket's given me a headache. Guess you'll have to make your own birthday supper, Samantha."

When Daddy came in from outside, we had sauerkraut and weenies, and I washed the dishes. It reminded me of when Mama was gone to the hospital. Just Daddy and me.

He had the backgammon board set up by the time I finished the dishes, and we played for three hours straight. I kept trying to bring up Mrs. Gray, but I could never get the right words in my head, and then it would be my turn to throw the dice. Bringing up the part about Aunt Vadine slapping me didn't seem right either, since it was my birthday and all, and it was *her* idea to get me the typewriter. Daddy took a thirty-minute nap and went off for his graveyard shift. I wanted to kick myself for not saying something.

Tuwana would barely speak to me when she got home from Amarillo. She didn't even look at me when I asked about her dad. "He's got second- and third-degree burns on his neck, face, ears, and hands. Now beat it. I don't want to talk about it."

I tried again the next day.

She put her hands over her face and cried. "Leave me alone! Can't you see I'm dealing with all I can?" I patted her on the arm and told her I would listen anytime. She knocked my hand off her arm and walked away. It was like after Mama died, when I didn't want anyone touching me. That dirty feeling of people's hands on me trying to make me feel better but making me sick instead. I left her alone, hoping someday she would tell me what happened in Slim's front room.

Every weekend, Tuwana went to Amarillo to see her dad, so I spent as much time as Aunt Vadine would let me practicing on my new typewriter. Thirty minutes. That was her limit, and even then she gave me a sour-lemon look every time I got it out. She kept an eye on the clock and yelled, "That's it. Time's up." Even if I was in the middle of a sentence, I stopped and put everything away. While I typed I let my imagination run free. What would it be like if Aunt Vadine went home to Midland? What if I interviewed the man with no legs I'd once seen begging on the sidewalk in Amarillo? What kind of story would he have? What if Daddy decided to get married again and it *wasn't* Aunt Vadine?

The more I wrote, the more I wanted to be back on the school newspaper and close to Mrs. Gray. I thought about bribing Aunt Vadine by telling her I'd give back the pearls if she would tell Mr. Howard to put me back on the paper, but then I got mad all over again at her taking them from me in the first place and kissing Daddy the way she did. She gave me fiery-eyed looks that straightened the hair on the back of my neck. Then she went back to her latest crochet project—baby booties. Every Wednesday on double Green Stamp day she drove to Mandeville and bought our groceries and a new supply of crochet thread. Now she had a dozen baby booties lined up on top of the dresser. Sorta creepy, you know?

Actually, I was sick of myself. Was this how Mama felt? Always hoping things would take a turn for the better? I looked up *depression* in the dictionary. *A neurotic disorder marked by sadness, inactivity, lack of concentration. Dejection. Hopelessness. Sometimes suicidal tendencies.* It sounded like Mr. Webster had taken a look at Mama when he made up the definition. But I wasn't like Mama, was I?

No. I had my New Year's resolution. I gritted my teeth. I

would face my problems. But why couldn't I get up the nerve to tell Daddy why I wasn't on the school paper anymore? Or shake Tuwana and make her tell me what was in Slim's Bible? I even tiptoed around Aunt Vadine like a spooked bunny rabbit.

Cly picked up on my moodiness right off when he came by one Saturday and wanted to go for a walk.

"You aren't yourself, Sam. What's wrong?"

"Nothing. Why would you think that?"

"Hey, don't bite my head off. Everything's cool, you know."

"Sorry, I'm just sick of Aunt Vadine and all that."

"You've been moping around for more than a month. At least your aunt hasn't threatened to send you to an orphanage. My old man did that once." He kicked a rock like he meant to send it into orbit.

"How awful. But it does sound like something Aunt Vadine might pull. Then she could have Daddy to herself."

"Well, why don't you do something about it?"

"Like what?"

"Beats me. You should do something though. Get out of this funk you're stuck in. Why don't you ask Slim? He's tight with your dad. Maybe he can give you some pointers. Look how he helped me patch things up with Norm."

"Norm is not Aunt Vadine. But there is something I've been wanting to ask him. You want to go over there?" Maybe with Cly backing me up I could find out if Mrs. Gray ever dated anyone. *Is that what older people call it?* And given half a chance, I would look in Slim's Bible.

We found Slim on his porch, banging the dust off his work gloves against his knee.

"Hey, kids, look at that sun, will ya? The almanac said April would start out sunny. Why it's plumb near eighty-five degrees today. Perfect day for getting the garden ready."

"Want some help?" Cly asked.

"Never turn down an offer like that," Slim said.

We helped him get a three-tined soil tiller, a hoe, and a rake from the garage. Soon the smell of the freshly turned ground filled our noses—the earthy humus tickling the backs of our throats. I waited for the right minute to ask Slim how Mrs. Gray was doing, and if she'd been over to see him lately.

"You can almost taste those 'maters, can't you?" Slim leaned against the wooden handle of the tiller. Beads of perspiration broke out on his forehead, and his breath caught.

"You okay, Slim?" Cly asked.

"Ain't no work worth doing but what comes from a little sweat." His face, though, had paled to the color of a cinder block, and he blew out his breath through pinched lips.

"Come on over to the porch," I said. "Let's take a break."

When he didn't argue, a queasy feeling came in my stomach. Like the day I'd found Lady Aster. Pushing it from my mind, I helped Cly sit Slim down on the porch, and I went in the house to get him a drink of water. *Call Daddy. He'll know what to do.*

I dialed our number, and when Aunt Vadine picked up, I told her I needed to talk to Daddy.

"He's asleep. You know he worked an extra shift last night."

"Slim's not feeling well. Get Daddy up and tell him to come over here. Right now." The authority in my voice scared me, and when I hung up, I went to get the water. My hand shook so much, half the water sloshed out when I carried it to the porch.

"Do you need to lay down?" A little color had come back in Slim's face. Just a pale blue ribbon remained around his cracked lips.

Cly sat beside him, worried, I could tell.

"I'll be fine. You two are as fussy as that girl o' mine." He sipped the water and winced, a breath of air escaping his lips.

"Are Norm and Eva home?" I asked Cly.

He shook his head. "Gone to town."

Perspiration shone on Slim's face and neck as he unbuttoned the top button of his shirt.

*Hurry up, Daddy.*

It seemed an eternity, but in a few minutes, Daddy pulled up in the Chevy, still buttoning his shirt, the tail flapping. He hadn't even bothered to tie his work boots. Thank goodness Aunt Vadine knew I meant business.

"Joe, these kids are fussing over me like old wet hens." Slim's voice trembled ever so slightly.

"What happened?"

Before Slim answered, he pulled his hand up to his chest and let out an "Uuugh."

"Quick, help me get him in the backseat. I hope one of you two scamps can drive. I'm sitting with Slim." Daddy opened the car door.

Cly crawled into the driver's seat and took off.

"Don't worry 'bout no speed limits, son," Daddy said. "We need to get Slim to the hospital. Looks like he's having a heart attack."

Slim didn't argue, but rested his head against the back of the seat. I watched the speedometer climb to sixty, then seventy, then I closed my eyes. *God, get us there safely.* A couple miles outside of Mandeville, Slim opened his eyes, looked sideways at Daddy, and started to say something.

"Don't talk. We're just about there."

"Have to. Call my girls. Gotta tell 'em good-bye."

"I'll call Olivia right away," Daddy promised.

"Alice, too. Call her."

"Alice? Do you have her number?"

"You know it. Alice Johnson. She's my daughter too." Tears

streamed from his eyes like water trickling down the face of an old mountain.

My head felt like my brains were pressing against my eyeballs. *Alice Johnson?* The one who called Slim a murderer? The facts started popping into my consciousness—Slim's Bible, his two daughters, a dead wife. Before I could sort it out, Cly pulled into the hospital parking lot and stopped the car at the red emergency room sign.

"Sis, run in and get someone to bring a wheelchair."

Nurses in starched white, with cowbird-looking hats perched on their heads, whisked the wheelchair into a curtained cubicle. Slim let out a moan when they hoisted him onto a stretcher. A soft hissing came from a green cylinder tank, connecting a long clear tube to a mask one of the nurses held over Slim's face.

"You kids need to get out of the way," the other nurse barked at Cly and me. "There's chairs in the lobby." She pointed down a long hallway.

We walked down the hall, which smelled of bedpans and iodine and rubbing alcohol, and found the lobby. Stiff, wooden folding chairs, the kind we had at the community hall, lined two walls with a low metal table between them stacked with *Western Horseman* and *Field and Stream* magazines. Cly and I sat down and stared at each other.

"Did you know about Alice Johnson?" Cly finally asked.

"No, but…" I told him the stories Tuwana had told me and what had happened the day Mr. Johnson caught fire in the explosion. Piece by piece, we put it together, and I didn't know whether to laugh or cry. One thing I did know. Heart attacks could be fatal, and my heart prayed Slim would survive to tell his daughters, *both of them*, that he loved them. He just had to.

## THIRTY-SEVEN

DADDY AND MRS. GRAY came into the waiting room carrying cups of coffee. My fingers curled into fists, and I swallowed hard, waiting for them to tell us about Slim.

Mrs. Gray smiled and sat on the edge of a wooden chair. "He's stable right now." Her hair, pulled back into a ponytail, sagged in loose waves around her neck and shoulders.

The breath I'd been holding swooshed out.

"And?" Cly's question filled the empty waiting room.

"Doc Pinkerton says he's had a mild heart attack. The next forty-eight hours are critical. A second one could be fatal...." She worked the cup around and around in her fingers.

Daddy stood beside me, legs apart, one arm crossed to prop up the other, which held his cup. He took slow sips as Mrs. Gray talked.

She looked at Cly and me. "Have you seen Alice yet?"

We shook our heads. Thinking of Mrs. Johnson and Mrs. Gray as sisters hadn't had time to gel in my head.

"She was with the girls in Amarillo when your dad got in touch. The nurses here had the number of the hospital in Amarillo." She looked at Daddy. "How did she seem?"

"Couldn't say, really. Upset, I know that. Tried to tell me I had the wrong number at first. I told her to get over here and see her pappy. Didn't know yet if he'd pull through or not. Seems she mighta been crying, something about Benny Ray, but she said she'd try."

"Let's hope she comes to her senses."

Daddy stepped outside to smoke, leaving us sitting in our rigid seats, staring at the toes of our shoes. A commotion started at the other end of the hall, jerking us all to attention.

"I want him transferred to Amarillo as soon as possible." Alice Johnson's voice bounced off the tiled walls of the hospital. She and Doc Pinkerton walked side by side, the Johnson girls trailing behind like loose apron strings.

The doctor didn't speak until they reached the lobby. By then Tuwana had seen Cly and me and ran over to us, her bottom lip quivering.

"Hello, Alice." Mrs. Gray stood up.

Alice straightened her shoulders, her lips as straight as a pencil across her face. "Olivia. It's come down to this, has it?"

"Now, Alice, please think of Slim."

"I am trying, forevermore. You don't just waltz in after twenty years and act as if…" Alice looked around at all of us in the blue haze of the hospital lobby. Cornered, like a wild animal.

I felt sorry for her.

Mrs. Gray held out her arms and Mrs. Johnson took a step, then two, and they embraced like cardboard paper dolls.

"You've not seen him yet?" Mrs. Gray asked.

Tuwana's mom shook her head. "I don't know if I can."

"We'll go together. That would be the best medicine for Slim."

"Doc, I still want him transferred to Amarillo." Mrs. Johnson pursed her lips, determination in her look.

"We'll see. Right now he's too critical for an ambulance ride. He's got fluid in the lungs from that pneumonia a while back. Could go into congestive failure. Let's see how he does tonight."

The two women—Slim's daughters—went off toward Slim's room, arm in arm.

Words spewed from Tuwana like the Hoover Dam had burst, telling us how she had figured out Slim was her grandfather when she read the marriages and births page in the front of his Bible. Slim and Dottie had two girls: Alice and Olivia. Something just clicked when Tuwana saw Alice's date of birth. And she recalled she had an Aunt Olivia, who her mother had told her moved off and didn't keep in touch.

Tuwana had kept it all to herself until my dad called the hospital in Amarillo. Now I understood why she'd been so weird the last few weeks. Tuwana, who never held anything in, must have felt like a volcano ready to blow. I felt as sorry for her as I did for Alice.

Tuwana sniffled. "I confessed to Mama on the ride here I knew all about her big secret. I asked her how she could just live her life in a big, fat lie. She was too upset to lecture me and started bawling so hard she had to pull off the road. She said she never meant to hurt anyone, that her grandmother *did* say all those things about Slim killing his wife and not being worth a hill of beans. Mother just kept on believing it even when Daddy moved her here to the very same place where Slim lived and Slim turned out to be a perfectly respectable citizen. She quit speaking to her sister when Olivia made up with Slim. I'm not sure, but I think that's why she hated living at Graham Camp. Too many lies and secrets."

Tuwana threw her hand over her mouth. "Slim is my grandfather! And not once have I ever called him Grandpa or Gramps or Big Poppa. Now he's going to die." Tears rolled down her cheeks. Her whole body started shaking and sobs poured out.

I put my arms around her and muttered something about Slim getting better. He could have been having another heart attack and dying at that very minute, but I had to say something for her sake. I gulped in big breaths to keep from shaking. *Slim could die.*

Then Mrs. Johnson and Mrs. Gray came back down the hall, sniffling and wiping their eyes with tissues. And smiling. My heart swelled with happiness for Slim, that he got to see his daughters. Both of them.

"I forgot to tell you all the good news." Mrs. Johnson looked at all of us. "Benny Ray will be home week after next. He's still got weeks and weeks of therapy, but it will be so nice to have all of us together again. At home in Graham Camp."

The way she said it sounded like she was talking about heaven.

At church the next day, we found out Slim had another heart attack around midnight. Weakness and the danger of further damage meant he had to stay in Mandeville, so Doc consulted by phone with a heart specialist in Amarillo. I wanted to go back to the hospital on Sunday afternoon, but the hospital didn't allow visitors under fourteen, so Daddy went in my place. That day and the next and the next. Slim needed complete bed rest and oxygen to recover and would be in the hospital for at least two weeks.

The week after Slim's heart attack, Daddy told Aunt Vadine and me that Fritz Brady took over Slim's job of driving the truck for the maintenance crew—"the gang hands" Daddy called them. "Slim won't be back at work for a while. He has night sweats, and Olivia worries about leaving him by himself all night. I'm off the next couple of days, so I'm going to sit up with him. Give Olivia a chance to get some rest."

My skin got an electric feel to it at his talking about Mrs. Gray. "So you see Mrs. Gray when you visit Slim?"

"She seldom leaves the hospital. She's mentioned you.... Says she misses you working on the school newspaper. I thought that was why you wanted a typewriter."

"It is." I glanced at Aunt Vadine, who had suddenly become engrossed in the pork and beans on her plate. "Did she happen to mention why I'm not working on the paper anymore?"

"No, can't say as she did. Is everything all right?"

"I would still be on the paper, but Aunt Vadine had Mr. Howard take me off." A ripple went through me. All this time I'd been worried about talking to Daddy, and now I blurted it out like an idiot. I glanced at Aunt Vadine.

She jumped up and grabbed the tea pitcher. "Here, Joe, let me refill your glass." Her hands shook as she poured the tea. "Anything else I can get for you?"

"No. Just curious though. I didn't know you knew Sammie's principal. When did this all happen?"

Aunt Vadine didn't answer, so I did. "Right before Christmas, but I didn't learn about it until after the holidays. Mr. Howard told me Aunt Vadine didn't appreciate what I wrote in the school paper about Mama. Tell him, Aunt Vadine, what you said to Mr. Howard."

She sat back down on the edge of her chair. "You know, Samantha, I was worried about you. Losing your mother was such a tragedy and dwelling on it like you have just can't be healthy." She patted Daddy on the arm. "I want to be here for the two of you. I know you have a lot with work and all. I just wanted to ease the everyday strain of raising a child, Joe. I merely mentioned to Mr. Howard how concerned I was about Sammie. I didn't mean any harm, you know that." She leaned back and took a bite of her buttered bread.

*Concerned? No harm?* My face got hot.

Daddy asked for the salt shaker. "You do have a point; I can see that. Even though I still miss Rita something fierce, we have to move on. Just yesterday Slim said, 'You can't relive the past; just make the most of today.' 'Tain't easy, but there's wisdom in that. He ought to know."

I wanted to scream. I might have if I hadn't been shaking so hard. He had missed the point completely. "It's not that, Daddy. What I wanted you to know is Aunt Vadine had me kicked off the newspaper even though Mrs. Gray and everyone else thought my article about Mama was fine."

"Mr. Howard didn't think it was fine." Aunt Vadine's nostrils flared.

Daddy swiped a napkin across his mouth. "Guess it don't matter one way or the other right now. Olivia's not planning to go back to school until Slim gets out of the hospital. I don't suppose there'll be a school paper with her gone."

"At least talk to Mrs. Gray. She said she wanted to talk to you about it. Then when Slim gets better, maybe I can go back to work on the paper. That's practically my favorite part of school. Working with Mrs. Gray. She's one of the nicest people I know. Don't you think so too?"

Daddy nodded. "Spunky thing too. I've been giving her a hard time about those sticks she pokes in that topknot of hers. Don't hurt to give her a laugh now and then."

My heart skipped a beat. He was interested in Mrs. Gray. I could just tell. I could also tell Aunt Vadine got really still, and when I looked at her, her eyes had narrowed. The gold flecks in them shone like fiery darts.

She blinked and said to Daddy, "You know, I like what you said about moving on. I've been thinking about having a few of my things sent here from Midland. I have some nice antique pieces that would be right at home here."

He frowned. "I don't know...."

"I could get a friend of mine to put them on a Mistletoe truck."

"Your boyfriend, Bobby?" It just popped out.

Aunt Vadine's head jerked toward me. "Samantha, he's not my boyfriend. He's an acquaintance from work."

"Bobby who? What are you two talking about?"

"Her *friend* Bobby called here. I think he offered her a job."

"You know your daughter has quite the imagination. Also the tendency to eavesdrop. Bobby called me a while back, just filling me in on the news back home. Samantha thought...well, I don't know what she thought. At any rate, I could have him send a few pieces of furniture over. Nothing fancy, but..."

The swallow of milk I'd just taken went down the wrong way when I started shaking my head. *No! No furniture.* If Daddy let that happen, it would be impossible to get rid of Aunt Vadine. I coughed and milk sprayed all over my plate.

"You okay, Sis?"

Phlegm stuck in my throat. Aunt Vadine reached over and whacked me on the back. Not a pat. *Whack!* Like she meant business. And not the kind to help my cough. My eyes teared up, and I cleared my throat. "I'm okay...."

"All right then. If no one objects, I think I'll give Bobby a call."

Daddy shrugged and rose from the table. "I need to get into Mandeville and check on Slim. Y'all don't wait up."

"Daddy, wait. About Mrs. Gray. And Slim. Could you check and see if I could visit him in the hospital?"

"He's been asking to see you and Cly. I'll see what I can do. Might be the best medicine for him right now." When he gave me a peck on the cheek, I caught the scent of Old Spice. Then he put on his good hat—the one he wore to church—and left.

## THIRTY-EIGHT

SLIM LOOKED BONY AND PALE against the white hospital sheets when Daddy took Cly and me to visit him on Saturday. The road-map lines in his face had deepened, and his eyes had sunk under his bushy eyebrows. The only parts of him not shrunk were his feet and ankles, which angled out from the bottom of the sheets. The skin puffed and looked transparent like if you stuck a pin in it, it would pop.

His face lit up when he saw us. "I'm glad you two came. Staring at these four walls has got me as keyed up as a caged tiger." He winked at Mrs. Gray, who adjusted the pillow under his head and then cranked the head of the bed up a little higher. Clear tubing ran from a tank beside the bed up to his nose.

"Hey, man, we've been missing you." Cly lifted Slim's knobby hand in his. "Graham Camp's a bust without you."

On the other side of the bed, I held Slim's other hand, wrinkly and soft like my hands after doing the dishes. "We brought you something." I handed him a new copy of *The Old Farmer's Almanac*. "We thought you might need something to keep you busy."

He took it, his eyes clouding over with tears. "You kids is something, all right. Before you know it, it'll be time to get those 'maters planted."

We promised we'd help him with the garden and told him to behave himself. Talking drained all his energy, and after a few minutes, Daddy nodded toward the door. "Slim's still got to rest. Can't have you tiring him out."

I kissed Slim on the cheek and looked over at Cly. His Adam's apple bobbed up and down, and his eyes had a wet look. "We'll come back," we both said at the same time. Then we followed Daddy out into the hall.

Mrs. Gray came with us. "Thanks, Joe, for bringing them. These kids mean the world to him. Alice is bringing the girls up later. Slim's been fretting about seeing his granddaughters."

Daddy draped his arm around Mrs. Gray's shoulders. "You take care. I'll be back to spend the night when I get off at eleven. You look like you could use some sleep."

She nodded, her hair spilling out from the rhinestone sticks on top of her head.

On the way home, Cly and I decided we'd get Slim's garden ready and surprise him. Daddy thought it was a great idea. Neither of us knew beans about how to do it, but we worked all afternoon taking turns behind the hand plow, raking out the dead weeds and grass. We stopped every so often to throw dirt clods at each other and take long drinks of cold water from the garden hose. George Kuykendall stopped by in the late afternoon with warm brownies wrapped in tinfoil.

"A treat from Goldie. I seen you two out here slaving away, and wouldn't you know? Goldie had just pulled these out of the oven. You kids take care now." He got in the Buick and waved as he puttered down the street.

Sitting with our backs against the apricot tree beside the garden, we gobbled the brownies.

"What should we plant?" The smell of chocolate hung in the air, swirled together with the scent of fresh-turned soil.

"You're asking me?" Cly's face was turned up toward the sky, which had turned gray, hiding the sun. "I ain't never planted a garden."

"Don't use double negatives."

"Huh?"

"Ain't never. You talk like a hick."

"Reckon that's what I are, now that I'm a Texan."

I threw my balled-up tinfoil at him.

"You'd better watch it, cat. I can swing a mean hoe."

"I am soooo scared." We laughed until our bellies hurt. "Seriously, what shall we plant?"

"All's I know is Slim reads that almanac like it was the bible of daily living. He told me the only two books worth reading were *The Old Farmer's Bible* and the *Holy Almanac.*"

"You goon. I think we'd be safe with green beans, tomatoes, squash, and cucumbers. Maybe onions. The question is, when do we plant them?"

"Guess we shoulda bought two almanacs. I think we've done all we can today. Besides, I promised Norm I'd trim some bushes out back."

I gathered up the tools while Cly wheeled the plow over to Slim's garage. Then we went back and washed the dirt off our hands in the garden hose. Cly shut off the water. "Say, Doobie says there's a recital or something starting at the church tomorrow. You going?"

"Revival, not recital. And sure, I'm going. Brother Henry's hoping a lot of kids will come since the visiting preacher used to play pro basketball. It ought to be interesting."

"Doob says he's about eight feet tall."

"I don't know about that." I wiped my hands on my jeans to finish drying them. "Since when did you get interested in church?"

"Since never. But Slim's been telling me I oughta check it out.

And after seeing Slim and all today...well, I thought...shoot, I don't know. Maybe I should go and say a prayer for him or something. Is that what you do there?"

"Sometimes. We also sing, and Brother Henry preaches. Most of the time I listen. You don't have to go to church, though, to say a prayer for Slim. I pray for him all the time."

"I'll see you tomorrow then. In church."

"Deal." We shook on it and went our separate ways.

Since all I had to look forward to was a long evening with Aunt Vadine, I took the long way home, past the playground. A bank of clouds had come up in the west, and I wished Slim were home so he could give us the latest weather prediction. The cedar trees that held Mama's pearls near their roots swayed in the breeze. *Mama.* Maybe Aunt Vadine didn't think I was moving on, but I was. I could tell. When I thought of her, I got a warm spot inside, not a stab like a knife. Well, most of the time anyway.

A shiver of excitement danced up my spine when I thought of the way Daddy put his arm around Mrs. Gray. Yes, we were definitely moving on. Can't say as I thought much about Aunt Vadine's idea of sending for her furniture, but she had been in one of her agreeable moods ever since she brought it up. Maybe Brother Henry had it right. If I trusted God, he would take care of the details.

When I got to my street, I remembered Mama's hatbox in the garage. Why not? Just because I wanted to look at Mama's things didn't mean I wasn't moving on. I lifted the latch and creaked the garage door open. I shut my eyes for a bit and then opened them to let them get used to the dark before going over to the metal shelves. Daddy's Coleman lantern sat at eye level next to his tackle box. The hatbox was where I'd left it. I scooped it up and took it to the front of the garage where the light was better.

Spiderwebs and a fine layer of dust covered the top of the box. I blew them off and noticed the faded paper on the box had lilacs on it. I took a deep breath and lifted the lid, hoping for a whiff of Mama's favorite scent. Knowing the box had been in the dingy garage all winter didn't stop me from wishing. The tiny green scrap of Mama's dress lay on top of the crocheted bonnet. Under that, two bundles of letters. I swooped them up and held them out to the light. The top bundle looked familiar. My handwriting on the outside. The letters I sent Mama in the hospital? I let the other set drop into the box. I would look at them later. All of a sudden I wanted to read what I had written Mama. I put the lid back on and returned the box to the shelf to keep Aunt Vadine from giving me one of her looks. Or asking a bunch of questions.

When I went inside, some Western flickered on the television, Aunt Vadine's eyes glued to the screen. I said hello and walked past her and into my room.

A tingle went through me. *Mama had kept my letters.* I wondered how they would sound now that Mama had died. Did I even want to know? Still, she had kept them.

The rubber band snapped when I took it off, stinging me on the wrist. I took the top envelope and turned it over to open the flap. *Weird.* It was sealed shut. My heart hammered in my chest as I turned over each of the envelopes. Sealed. Sealed. Sealed. Why would she do that?

Slowly, it hit me. Mama had not read my letters. All the hours I spent writing to her about my summer, the brownies I made, Cly coming to visit, baby Penelope. She had never read one word. Not one.

My fingers went numb. Then cold. Inside it felt like an ice pick went through my heart, lodged there so that every time my heart beat, it reminded me over and over—Mama had not read my letters. Not the funny jokes I poured out on the pages. None of the newsy things I wrote trying to cheer her up while she got shock treatments. Not one word.

Something else simmered, bubbling up. I couldn't explain it, but everything I'd done to protect Mama, to make her laugh and love me, flashed before my eyes. My insides felt electric, little pulses of energy that hummed along stinging me here and there, making my breathing short and huffy. My jaw ached from clamping my teeth together. Some fat good I'd been to Mama. She didn't even care enough to read what I wrote her.

I turned the envelopes over and over in my hands. I traced the letters of Mama's name on the front of each one. Every time I traced her name again, another stab of the ice pick went through me. I clenched my fist around the letters. How could I move on when my own mother did this? Pretended all those times she knew what I was talking about last summer like she had read them.

*Not. One. Word.*

I clutched the unopened letters, went into Mama's closet, and gathered up all her clothes piled on the floor. I marched past Aunt Vadine and out the back door, staggering under the weight of Mama's things. I stumbled toward the incinerator, dropped everything on the ground, and let out a long breath. One by one, I pitched every last stitch of Mama's wardrobe into the eternal fire.

A breeze caught one of the letters. I chased after it and then another one. My heart pounded in my ears. I scooped the last one up and threw them all on top of the smoking clothes. My knees had turned watery, and my eyes stung from the smoke billowing up. My muscles twitched with exhaustion. I slumped down and sat with my back against the warm cement blocks of the incinerator. Crackles and hissing filled my ears, and I imagined every single word I'd written in those letters being licked by flames. A fire burned inside me too. I pulled up my knees and wrapped my arms around them, waiting for something. Anything. What now? One thing for sure. I wouldn't cry any more tears for Mama. Not now. Not ever. I had moved on.

More pops and cracks came from the incinerator, creaking sounds like an old campfire nearly burned out. I stared off into the distance and then looked toward the house. There, Aunt Vadine stood on the back porch, her arms crossed, her face shaded by the house. She didn't move, just stood there under the eaves. I blinked trying to read her face, but nothing came. The only thing I could tell for certain, and this sent a chill clear to my toes—her eyes had the same look as in my dreams.

Blank.

Hollow.

## THIRTY-NINE

I JUMPED TO MY FEET and ran toward her. "What are you staring at?"

"You. Are you all right?" Her eyes had returned to their usual muddy look.

"Of course. Moving on, like you said. No more crying for Mama." As soon as I said it, tears sprang to the surface, fuzzing everything. I blinked and swallowed to keep from letting them fall.

"You don't sound all right." She took my arm and led me into the front room. "I'm here to listen; you know that. Something has upset you, I can tell." She gathered me in her arms, guiding my head to rest on her shoulder.

I pushed her away. "Nobody listens to me. Why should you?"

"I've had my share of regrets. Not being more sensitive to you. We've not given each other much of a chance, have we? Me and my being so bossy. It's no wonder you don't trust me. And it's something I would like to change, if you will let me. I'm listening to you now." She smiled at me, not in her normal sarcastic way, but like she meant it.

"Well, try this out then. I just found out Mama didn't love me. How would you like it if you found out after thirteen years your mother never loved you?" I scooted away from Aunt Vadine on the couch.

"Of course your mother loved you. How on earth did you come up with the idea she didn't?"

"The letters, for one thing. She never read them."

"Letters? What letters?"

"Nothing I want to talk about."

"Sammie, I know it's hard to talk about our hurts. Keeping them bottled up, though, will only make it harder for you in the long run. If she wrote you a letter, maybe it would help to tell someone about it."

She called me Sammie, not Samantha. *Maybe she is trying to change. No, she won't ever change. She's just trying to trick me so she can bring it up later.*

"She didn't write me. It's the ones I wrote her." The sound of Mama's letters crackling in the fire filled my head. "Nothing that concerns you."

She smoothed a wrinkle in her dress. "I know it's hard being a teenager. I had my share of traumas during those years. Nothing like what you've been through, but I know how emotional this time can be. You think a certain way one day, another way the next. That's one reason I've stayed at Graham Camp as long as I have. For you. To get you the help you need for your irrational behavior."

"What kind of help?"

"Counseling. A juvenile program. I understand they have one in Amarillo."

The hair on my arms stood up. "You think I'm a juvenile delinquent? I haven't broken any laws or stolen hubcaps."

"Of course you haven't. It's a program for those with emotional struggles. A place where you can talk out your problems. I've tried to provide the stability you need, but I'm just so inept." A sigh escaped her lips. "Still, I'm willing to stay until you get back on track."

"I thought you were waiting for Daddy. To become his new wife."

Her arms twitched ever so slightly, but her face looked pleasant. Calm. "Oh, in the beginning I suppose I entertained those ideas, seeing him so needy and all, but I know now that's not going to happen."

"You said you believed in second chances."

"Funny you should say that. I didn't see it at first, but in the last few weeks I've come to realize my second chance is with you."

"I don't get it."

"The thing is, I had a baby once." She had a faraway look in her eyes. Sad, like I'd seen sometimes in Mama.

"What happened?"

"He was stillborn. My marriage didn't work out, and then I never married again. I was thrilled when you came along. A niece I could love on."

"You said I was a nuisance."

"You were." She wrinkled her nose and patted my knee. "All children are. That doesn't mean we don't love them. I didn't have the opportunity to raise my baby boy, so I have no real experience. Being here at Graham Camp has been good for me, seeing how young people act and talk. I'm willing to make a go at being the aunty you never had. If we work together, you might not even need professional help. I know I can't replace your mother, but maybe we could be friends, confide in one another."

"I don't think I'm ready for that." After all she'd done, why should I trust her now?

"I understand. I have a lot to learn, some old habits to get rid of. Your daddy told me about Alice and her change of heart about Slim. Now that was something, you know."

The muscles I'd kept bunched up relaxed a little. Maybe I should give her another try. It was either that or get shipped off. I looked at her and shrugged. "You're right. Mrs. Johnson is like a whole different person."

Aunt Vadine made a little O with her mouth, and her eyes widened. "I've been meaning to tell you. Actually, I wanted it to be a surprise. After hearing you tell your daddy how much you wanted to be on the paper, I called Mr. Howard yesterday. Told him I thought you were ready to come back."

"Really? You did that?" *No way.* Not after all the stink she made. Still...

"Sure did. Now, I'm still not crazy about all that pounding you do on the typewriter, but maybe it's something I'll get used to."

She sounded sincere. Maybe it was me who had a problem with trusting people. When I looked at Aunt Vadine, her eyes sparkled. She had made the first step. Now I had to decide. I told her thanks and let out my breath.

She held out her arms, and I let her hug me. A nice soft hug that had a familiar smell when I closed my eyes and breathed in through my nose. Not Juicy Fruit, something faint and sweet.

"I don't suppose you'd like some supper? You've had a long day."

"I'm starved."

"Filthy too. Look at all that dirt on your clothes. Why don't you go take a bath while I cook us something?" Her voice had a teasing ring to it. Besides, she was right—I was a mess.

I hurried off and took a bubble bath, washed my hair, and put on clean clothes. Aunt Vadine had potato soup ready when I came out of the bathroom. She asked about Slim, and I told her about Cly and me working on his garden.

"That's lovely, dear."

Lightning started flashing through the window while we watched television. I thought about Slim and wondered if the almanac predicted rain for mid-April. Once in a while Aunt

Vadine tilted her head toward me and smiled, and not once did she pick up her crochet hook. Personally, I couldn't get used to this new Aunt Vadine and thought any minute the bubble would break and we'd be flying off the handle at each other again. I yawned and stretched.

"I swan, I bet you're plumb worn out. Working outside all day. I'm a little tired myself. What say I make us both a cup of hot chocolate before we turn in?"

She whisked into the kitchen and rattled a pan. After a few minutes, she called out, "You know, tomorrow we should bake some peanut butter cookies. Would you like that?"

It was a start. Maybe she *was* trying.

We sipped our chocolate and listened to the rain hammering the roof. When my cup was empty, I took it and Aunt Vadine's to the kitchen and rinsed them in the sink. I yawned again and said good night.

When I slipped under the covers, Mama's robe rubbed against me. How had I forgotten her robe? Repulsed, I wadded it up and threw it off the bed, then curled onto my side. The ice pick feeling came back inside. *Mama didn't read my letters.* I gritted my teeth and forced it out of my mind. A streak of lightning lit up my room, and I saw Aunt Vadine standing in the doorway, her lips tilted into a smile. *Lilac.* That was the smell I couldn't identify earlier. When had she started using Mama's lilac water? A fuzzy-headedness came over me. Another yawn.

*Dear God, please watch over Slim. Help him get better. Tell Mama she should have read my letters. . . .*

Rain beat on the roof, sharp pinging sounds. Hail? No, a different sound—louder—more metallic sounding. My body felt stiff from sleeping too long in the same position, but when I tried to move,

I couldn't. My arms seemed locked at my side, tangled in my covers. I twisted, thinking how hard my feather mattress had become. Had I fallen out of bed onto the floor? Or gone to the closet in Mama and Daddy's room? That would explain the blackness when I squinted my eyes trying to make out where I was.

Had I dreamed of the black hole again? This time I wasn't being sucked into the swirling dark pit. No, definitely not a dream. But where was I?

The smell of dirt mixed with oil and dampness in the air came to me. I tried to lift my head and get a better whiff. No pillow rested under my head. I turned my face and felt the grit of dirt on my cheek. My heart pounded in rhythm to the rain. *Take off the covers!* Squirming, I worked one arm up across my belly and then the other one. *Where am I? How did I get here?*

Had I spoken the words or was my mind playing tricks on me? My throat got a tight feeling. Again, I twisted my head and saw a tiny sliver of light, as thin as a pencil, stretching from one side of the room to the other down low, next to the floor. The garage. I must be in the garage, but why?

A scuffling noise came from one corner. I shuddered. *What if it's a mouse? Or a* rat?

*Don't be silly. You've never seen a rat at Graham Camp.*

Shivers zinged along my legs still tangled in...in what? A blanket of some kind. I took a deep breath and heaved my body over to my stomach. Maybe I could free my arms and legs that way. The hard surface of the garage—I knew now that's where I was—pushed against my arms. Sweat popped out as I lunged to make another roll. And another. I felt the blanket loosen as cold hit my arms and legs. A clap of thunder shook the air. I drew myself into a ball and covered my head with my arms. *Click. Screech.* The familiar creak of the garage door opening. When I lifted my head, Aunt Vadine stood against a gray sheet of rain, the wind whipping her thin robe like a ghost costume. She stepped inside. The wet nylon of her robe clung to her, outlining the bulges of her hips and breasts.

"Samantha? Are you in here?"

I edged toward the wall, pulling the blanket with me. *Mama's quilt?* I knew it was. More light came into the garage, faint and shadowy. I looked again at Aunt Vadine, but something else caught in the corner of my vision. A figure hung from the ceiling, sway-ing...swinging.

I screamed. And screamed again. More screams, but I didn't know if they were mine or Aunt Vadine's. She rushed in and knelt beside me. "You poor child. What are you doing in here?"

"What is *that* doing in here?" I pointed to the hanging figure. "*Who* is that?"

The stepladder lay on its side in the dirt slightly away from the center of the garage.

She turned her head and gagged. "Oh dear. What the devil?" She pulled me to my feet and dragged me to the ladder. She uprighted it and said, "Help me! Hold it steady." She climbed onto the first step, then the second. I didn't want to look, but I couldn't help myself. I wanted to throw up, the phlegm rising but stuck in my throat.

"Oh, Samantha. Look at that. There's not a body in here at all."

I forced myself to look. No legs dangled down. But what I saw did make me throw up. Vomit spewed out of my mouth, splatting on Aunt Vadine's ankles.

Mama's robe dangled above us, stuffed with something, and tied with a rope in the spot where I imagined Mama hung herself.

Aunt Vadine stepped down and pulled me to her chest. "Oh, you poor dear. You must have thought..." She leveled her gaze at me. "You. You did this? How could you?" She turned away, hid-ing her face. "All your cries of desperation, and now this?"

The folds of her saggy body enveloped me. I wrenched my head back, her fingers like claws in my back. "What? You...you think I did this? No. No. No! It's sick. A sick joke. I swear...there's no way...I couldn't have."

*Could I?* I had been so upset about Mama. Had I slipped over the edge and done this horrible thing? I closed my eyes and tried to think. To remember.

Aunt Vadine's talking kept my thoughts from coming. "I worried myself plumb sick about you last night. Moaning in your sleep. Thrashing around. I tried to stay awake, but I must have drifted off. When I woke up, you were gone. I turned the house upside down looking for you. In the closets, under the beds, everywhere I could think to look. I felt close to having a heart attack myself, worrying that you had run off. Thank the Lord you're safe, where we can get you the help you need." Her palm pushed the back of my head into her shoulder.

I pushed away from her. "Take that thing down. I didn't do it."

She held her hand over her heart. "I pray your daddy will be home soon. He'll have to see it. He'll be as desperate as I am to get you help."

My head cleared a little. I turned away from the swaying robe, limp, lifeless like Mama. I knew I hadn't hung Mama's robe from a rope. But if I didn't, who did? Only one person came to mind. Aunt Vadine. She was the one who was desperate. All that talk about confiding in her. I knew it was a lie.

*Think.* I had to think what to do. The smell I noticed earlier came to me—the smell I thought was oil. It wasn't. It was Daddy's kerosene lantern—the Coleman we took fishing. Whoever did this had to have a light. A flashlight wouldn't have worked with just one person. But Daddy's lantern would have. I had an idea.

"Can I ask you a question?"

"Sure, dear. Anything."

"How do you think I did this"—I pointed behind me in the general direction of Mama's robe—"in the dark?"

"I have no idea. A flashlight maybe. Or your daddy's kerosene lantern. I know I've seen one around here somewhere." She craned her neck and looked around. "Over there. On the workbench. Isn't that your daddy's lantern?"

It was. And it wasn't where I'd seen it yesterday. Was it only yesterday I found the letters? My stomach tightened. How could I call her a liar? Something else. *Think. Think. Think.*

"How did I wrap myself up tighter than the husk on a corncob in that old blanket?"

"You call the quilt your grandma Grace made an old blanket?"

"How did you know it was that quilt?"

"It's laying right over there, sweetie. Any fool could see what it is."

"Why would I do that? Wrap myself up in it?"

"Samantha, I don't know why you do most of the things you do. No matter how hard I try, I just can't imagine what demons you fight every day in your mind."

"Another thing I've been wondering. Why did you pick now to be so nice to me? To be so concerned about helping me? Are you afraid Daddy and Mrs. Gray might start liking each other? That she might take Daddy away from you like my mother did? She's pretty like Mama, you know."

More light came into the garage, and I noticed the rain had almost stopped. Daddy would be coming back from Mandeville soon. I prayed he would hurry. What if he believed her and not me? I tilted my head and looked at her. Her eyelids twitched, tiny jerky movements.

"Pretty? She's a floozy, just like your mother."

My ears pounded in fury. The fact that Mama didn't love me didn't make her a floozy.

"What if Daddy fell in love with Mrs. Gray?"

"He's only helping her out because she's related to that nasty Slim."

"He's not nasty. He's one of the kindest people I've ever known."

"And it's all because of your little friendship with him that your daddy's involved anyway. You running wild all over the neighborhood, going into strangers' homes. Heaven only knows what goes on over there. Nothing would surprise me. Not after that outburst you had yesterday. You were over there with that boy, weren't you? Doing what?"

"Plowing a garden, like I told you. For Slim, because people at Graham Camp care about each other and stick together."

"I can tell what a lot of good it did your mother." Her face had a twisted look. She stepped over to the wall and picked up a piece of wood, a leftover two-by-four, that's what Daddy called it. "I'm afraid with this latest escapade you've gone too far." She jabbed the end of the board toward me.

I jumped sideways and looked out at the driveway. *Hurry up, Daddy.* She stood between me and the garage door. I would have to distract her and make a run for it. That or let her attack me. She seemed to read my mind.

"Don't get any ideas, missy. Your daddy needs to find you in here like I did." She pointed with the wood toward the swaying robe. "With this." She swiped through the air like she was swinging an ax. "Go over there and sit down." She pointed to Mama's quilt.

I backed up two steps, not taking my eyes from her. "You know Daddy is not going to believe you."

"I've already talked to him about your throwing your mama's things in the incinerator. He came home to change clothes last night before he went to the hospital. I had to tell him, don't you see? Or else how would he know how sick you are?"

Her voice sounded tinny. I didn't know whether Daddy would believe me or not, but I had to keep her away from me. She had a piece of wood as long as a yardstick in her hand. Not something I wanted to get whacked with.

*Calm down. Get her to talk about something else. But what?*

"I have an idea. Let's go in the house and wait for Daddy. You can show him the garage later. Besides, I need to go to the bathroom."

"You'll run off if I let you out of here. You've proved that time and again."

Goose bumps covered my arms and legs, whether from fear or the cold, I couldn't tell. "Fine. Then we'll wait here. It's kind of chilly in here though." I stepped back and dropped onto Mama's quilt. I pulled a corner up around my shoulders, wiggled around, and found another corner. Mama buried her problems in here, waiting, always waiting for a better day. Now I was waiting for Daddy to get home. Would he believe me or Aunt Vadine?

My stomach churned as I drew the quilt closer. Its soft folds hugged against my bare arms, and I thought I felt Mama's arms around me, caressing my shoulders. Sweet, whispery touches. My eyes closed without me willing them to, and a thickness came to my tongue, filling my mouth, yet allowing me to breathe normally. Heat radiated around me, so close I thought I could touch it like a real thing. I'm not sure when I knew it wasn't Mama there with me but something more, bigger than I could imagine, yet stroking me like a feather. A swelling came in my chest like I'd had before on that long-ago morning in my church pew. The day I'd given my life to Jesus. And once again, he didn't call my name, but words appeared in my head, not in my voice or Mama's.

*Say something about the pearls.*

The words startled me, brought me back to the garage and the hulking figure of Aunt Vadine. She fiddled with the edge of her nightgown, which seemed to have snagged on the two-by-four she wielded. What did the pearls matter if Aunt Vadine sent me away and got Daddy anyway? *Please, God, if this is really you, help me be brave.*

My shaking turned into a slight tremor. *Breathe. Stay calm.* My head cleared, and a voice inside told me what I had to do.

"If you send me off, you'll never see Mama's pearls again, you know."

She stepped toward me, hitting the end of the two-by-four on the dirt. "Just another of your hateful little schemes."

"I could show you where they are."

She scrunched her eyes up. They darted around the garage and stopped at the metal shelf in the corner, a few feet from where I sat huddled in Mama's quilt. I could tell she was trying to decide whether or not to go to the shelf. If she did that, I could make a dash for the door. Her eyes lit up.

"Hand me that box off the bottom shelf." She pointed with her finger.

I didn't move.

"Now." She poked me with the wood, but the quilt protected me from it. She slashed through the air again, bumping the side of my head.

Stars danced before my eyes, but still, I didn't move.

She inched closer and glared at me.

I looked the other way, craning my neck like I'd seen someone in the drive.

She spun around to look, and when she did, I grabbed the box and tucked it inside the quilt. Working under the folds, I lifted the lid off and reached in until I felt the baby bonnet.

"I have something for you." I wadded the bonnet in my hand and acted like I was going to pull it out from under the quilt.

Suddenly, she lunged for me and grabbed at the quilt. She

twisted my wrist in her iron-like fingers until I opened my hand. Eyes wide, she flinched back, then flew at me, off balance. I held the hatbox up like a shield and it connected with her knee. I heard a crack like a stick breaking. The lid flew off, scattering the contents across the dirt. She screamed a string of curse words and collapsed on top of me.

"You tricked me. Just like your mother did. Taking Joe away from me." Sour morning breath poured out of her as she tried to get up. The weight of her on me made it hard to inhale. I straightened my legs and tried to push her off, but she yelled again and grabbed her lower leg.

"That's not what Daddy says."

"She always got what she wanted from the day she was born. All that red hair. Naturally curly. Never mind her face had more freckles than a speckled chicken. One look at her and no one knew I existed." Short, raspy breaths huffed from her twisted mouth.

"You mean Daddy?"

She groaned again and tried to move. "Having your daddy wasn't enough. Oh no, she had to throw it in my face ever' chance she got. Joe this. Joe that."

My legs grew numb pinned under her weight.

"Well, she can't have him now, can she? But I will. As soon as we cart you off to that sanatorium and shock your brain a few times, you won't be able to stop me. I should have hung you up there instead of your mother's robe. Put an end to you forever. No one would have been surprised, you know. Like mother, like daughter." Her eyes had a strange, empty look.

Like my dream.

I wiggled my legs once more and got out from under her. When I looked up, Cly stood over me, his mouth open, his eyes as big as golf balls. Aunt Vadine reached out and grabbed my arm, yanking it out of the socket, it felt like. When I fell on top of her, her hands went around my throat.

Cly kicked her and pulled me away. I landed with a thud on my bottom.

"Sam, what's going on?"

"I don't know. I honestly don't know." My shoulders shook, and I pulled my gown down around my legs. "What are you doing here?"

"Slim."

My head spun, and I waited for him to tell me what I already knew in my heart.

"Your dad called, said he'd been trying to call you. He asked me to come over." His lips trembled, and he clamped his eyes shut. "Slim died this morning."

I toppled over on the cold dirt of the garage.

## FORTY

CLY ROLLED HIS JACKET UP and put it under my head. I told him to go get help. "George and Goldie. Brother Henry. Anybody, just go."

"I can't leave you here."

"I'm fine. Hurry."

Numb, I looked around. In the corner Aunt Vadine lay curled on her side, moaning but not moving. Mama's hatbox lay on its side, with the other bundle of letters and a thin, flat book I'd not noticed before. I raised up and tried to reach them, but it took too much effort, and I collapsed back onto the dirt floor and waited.

George and Goldie came first, and when I saw them, my heart raced. Behind them the clouds had parted and sunlight lit up the outside world like a thousand carnival lights, dancing off the trees, the grass, the world of Graham Camp.

Just like before when Mama swallowed the pills and Mr. Johnson caught fire, our friends and neighbors ran from every direction and swallowed me up with hugs and questions. Cly stood beside me and told them he saw Aunt Vadine trying to strangle me. Goldie brought a bag of ice for the goose egg on my head. When Norm MacLemore and George loaded Aunt Vadine into George's Buick, she raised up and called me *despicable* and *vile* and some other words that burned my ears. Cly put his jacket around me and took me into the house.

The next thing I knew, Daddy came and swooped me into his arms. Someone outside had told him part of the story. He wanted to know the rest, but I made him tell me about Slim first.

"He had a big day yesterday seeing everyone, said it was the best day of his life. We talked until the wee small hours. He finally went to sleep, a grin on his face, and he...he just didn't wake up." Daddy's forehead wrinkled, and sags drooped around his mouth. He drew me close to his chest. "It happened around six this morning. I'd stepped out for a cup of coffee, and when I came back, he was gone. It ain't fair, Sis, that's what. Just getting his life back on track with his girls...his grandkids."

My chest felt heavy, not like when Aunt Vadine lay on top of me, but something inside swelling up. I wanted to scream and cry, but nothing came out. I looked at Cly sitting in Daddy's chair, his hands folded. A tear ran down his cheek. I held out my hand to him, and he came, the three of us holding onto one another. Then a thought flashed through my head.

"Tuwana. She'll need me. Slim was her grandpa. I have to get cleaned up—"

Daddy held up his hand. "Not until you tell me what happened. Every single detail."

The words tumbled out, bits and pieces of what I could remember, but I didn't know if any of it made sense. Daddy's face turned purple, and he stomped across the front room, telling me how sorry he was, that he would make sure Aunt Vadine never saw me again. Cly told him what he saw and heard, which made Daddy madder than ever.

"How the devil did she do all that? It rained all night."

I shrugged. "She acted so nice, fixing me supper and then hot chocolate before I went to bed. She said she wanted to change, and I believed her."

Daddy's eyes squinted, then got fiery again. He stormed into my bedroom and came out with Aunt Vadine's purse. He dumped it on the floor and pulled up a brown pill bottle. "Bingo." He read the label. "Chloral hydrate. Take one capsule at bedtime." He looked at me. "I'd say your dear aunt slipped you a Mickey. Knocked you out cold. Which she had already done when I got home from work, and she told me some tale about you and the incinerator."

I cringed. It wasn't a tale, and I didn't know what to say to Daddy about that. Later I could tell him about Mama and the letters.

He stuffed everything back in her bag, including the pill bottle. "One thing about Vadine. She was no lightweight. My guess is as soon as I left last night, she dragged you out there, maybe wrapped in the quilt. There's an awful mess on the back porch, mud everywhere, trailing all through the house. Then she made that rigging in the garage. No doubt she intended to blame you, make it look like you'd gone nuts or something. Goldie said she found Scarlett tied up in the doghouse. Not even your pooch could help you." He buried his head in his hands. "That blasted woman. I'll take care of everything, Sis. You can bet she won't be messing with you anymore."

Cly had an anxious look on his face. "Uh...I need to get going. Doob said church starts at eleven."

Daddy looked sideways at him.

Cly cleared his throat. "Somebody named Dunkin' Don's doing a revival."

"He used to be a pro-basketball player, Daddy." I motioned Cly to the door. "Go. You don't want to miss that. And say a prayer for Mrs. Gray and Tuwana's family."

"I already did. For you too." His face pinked up as he stared at the floor.

"Good for you." Daddy clapped Cly on the shoulder. "Best if

we all did more praying." He held the door for Cly. "Sis, I need to take a nap if I'm gonna be worth my salt at the plant this evening. I'll call and check on Aunt Vadine while you take a bath. I'll make sure they keep her in the hospital until I can make some arrangements." I could tell he meant business.

From head to toe, I felt like I'd been run over. In a way I had. I been dragged from my bed to the garage, not to mention being hit in the head and having Aunt Vadine land on top of me. I poured a double dose of lilac bubble bath into the bathtub and soaked until my skin wrinkled. When I came out, Daddy snored from his bed. I slipped out and ran over to Tuwana's.

"It's not fair." Tuwana's face had streaks running down. "I just find out I have a grandpa living two streets over. And now...now he's gone."

"I'm sorry. We're all going to miss him." I pushed my toe against the dead grass in front of the glider, squeaking it back and forth. "Daddy said Slim wouldn't quit talking about you and Tara and Tommie Sue. He loved you, you know."

"I guess. Tell me again what happened with your aunt. I heard she went berserk and tried to hang you from the rafters."

I smiled. "Not exactly. But *berserk* about sums it up. At least she didn't get to make her move on Daddy."

"What will you do now? You won't have Aunt Vadine to complain about. I won't be avoiding Slim all the time...." Her eyes filled with tears, and we grabbed hold of each other.

I sniffed. "Guess you're just stuck with me." We scritched back and forth in the glider and let the sun warm our faces. Irene Flanagan marched up the sidewalk carrying a cake. I knew it was coconut. I hoped Alice remembered to number the dishes and write down what everyone brought.

"Oh, I forgot to tell you!" Tuwana jumped up. "Daddy's coming home tomorrow. He'll be here for Slim's funeral on Wednesday."

*     *     *

After Daddy went to work that afternoon, I stuffed all of Aunt Vadine's things in her suitcases and lined them up by the door. I folded up the army cot and took the feather bed topper to Scarlett's doghouse. She nosed around and curled right up on it. I looked toward the garage. Would the hatbox still be there? I took a deep breath and walked slowly toward it. I flipped the latch and opened the door. I closed my eyes and stepped inside, squinting to make sure nothing swung from the rafters. So far, so good. The box sat on top of the workbench. I hurried over and lifted the lid and found the bundle of letters and the thin book I'd seen earlier—was it only that morning? The side of the box had a dent where I'd shoved it against Aunt Vadine's knee, but otherwise it looked okay. I carried it back to the house.

On the couch I sifted through the letters first. Most of them had our address and were from Grandma Grace. One, though, had a thin yellowed envelope with an Atlanta, Georgia, postmark. I removed the single sheet of paper.

> My dearest Rita,
>
> I'm grieved by the loss of your aunt Faith. She was a lovely woman whom I had the pleasure of knowing. I enjoyed our visit on the bus and pray that all is well with you. Please give my regards to your mother.
>
> Your friend,
> Margaret Mitchell

The name rang a bell. *Margaret Mitchell. The* Margaret Mitchell? I turned the envelope over and read the postmark again. *Atlanta, Georgia.* Shivers went through me. Mama had met the woman who wrote *Gone with the Wind*. No wonder she loved the book so much. But who was Aunt Faith?

I grabbed the slim book, looking for a clue. Mama's journal. On the third page she wrote about taking the train to Atlanta to see Grandma Grace's twin sister in the hospital. On the city bus, Mama and Grandma rode next to Margaret Mitchell, who sat with people at the hospital. She knew Grandma's sister, Faith. My heart raced as I read what Mama wrote about her trip and ended with a note that said, "Vadine couldn't go with us. She hasn't recovered from losing the baby, nor her injuries from that awful beating she took from Wayne Cox. I am, quite frankly, worried sick about Vadine."

Something pierced my heart. *I had a boy once. Stillborn. My marriage didn't work out.* Aunt Vadine's face, the empty look in her eyes, rushed into my mind. I shuddered and thought about her loss, the awful way her life had turned out. And Mama's. She'd lost baby Sylvia. And I had lost Mama.

Page after page, I devoured Mama's words, the loopy way she ended her letters, the tiny circles she made to dot the *i*'s in my name. Each page drew me to the next one until at last I had read her entire journal. I went back and reread what she wrote on June 5, 1950.

In all my born days, I would have never dreamed I could love another human being the way I love Sammie. Every day she asks a million questions and pesters me till I'm blue in the face. Already, she knows how to write the entire alphabet. Today she wrote "I love Mama" in perfect penmanship. She's really something for a four-year-old.

I closed the book and hugged it to my chest. Mama loved me. She always had. And now I had it in her own words. Another thought came. Mama had kept her favorite memories in this hatbox. Her journal. Special letters. Sylvia's crocheted bonnet. The letters I had written her. The empty place inside me grew warm with memories of Mama. The two of us chasing dragonflies at Red River. Her laugh when we pored over the Montgomery Ward catalog picking out my school clothes. The way her hair swirled in the breeze riding in the Edsel. *She had kept my letters.*

I went back to the day she died, the day that I might never understand completely. She must have brought her memory box into the garage and put it on the shelf in the corner. Maybe she thought of me and wanted to tell me somehow she loved me. As sure as my name is Sammie Tucker, I knew she must have pulled her New Testament and the leather case with her pearls out of the hatbox and run back into the house and put them where she knew I would find them. Whether she remembered the words in her testament, *Seek and ye shall find*, I don't know. Only that somehow those words brought me to today. She did love me. A fire burned in the deepest pit of my stomach. Mama loved me!

From my purse, I took her New Testament. I put it in the hatbox along with her journal and letters. The tiny scrap of green material had wedged into a torn corner of the paper lining. I lifted it out and rubbed it between my fingers. Then I added the sliver of lilac soap I had saved and her hairbrush. The glove filled with dirt from Mama's grave stayed in my purse. I had another idea for it. Only the pearls were missing, and Tuwana would have to help me with that.

It didn't come as a big surprise to find out from Mr. Howard that Aunt Vadine had not called him about me being on the paper. What did surprise me was that Daddy had called him.

"I'm sorry things didn't work out with your aunt. Your father told me she would be moving on." He cleared his throat. "Sammie, not many students go through what you have and come out on top. I'm glad I kept my eye on you. And I'm sure Mrs. Gray would love to welcome you back on the school paper."

I floated through the rest of the day. That night I got out my typewriter and rolled a sheet of paper into it. Then, beginning with the day Mama swallowed the pills, I started writing our story.

George, Norm, Cly, and Daddy carried Slim's casket from the Hilltop Church to the waiting hearse. From there, cars with their headlights burning made a long snake to the cemetery. Brother Henry read from the Psalms and prayed. After the amen, I stepped to the casket and broke a rose from the arrangement. One for me and then three more that I gave to Tuwana and her sisters.

Daddy and I stood to the side while people shook hands and whispered. After a while Daddy nodded his head in the general direction of Mama's grave. Hand in hand, we walked, not saying anything. A simple stone jutted from the ground where Mama was buried. *Marguerite Samuels Tucker* was chiseled in thick letters above the dates of her birth and death, and below that the words, *Beloved wife and mother.* Tears ran down my face as Daddy squeezed my hand. He sniffled a few times too. Neither of us was in a hurry to leave.

The cemetery stood empty then, except for Daddy and me. A hawk swooped and picked up a mouse near the wire fence a few rows over from where Mama rested. A breeze brought the scent of sage, but up above the sky was a blinding blue, the same color as Mama's eyes.

Daddy took in a deep breath and stepped back from the stone. A toothpick bobbled up and down between his lips. I was glad he'd given up smoking again. He cocked his head one way and then another.

"I've been thinking we ought to plant a lilac bush or two here for Mama. What do you think, Sis?"

"Mama would love that." I smiled up at Daddy. I opened my purse and pulled out a silt-filled glove, unwound the rubber band, and let the dirt drift like brown snow onto the top of Mama's grave.

"You okay?"

"I will be. I just keep having a weird thought."

"What's that?" Daddy put his arm around me.

"You'll think I'm crazy, but sometimes I think about Aunt Vadine. Even though she lied about talking to Mr. Howard and made my life miserable, I don't hate her for what she did."

"That's good. She's had a tough life—most of it her own doing."

"Do you think she'll be all right?"

"Don't rightly know. All this time, I thought we were doing Vadine a favor, giving her a place to stay until her life straightened out. I called that fella Bobby in Midland. Seems she lied about him too. Got herself in a spot of trouble it sounds like."

"Was he her boyfriend?"

"No way of knowing. He told me she was the one who took the money from the truck stop, and he talked her boss out of pressing charges by selling all her furniture to pay him back."

"So we won't be getting a truckload of her stuff like she wanted?"

"No. Could be that was another thing that set her off. All I know is we gotta pick up the pieces and get on with our lives, Sis."

"I'm ready. I love you, Daddy."

He thumped me on the arm and said, "I love you too."

## FORTY-ONE

ON FRIDAY NIGHT, Daddy took Mrs. Gray and me to the Dairy Cream for a hamburger.

Mrs. Gray nibbled at her burger. "The plant superintendent says we can take our time with Slim's things. I think it's best to get it over with though. Next weekend Alice and I will start packing everything up."

"I'll be glad to help, Mrs. Gray." I dipped my French fry in a dollop of ketchup.

"Count me in," Daddy said.

"Please." Mrs. Gray looked sideways at me, the bun on top of her head slightly off center. "I want you to call me Olivia. And I want to thank you both for all you've done, what you meant to Slim. . . ." Between her fingers, she turned the paper cup, glistening with the sweat cups have in the heat. Around and around.

Olivia invited us into the house when we took her home, but Daddy wanted to sit on her porch, where a slatted swing hung on thick chains. They sat beside each other, swinging gently like a couple of old grannies. Daddy fished in his pocket for his knife and began whittling on a tree limb he'd picked up nearby.

"I didn't know you whittled," Olivia said like it was the most interesting thing since the invention of ice cream.

"Oh yeah, I'm a whittler from way back." Thin slivers of wood curled at the blade of his knife.

"He whittles, all right. He just hasn't figured out how to make anything." I rolled my eyes at him.

"I'll have you know this is a very handy item I'm working on right now. You'll see." He continued shaving the stick while I wrapped my arms around my knees and gazed off into the heavens. The Milky Way seemed close enough to touch, hugging us somehow. A firefly or two lit up the bushes near the porch, and I was trying to guess where they would pop up next when Daddy announced he'd finished his project.

"It looks remarkably like a stick, Daddy. How clever."

"This, dear ladies, is not just a stick; it is a hair stick." He reached up and poked it through the wad of hair on top of Olivia's head.

We all laughed until the moon smiled through the trees and Daddy said we ought to be getting back.

The next day I called Tuwana and asked her to meet me in the middle of camp.

The bounce in her step had come back. And her attitude. "What's going on? Why all the mystery?"

"Unfinished business." I started toward the playground, gripping the paper sack I'd brought along.

When we came to the cedar trees, I held back a heavy branch and motioned for Tuwana to enter. I opened the sack and took out an old tablecloth, which I spread on the ground. "Sit down, please."

We sat cross-legged, and I pulled out Mama's journal.

Tuwana scrunched her eyebrows together but didn't move.

"Listen to this." I turned to a page in the middle.

Tomorrow Joe and I will be married. The pearls Mother gave me look beautiful with my dress. I could just pinch myself I'm so happy. I can only pray someday I'll have a little girl to pass them on to.

Tuwana studied her fingernails.

I closed the book. "Mama did want me to have her pearls. And thanks to you, they're safe." I took out the red-handled serving spoon and a meat fork. "Ready?" I handed Tuwana the fork, and together we scooped the dead needles away and dug until we heard metal scraping the cocoa tin. My heart rose in my throat as I lifted it out. I used the edge of the spoon to pry the top off, pulled out the rolled- up sock, and then held Mama's pearls in my fingers. I closed my eyes and counted each one. Eighty-four. A fresh breeze kissed my face and the scent of lilacs tickled my nose. *Mama. She's here.*

Tuwana smiled, then fastened the pearls around my neck as I held up my hair. I gave her a quick hug. "You were right, you know."

"How's that?"

"Everything has turned out fine. Just fine."

"I said that?"

"Indubitably." I laughed and helped her up. "Another thing. I've started typing everything that happened since last summer. It will probably be a never-ending story, but I think there just might be a chapter about Tuwana becoming a cheerleader. It's time for you to start practicing, and I'd be glad to help."

She wrinkled her nose, and together we walked arm in arm back home.


When the Saturday came to clean out Slim's house, we had more help than we knew what to do with. Mrs. Johnson brought her girls and Mr. Johnson, who could only give advice and moral support. Cly came with Norm and Eva. Daddy and I helped Olivia pull things out so Tuwana's mother could see them, and then Olivia directed which pile they went into. The furniture was up for grabs, except for Slim's rocker, which Tuwana's dad had taken a shine to.

"You know it doesn't go with our décor," Mrs. Johnson said.

"Hell's bells, woman, a man's home is his castle. That'll make a nice throne." He winked at his girls.

"You're the king, all right." She touched him lightly on the cheek, then went into the kitchen and started pulling things from the cupboards.

Slim's Bible went to Olivia; Norm got twenty years' worth of *The Old Farmer's Almanac* when he said he'd been thinking about taking over Slim's garden—something he and Cly could do together. We set the Last Supper painting aside to donate to Hilltop Church.

At noon Irene Flanagan brought ham and cheese sandwiches for everyone. And a coconut cake. Goldie dropped off a plate of cookies and hugged me. Doobie and PJ came by to eat a sandwich.

Fritz Brady took two pickup loads of boxes and assorted furniture to the VFW, giving the veterans a boost for next year's sale. When Mr. Johnson grew tired, Tuwana's mom drove him and the two younger girls home in the Edsel. Olivia wanted me to have Slim's walnut desk from the spare bedroom so I'd have a nice place to write. At Olivia's insistence, Daddy agreed to take Slim's braided rug, and somehow it just felt right.

"Slim would want you to have this." Olivia handed Cly the backgammon board with the worn-smooth playing pieces. I could see his Adam's apple bobbing up and down when he thanked her.

The rooms echoed now that they were empty. I ached to hear Slim tell us another story or play another game of dominoes. To hear his teakettle whistle on the stove and sniff the steam from a cup of Ovaltine. As I fought back tears, Daddy winked at me and guided me toward the front door.

"Sis, I think we need a break." He dug in his pocket and handed me a fistful of quarters. "Why don't you and Tuwana run over to Willy's and get us all a Coke?"

The sun beat down on our backs as Tuwana and I walked up the center of the camp, our faces smudged and grit under our fingernails. If normal had a name, this would be it. Tuwana and me, being ourselves in spite of everything. Every day a new beginning without knowing what might be around the corner. Maybe something exciting. Maybe nothing. Goldie had been right. The Almighty had seen us through some tough times.

Instead of reading *Gone with the Wind*, I had taken Mama's New Testament from the hatbox and started reading the first chapter. With the whole summer ahead, I'd have it read in no time. And I couldn't wait.

After getting the Cokes from Willy's, we headed back.

Graham Camp. Not even a dot on the map.

Under the shade of an elm tree, Daddy and Olivia sat in webbed folding chairs. Daddy whittled a long stick while Olivia watched, her honey-colored hair escaping in loose strands from her topknot. No wonder. The only thing holding it was the stick Daddy had given her a few nights ago. Now he was apparently making one to match it. Across the street Cly pointed out to Norm the various rows of the garden while Norm nodded his head up and down.

"Here you go." I handed over the ice-cold bottles.

Daddy pried off the tops with the hooked blade of his knife while Tuwana and I settled on the tickly grass. When I tilted the bottle up, Grapette soda fizzed all the way down to my toes. I ran my hand across the top of the grass looking for four-leaf clovers, but all I came up with was a dandelion tuft. Twirling it in my fingers I puffed out my cheeks and blew the snowy top. Fuzzies floated in the air.

"You know, days like this don't come along too often," Olivia said. "Friends, neighbors, family. All of you helping out. I'll savor this moment a long time. A dandelion day, that's what I call it." She smiled at Daddy, who reached across and took her hand in his.

My heart did a little skip as I watched them. *Daddy and Olivia holding hands?*

"I wonder what they'll be like?" Tuwana said out of the blue.

"Who?" I asked.

"The people who move here. Daddy said the new family would move in July the first. You know we really do need some excitement, something fun and totally cool."

"Tuwana." I planted my hands on my hips. "You are nuts! Totally."

But my mind spun with possibilities.

DISCUSSION QUESTIONS

*Chasing Lilacs* by Carla Stewart

1. Both in the beginning and after her mother returns from the hospital, Sammie is torn between caring for her mother and having fun with her friends. Do you think this is a normal response for a twelve-year-old girl? Have you ever been torn between duty and pursuing your own interests? How did that make you feel?

2. When did you first suspect that Rita (Sammie's mother) might still have "nerve" problems? What was the source of Rita's inner turmoil?

3. Tuwana has been Sammie's best friend since first grade. Cly appears during the summer the story takes place. How are these friends different? What role do they each play in the story? Which friend do you think was closer to being a soul mate for Sammie? Do you find in your circle of friends those that fill different needs for you? Do you have a best friend? A soul mate?

4. What clues were given about Rita's inner struggle? Could her suicide have been prevented? Were you able to identify the stages of grief Sammie went through following her mother's death? How did Sammie and her father grieve differently?

5. The story is set in the 1950s. Does this era hold any special memories for you? How does the intimate setting of the petroleum camp affect the story? Are small, close-knit communities

the same today as they were fifty years ago? How has our need today to encourage kids to be cautious with adults changed our view of community?

6. Goldie and Slim are two very different adults who embrace Sammie. How have their own past experiences with grief and loss equipped them to be wise mentors? Have you had an older person mentor you? Have you ever mentored another person?

7. Sammie's aunt Vadine is a difficult person to like from her first appearance on the page. Did you think Sammie tried hard enough to get along with her aunt? Have you ever had a difficult person in your life? How did you handle it? What was the outcome?

8. What was Sammie's relationship like with Joe, her dad? Why do you think he was unable to see what was happening between Sammie and Vadine? Do you think fathers today are more sensitive to their children's needs? How have parental roles changed in recent years?

9. Brother Henry's response to Sammie about her mother's suicide wasn't definitive. Do you think suicide is the unforgiveable sin? Have you ever been close to someone who committed suicide? What words of wisdom did you receive? Discuss what steps you took to reconcile the tragedy.

10. Rita had many of the things Vadine felt were rightfully hers— Joe, the pearls, a child who lived (Sammie), even the experience of meeting the author of *Gone with the Wind*. When did you first suspect Vadine had deep-seated jealousy and pain? How did she act this out? Were you surprised by her final act of desperation toward Sammie? Were you able to sympathize with her by the end of the story? Do you think Sammie forgave her?

11. Have you ever longed to feel loved by someone you weren't sure loved you back? For Sammie, healing hinged on finding

out if her mother loved her. What was Rita telling Sammie by putting the pearls and New Testament in her chest of drawers?

12. The scent of lilacs occurs frequently in the story. How was this used as a literary device to tie Sammie and her mother together? Are there any smells that evoke specific memories for you?

13. Tuwana was fond of predicting who would be Sammie's new mother. Do you think Joe and Olivia, Sammie's beloved teacher, have a future together? What do you predict will be the outcome? What problems might arise?

14. Both Sammie's mother and aunt had psychological problems based on inability to deal with traumatic events in their lives. What are the chances of Sammie having the same kinds of problems? What does the future hold for Sammie? Is she stronger or more vulnerable because of what happened in the story?

15. What role does faith play in dealing with psychological issues and/or the effects of past traumatic events?

# ABOUT THE AUTHOR

In her life before writing, Carla Stewart enjoyed a career in nursing and juggling the adventures of her four rambunctious sons. She believes her experiences prepared her to write novels that answer some of life's tough questions and offer hope in our skid-marked world.

Carla launched her writing career in 2002 when she earned the coveted honor of being invited to attend Guideposts' Writers Workshop in Rye, New York. Since then, her articles have appeared in *Guideposts*, *Angels on Earth*, *Saddle Baron*, and *Blood and Thunder: Musings on the Art of Medicine*.

Most recently, Carla won two ACFW Genesis contests: one in the Historical Fiction category in 2007 and another for her Young Adult entry in 2008. *Chasing Lilacs* is her debut novel.

She enjoys a good cup of coffee, great books, and weekend getaways with her husband. They live in Tulsa, Oklahoma, and are somewhat partial to the little people in their lives—their six grandchildren.

Carla loves to hear from readers and invites you to contact her and learn more about her writing at www.carlastewart.com.